SHORTS

5

SHORTS
5

The Macallan/
Scotland on Sunday
Short Story Collection

Edited by Suhayl Saadi

Polygon

First published in Great Britain in 2002 by Polygon
an imprint of Birlinn Ltd, West Newington House,
10 Newington Road, Edinburgh EH9 1QS
www.birlinn.co.uk

Editorial arrangement and Foreword © Suhayl Saadi, 2002
Contributions © the Contributors, 2002

Typeset in Galliard by Hewer Text Ltd, Edinburgh,
and printed and bound in Great Britain by
Bell & Bain Ltd, Glasgow

A CIP record for this book is
available from the British Library

ISBN 0 7486 6329 0 (paperback)

The publisher acknowledges subsidy from

Scottish
Arts Council

towards the publication of this volume

CONTENTS

Contents

FOREWORD

A t heart, every writer is a necromancer. She or he would just as soon be stirring a small cauldron as dripping ink onto a blank page. It is this lure of the unpredictable pen, and the hope that the resulting piece of artifice will be realised effectively enough to entice other readers into its world, that at base drives many writers. To write a very short story that works may be an exercise in simplicity, but like the construction of a tiny engine, it is far from easy. A writer does not have the luxury of space in which to deploy the paraphernalia of the novelist in pursuit of character depth, credible narrative and convincing atmosphere. The lower the word-limit, the more tricky it gets. And yet all you need, really, is one powerful idea, enunciated with the clarity of pure music. Hey – that's about it! Like Theseus and the ball of string; simple, not easy.

In this hopscotch spirit, I shall discuss the stories following thematic lines, rather than adhering strictly to the order in which they appear in the book. And plenty of conjuring and seduction, Mittel-European style, is going on in 'Moon and the Spy Pencils'. In this splendid story, which kicks off this year's *Shorts* collection, Hannah McGill creates a British office-factory where pencil graphite is replaced by miniature spook maps. Then one day, the shortest worker in the place, Moon, begins to draw something else . . .

'All things are by their opposites known', goes the Sufi line.

So before we delve further into the excellent stories in *Shorts 5*, let's look at some pitfalls into which many of the less successfully realised stories submitted for this year's Macallan/Scotland on Sunday competition fell, and indeed which I have observed when assessing prose written for other competitions, as well as writers' group work, and so on. A common theme, this year as always, was relayed in stories about sad but plucky, elderly folk, particularly characters who spoke in a kind of couthy Scots-English and who seemed to talk largely in rather predictable aphorisms. The point to remember here is that people who happen to reach a certain age do not automatically turn into brass cylinders. That might be what some individuals appear to be (to writers younger than themselves), but it's just a surface reflection; the point is to get beneath that and into what they really are, and to do it through the writing. Sometimes, it's worthwhile slipping into first person when attempting this: imagine how you might be, in several decades' time, say, and given a different body, skin, locus.

In some senses, it is a kind of vicarious method-acting. The same applies to the avoidance of regurgitated stereotypes, be they of gender, ethnicity or whatever in even minor characters, unless such a type is there for a positive artistic purpose and not merely through the writer's laziness. They don't ring true, you see. Such people may exist, but in fiction we are not reproducing the physical world; deeper levels of engagement with the subject are required, and readers rightly demand much more than just a literary version of the so-called 'reality TV'. 'The Strechle', by Iain Bahlaj, cleverly avoids such pitfalls. Here, an old woman recounts to a young girl the story behind a painting of the sea which depicts something odd rising from the surface of the waves. This story takes two potentially very risky areas for writers – childhood and old age – and turns them into a work of terror and wonder, a melange of Kafka, Lovecraft and good, old-fashioned Goidelic darkness. Speaking of which, another excellent childhood story set in Scotland, Linda Saunders's 'The

Sheep', is penned in the unpretentious yet unsentimental manner of a boys' weekend trek up a hillside, yet something very strange is happening. To complete this particular Alban triumvirate, Angus Dunn sculpts 'Scrimshaw' into a tender, powerful and emotive story delineating the relationship between the narrator and his grandparents around love, devotion and . . . bones.

Okay. Next.

There is a trend right now for stories which seem to function as a substitute for a long, male moan. It's fine – indeed essential – to take cracks at society, but if it's to be interesting, more is required of the protagonist than simply to complain. If something dramatic were to happen to the character, now that might be different. Cathy McSporran's 'Alasdair's Angel' takes this stance of the 'unrequited man' and turns it into an edgy, fragile and immanently violent tale of redemptive masochism. 'The Last Day of the Year', by Alan Bissett, deftly transfigures a frozen-frost hogmanay graveyard stroll into a harrowing reckoning with sexual guilt and personal responsibility.

A whole batch – or, one might say, brood – of stories dealt with the experience of new parenthood. In these cases, it was usually a professional woman in her twenties or thirties who was feeling existentially dissociated, both from her previous existence and from other people, through the arrival of her first baby. In order for such a valid and powerful experience to be rendered in an effective way in fiction the writer really has to develop this starting point into something more, perhaps as Ruth Thomas does in 'Precious Cargo' by stretching for a suburban hyper-realism redolent of John Cheever or of the 'mute and luminous desolation' of Juan Goytisolo. An alternative handling by the same writer, this time from the male point of view, is presented in 'Wonderful Age' which is the hilarious story of a toddler's father at a child's birthday party who is desperately, comically, embarrassingly clinging to his pair of snazzy, maroon loafers as the sole remaining symbol of his previous, freebooting existence. Both stories derive their power from an analysis of the political into the personal through the protagonists' struggle to escape the contemporary ruthless, yet insidious, commodification of infancy and parenthood.

And as in the theopoetic architecture of the corpus of San Juan de la Crux, the closer one gets to perfection, the more insidious the pitfalls become. There is a type of competently written fiction which emerges straight from the shamanism of creative writing courses (while being a keen exponent of such literary interactions, I am not blind to their limitations). These narratives represent the socially engineered flipside of sub-Welshian story-clones; whereas the protagonists in the latter tend to be male, insensitive, contemporary and working-class, in these more self-consciously literary stories, the main characters are almost invariably highly-educated, narcissistically sensitive, middle-class contemporary women. Sometimes, such stories are almost perfectly executed (in technical terms of phrasing, etc.), but they tend to lack something vital: voice, maybe, or animation. Soul, perhaps. Many writers go through this kind of phase, but it must be got through. Rachael McGill demonstrates that she has got well through it in 'A Tasmanian Tiger in London', where with skill, poise and a sinuous sense of rhythm she leads the reader right inside the head of a woman who is having difficulty making connections with other human beings while attempting to harness her own erotic beast. Ferocious stuff.

Hallucinatory urban realism; the Turkish coffee of short fiction. Reading like a *hommage* to the works of writers such as Ann Donovan and Janet Paisley (and indeed, who better?), Carol McKay's 'Unrestricted' paints a picture of a heavily pregnant woman who risks either going into labour or else being beaten to a pulp by her psychopathic criminal partner, beneath the starlet on the wall and amidst the barking trash of the Playstation. Bloody old Clyde, at its macho, patriarchal worst. A thousand years of history, pregnant in its denial, its restriction, its murder. Subliminally (the way fiction does), this story carries the torch once wielded by Marion Bernstein, Helen Crawford, Mary Armour, Rose Witcop and all those other women whose own stories remain almost untold, barely documented, uncelebrated, yet who were – and are – Glasgow. 'Unrestricted' is a story told at its very best.

Through the looking-glass, with Kath Murphy's 'Help' we swirl down the convoluted brain of just such a brutalised, incipiently violent male as he has a conversation with, and gets the shopping for, a once-fearsome neighbour. Late at night, in a lonely carriage on the Glasgow Underground line, these guys fade into the background as the scene is filled with Frances Sessford's supremely mystical, the pink and poignant 'The Carntyne Elephant' and the homiletic, under-the-skin angst of two passengers who quite literally are not what they seem. As The Woman says: *Love don't come easy* . . . Especially not self-love.

What's the difference between a tale and a story? Lorn Macintyre demonstrates admirably how one can be made to function within the medium of the other through the beautifully told, brutal 'Peaches', which is set in an unspecified Highland place psychologically 'beyond the Minch'. In its sub-textual amorality, it reads like a folk-tale. This ferries us conveniently into magical realism, a literary style which over the years has become steadily easier to do by numbers, often through a series of facile tropes, or else to death. Fiona Thackeray avoids both in her perfectly pitched evocation of Brazilian parasols and confit heaven in 'The Secret's in the Folding'. How many sins of the past have been beatified beneath just such battered canvases, I wonder? Only Dona Celestina, lately of the town of Bom Jesus, knows the answer. In 'Levitation', John Dodds tenderly invokes the ghosts of a Polish upbringing in a superb story of the loss of language, of the place of words in the midst of a world of joyless sex and solitaire. Then we're spiralling off with Angus Dunn again on an 'Unravelling', 'definitely antique' Persian carpet which over the years, strings out into a brilliant, flying metaphor for the slow disintegration of a relationship. For 'The Caged Bird', we're keeping company with Alan Mackay and an unascending lark in the intoxicated blaring emptiness of a Grecian quayside ouzeri. Same sea, different beach: Jules Horne's 'Radar Bird' cleverly distils the whisky from out of the schlock and pitch of a Hollywood film, all the while striving for that zero point of music and silence: the impossibility of real communication between one human being and the next: Poetry. Through the redemptive, frozen sands of 'Easter', David Pettigrew takes us to the lyrical edge of a relationship which is effectively wordless, but which re-animates through the creation and performance of a shared and painful love: Music. Tiny details, ghost duets.

Frances Sessford's 'Leaving Dan' is a moving, lyrical story, told from the inside, of a woman whose husband has just died. In a scene worthy of Joyce, the coffin – together with every single imaginable relative – are in the cramped house, and the holy waters are about to flow and to reflect the lightness of being, the weight of lives. Through the morning clarity of its perception, this intense sympathetic treatment is the very opposite of mawkishness. Still on the theme of loss, 'How She Came to Write a Poem Called "Apostrophe" ' by Dorothy Alexander is an intricately seeded narrative of a woman's attempt to pen an elegy of sorts for her close friend. Through the process of the poem's construction, we gain an intimate insight into the nature of their relationship. 'Shunting', a story written by Paul Brownsey from the point of view of a man at the crematorium who is waiting for the body of his once-vibrant friend to slide into the furnace, has a quite different feel and humour, but is an equally effective portrayal of the universal human need to transcend death.

With so many stories about funerals in this book, thank Brian Hennigan for 'The Selkirk Oscillation', a comic piece, which in a narrative voice worthy of a respected member of the local chamber of commerce, charts the supremely polite and totally reasoned bourgeois battle over the secret of the perfect and replicable scone (or should that be 'scoane'?). This epic story of the proud and independent city-states of southern Scotland rollocks along with perfectly timed ironic humour. Moving from the ovens of the Palace of Scone to the bonfires of the Piazza della Signoria, the burghers of Middle Italy feature in Clio Gray's 'The Caponisation of Edgardo De Pucci', the tale of an eel-catcher told with a wit and sleight of hand worthy of Marguerite de Navarre. As though to underline that writing is not just about storytelling, at the other end of things is 'The Tramway', an elegantly broken, triumphantly modernist edifice redolent of the 'Hopscotch' work of Julio Cortazar or the translucent, *Pittura Metafisica* surrealist narratives of painter-writer, Giorgio de Chirico. The whirlpool here is powered by insinuation and imagery rather than through conventional plot and characterisation. The exhibition is all. Hetherington. Alex. Finito.

So that's it: *Shorts 5*. Twenty-five stories from 2002, written by twenty-two authors. From the editorial point of view, the fact that three writers have between them, six stories in the collection was totally coincidental, anonymity being maintained until after the selection for the compilation had already been made. Also, as it happens, none of these three writers' work was known to me before being asked to edit this book. Once the identities of the authors were revealed, I faced a dilemma: either I would have to pick three other stories by other writers which I had previously considered not quite as well realised as the ones I had already chosen, or else I could just leave things as they stood, on the basis that with regard to the literary quality of a collection, it concerns us little who the authors happen to be. It is always the writing that matters. So I decided to let the work speak for itself, and I think it does that eloquently.

Each of these twenty-five stories has an idea, a certain music, a whirlpool and perhaps most importantly of all, unspoken words. To define a narrative as 'a perfect short story' is virtually an oxymoron. The best stories, the ones that on being read make the most impact, are those which hold the artifice of their possible imperfections close to their chests like plates of broken, luminous armour. It is in the reader's moment of realisation, of illumination, that one story becomes two, a nodal point which is held thereafter in the invisible, contrapuntal tension which marks great short fiction. Many masterpieces have flaws. Their authors took risks, of one sort or another. They put themselves, and their art, on the line and it didn't always come off. But to some extent, their greatness lies in their ability to make even the flaws work. It is partly the incipience of failure, of becoming Babel, which gives writing its edge. At some level, in the construction of every story, one must first almost fail as a writer in order to be able truly to respect, and recognise, writing which has transcended. One way or another, aesthetically speaking, all of the stories in this volume are transcendent. Necromantic, you might say. Yet even this cannot be set down as a recipe for complacency. The final mistake, the flaw of the virtuoso so to speak, is that you develop voice, character, music and the idea, and that you forge all of these elements into a unified and transmuting catalytic animator, which gets you in and back out again, intact. So then you do it again, and again, and again. It becomes a formula. Mind you, some writers have made fortunes out of it. Me, I prefer magic.

Moon and the Spy Pencils

Hannah McGill

Moon was such a small man that if he had been one of many trapped in a burning building, he would have been able to avert catastrophe by wriggling through a skylight or a heating vent. He thought about it sometimes in bed at night. He pictured himself squeezed bullet-shaped, narrow little shoulders working forth and back, face contorted, encouraging shouts and hands at his rear. Lying in his bed, he wriggled a little, strained his little shellfish muscles. He imagined popping through like a cork out of a bottle, and being cheered and applauded as he got to work freeing the others. Fast and dainty as a cat, he would remove a window frame or force a lock, to accommodate their bulkier bodies.

More than once since he reached his full height, Moon had been confidently informed that women went wild over tiny men. Other men – taller men – had told him with many a chuckle and wink that short men were known to be great lovers. Women, they said, could not resist short men. Look at Bogart! Look at Alan Ladd! And look at circus dwarves – they had beautiful full-sized wives *and* beautiful jealous full-sized girl-friends! The reason clowns were sad was because canny dwarves stole their women.

Moon had never stolen a woman. But now that the war was bad, he found he was one of very few young and able-bodied men in town. He couldn't go away and fight because he was too small and his breath came out rough and ragged. His mother had given birth to him too soon, which she still spoke of reproachfully as if it had been his fault, but which he privately considered a failure on her part. He had been born in a bloody wrangle in the kitchen, too little and surprised to breathe easily on his own. He had not got enough oxygen.

(He did wonder if this early experience of breathlessness might trouble him if he ever *was* called upon to wriggle through a skylight, or a heating vent.)

Moon had a number of skills, though his body was weak and stunted. He knew he was cleverer and more able than many people who had enjoyed a full gestation period. His brain must have been finished, perhaps already dreaming, when he was rudely awakened and forced out that day in the kitchen. Only his body had been interrupted, and left unfinished. Moon had looked at embryos in jars and seen that they were all head, with just the smallest apologetic flicker of a body behind. They looked calm and wise, as if they had been left alone to think, without the distraction of other physical demands. The important early work goes into making the brains; the limbs and torso are afterthoughts. So Moon was made. His head was beautifully, perfectly large, his brain worked well. Some days he even felt he was superior – part of a different, more cerebral breed, constructed to think freely without the burden of muscle and bones and fat. His hands were faster, too, for being small.

It could have gone another way. The lack of oxygen could have made him an idiot. For many months of his early life, doctors and other interested parties had watched anxiously at Moon's bedside for signs of strangeness. They expected that at any moment his tongue would loll or his eyes would lazily cross. But Moon was so alert that before they even knew he could speak he had secretly given them all names. He had also named his toys, his pillows and the three soft moles on his nanny's face. He hoarded words from stories and from conversations that he had overheard.

He revealed his abilities gradually to the people around his bed – starting, for tradition's sake, with 'Mama'. They kept saying 'Mama' to him, mugging with big eyes and flapping lips and wanting him to reciprocate, so he obliged. His own name for his mother, as it happened, was not Mama; it was This. His father's name was Out.

The company that Moon worked for had been an innocuous concern before the war, producing games and packs of cards and crossword puzzles. Now they had a new project and they felt more important. They collected together useful items that could be smuggled into prisoner-of-war camps, and packaged them up in pretend care packages. There would be food, socks, a pack of cards perhaps, cigarettes, small comforts. Each box got stamped with the name of a fictitious charity and then they were shipped out, rich with secrets and never to be seen again. Moon's particular job was to work on tiny maps that were inked on tissue paper, rolled as thin as hairs and stashed inside the wooden chambers of pencils, where the lead was meant to be. It was a delicate process. Moon would be given a map to copy out, and would sit all day frowning very close to his work, a stack of pencils next to him, their insides mutilated to make room. Moon alternated the drawing and the rolling and the poking, and got up sometimes to wash his hands, so his sweat wouldn't buckle the tiny slips of paper or smudge the pencil lines. On his way to the men's washroom he would pass the table where the young girls sewed codes into handkerchiefs and map references into the heels of socks. Sometimes he passed by unnoticed. Sometimes the girls nudged each other and made comments. One of them was called Hilda and had two red coils of hair and a wide red mouth. She was as broad in the flanks as a horse and had rough skin around her mouth.

'That's a wild one there,' said Harry, who had a withered leg and worked on tiny compasses, strong and resilient enough to be hidden in the heel of a boot. No-one knew how many of the little maps and other items actually got to their intended beneficiaries, or if they provided any help. But Harry and Moon and the girls all worked late into the night anyway, straining their eyes. Harry gained secret pleasure from not telling his wife anything about his new line of work, and she gained secret pleasure from not being told.

'That's a wild one there. Eat you for breakfast, Moon. Soon as look at you.'

Harry had a wife, a woman of virtue who was not to be discussed in the same terms as the working girls. Moon blushed when Harry talked that way. Hilda stood a full foot taller than Moon. Moon knew this because she'd once backed him against a wall and offered him a swig of something strong-smelling from a hip flask. His nose had come level with the imperious jut of her bosom. Too close to her body, he saw that it was really a collection of beautiful arches, like a church: her eyebrows, her feet in battered high-up heels, her front curved out under black scratchy heavy fabric. Her pelvis the doorway, her ribcage the rafters. Moon pitter-pattered like a rabbit, feet working for escape, heart fast. He felt the breath gather in his chest as if in a balloon.

'You're so LITTLE. It's sweet,' Hilda hissed before he got away. 'I could snap you over my knee like one of those pencils.' After that he began sneaking glances at her knees, which were as solid and lumpy as potatoes.

One of the things that Out did after Moon gratified him with the word 'Dad' was to provide Moon with books and paper. After the incident in the kitchen Moon's mother had made it very clear that she would not tolerate another pregnancy. She had found the experience uncomfortable, its culmination horrifying and its issue disappointing. So Out had to accept that his only heir was sickly and undersized. The only hope was to encourage the boy to use his big head and become a great thinker. Great thinkers, Out reasoned, could be peculiar in appearance; it was tolerated, in intellectual circles. Out ordered stacks of books on random subjects from geology to Greek architecture, in the hope that Moon would display natural ability in one direction or another. Moon, curled foetus-like on his bed, quietly read everything and told his father very little about what he thought. In private he drew on all the flyleaves of the books – pictures of himself, big-headed and serene, and of This, and of Out. Next to their heads he would write things that they had said to him or about him. ALWAYS WITH YOUR HEAD IN A BOOK! This said. MAYBE THE CIVIL SERVICE OR POLITICS, Out said. Because Out never looked at the books, he didn't know about the drawings and it seemed somehow necessary to keep them secret.

'*That* ain't a map,' said Harry, leaning over Moon's shoulder. Moon's map had turned itself into a drawing of Hilda, the dimpled side of her face and the heavy sweep of her hair. 'If you ever run short on dough, Hild, you could sell that hair,' one of the other girls had shouted once when Hilda was pinning it up. 'But if I didn't have the hair, I wouldn't get my drinks bought for me, and then I'd be even shorter on dough,' Hilda laughed back. 'Who wants to dance with a bald girl?'

'You're a dark one. Got any more?' Harry asked Moon, with surprising urgency. 'No,' said Moon. 'I just lost concentration for a bit.' He crushed the map in his hand – a waste.

'Draw us one,' urged Harry. 'Not Hilda, though, she's a cow. Draw us little Jean there, the blonde one.'

Drawing women wasn't unlike drawing maps. They had curves and fencing and wooded areas, too. Jean was smaller and sharper and Moon thought her geography far less intriguing than Hilda's, but he obliged Harry. Harry whistled appreciatively and Moon felt suddenly liked.

'Tell you what, mate. Most of those prisoners would rather see one of these than those bloody maps. Know I would if I was in the lock-up.' Harry paused. He had been in the lock-up, once, having been given to using his nimble compass-making fingers for the less noble purpose of breaking locks and opening safes.

Encouraged, though shy, Moon started using both sides of the paper. Waste not, want not. On one side the map; on the other, a version of Hilda, first based upon sneaked glances across to her laughing or frowning over her work, then as he grew bolder, in imagined poses and scenarios. Harry encouraged him but then betrayed him. Hilda came in for the day in a state of high excitement, her wide cheeks redder than black-market rouge. She came right over to Moon's desk and he felt littler than ever, as troubled as when Out had fired questions at him about his reading.

'Harry said you been drawing me!'

'No,' said Moon.

'Come on, show! No-one ever drew me before.' Moon was quicker but she was stronger, and with one tough move she whipped a pile of finished papers off his desk. The delicate paper crumpled in her grip. She held them too high for Moon to reach and he sat red and suffering as she looked at each one in turn. She seemed angry and then not angry. She looked at the pictures for so long that Moon stopped watching her and went back to his work.

'You been putting these in your little pencils, then?' she finally asked him.

'Yes,' he said, wretched.

'Show me.' She proffered one of the drawings.

'Show . . . ?'

'Put it in. Do what you do.'

Harry was watching from the other side of the table. Moon picked a pencil up. His hands trembled as he rolled the paper up tight and slotted it in through the tiny hole. Hilda leaned in close, and giggled.

'Look at the way you slide that in there.'

Harry let out a rude snort.

'I don't have any notion who's looking at me, do I? Don't you think you ought to ask a person before you send pictures of them across the bloody world, hmm?'

6

'Yes. I'm sorry.'

'Make it up to me, then.'

She placed the papers back on his desk with exaggerated care, patting them flat.

Moon watched, not understanding.

'Draw me properly,' she said. 'A big one, like proper artists do.'

'But how can I—'

Hilda leaned in again and took the completed, forgotten spy pencil out of his hand. She wrote an address down on one of the finished maps in front of him. 'That's where I live. You're going to come over and do my picture. Or I'm going to tell the supervisor about what you've been up to. Dirty little man.'

Hilda lived with Jean in a shabby two-room flat. There was just a bedroom, with twin beds, and a kitchen. There were dirty saucepans crowded by the sink, and stockings hanging limply over the doorframes like discarded skins.

'It ain't Buckingham Palace,' Hilda said, handing Moon a china cup with an inch of brown in the bottom. Moon touched his tongue to the liquid and it burned.

Outside work, Hilda seemed a little quieter and less aggressive. She was wearing a sober brownish jumper, assiduously darned at one elbow, and a grey skirt that didn't show her knees. Jean had gone out for the evening.

'You brought your stuff, then?' Hilda said, looking down on Moon with a smile that betrayed some nervousness or regret. 'We don't keep a lot of *artists' materials* around.'

Moon produced a sketchbook from his knapsack. Paper was so scarce that he had begun rubbing out old drawings and working over their remains. Some pages had four layers of faint lines on them. Moon still could not be sure if he was being punished, or befriended, but he suspected the latter.

'Come on into the bedroom, then. Jean's out for the night, and good luck to her.'

The thing about the bedroom was the beds, and the chamber-pot neatly stashed in one corner. There was a smell, too, of close-confined flesh and talcum powder. Moon was gripped by a sudden conviction that Hilda was going to dart back out of the room and leave him in there, locking the door behind her. He would have to sit down on the corner of one of the beds and wait, the chamber-pot horrifyingly close by and the smell of girls growing stronger as the night drew in.

But she didn't leave the room. She did something Moon had not even considered, something far more audacious and threatening.

'Oh come on, little man. Proper artists always drew women starkers. You know that.'

The brownish jumper with its thoughtful darn was on the floor, soon joined by the grey skirt, two discarded skins of stockings and a number of complex items that had long ago been white. Moon stared at the pile of clothes and then flicked his eyes up to Hilda's face, trying to avoid the skin in between. She was flushed and defiant-looking, glittering at him. The last thing she did was unpin her hair. Who *would* dance with a bald girl? Seeing that he wasn't going to speak, she sat down on the bed, and made an impatient gesture. *Well?* He had to look then, and saw the way her belly settled into comfortable folds, the sad tug-marks on her hips and breasts where the flesh had swelled too fast. The arch of her pelvis, the arch of her arm propped awkwardly behind her head in imitation of a pose she had seen in magazines, the arch of her foot pointed out. Moon sat on the other bed, and did as he was told.

'Can't believe I took all my clothes off and you never tried a thing,' she said when he had stilled his trembles enough to execute a competent sketch of her. He looked at her. She peeled the bedspread off her bed and wrapped it round her shoulders. 'Never say a word, do you? Just big eyes like an owl. Never ask any of the girls out for a drink. Nothing from you. You're a rare commodity, you know. Nice-looking bloke still at home. You ought to take advantage.'

'I'm so small,' said Moon at last.

'But it's nice for a man to be gentle, though. Makes a change.'

She reached over the gap between the two beds, and took the sketchpad out of his hands. 'Ever think about all them prisoners who might be looking at me and wondering who I am?' she said with a soft laugh.

'We don't know—' began Moon.

'We don't know if they get there,' she filled in, nodding, drawing him over to her bed. 'We just never, never – know.'

A hundred pictures of Hilda, wadded between socks and chocolate bars, inside pencils that had been part of trees, tumbling in luggage holds, handled by guards, confiscated, maybe, or never found. She unbuttoned Moon with the tender efficiency of a nurse.

'Like this.' she said.

'Like this,' he weakly echoed.

'Don't draw the others, Moon.'

'I don't.'

The Secret's in the Folding

Fiona Thackeray

From behind door jambs, suspicious eyes observed Dona
Celestina come to town. Her head held high, a canvas
bundle bumping her behind, creaky shoes pinching. Her stick –
a hoe-handle polished by sun and years and hands – thudded
the dust, leaving powdery dots. From her left hand swung a
crate with feathers protruding: the two guinea fowl who would
colonise the town of Bom Jesus with their squawking progeny,
and oblige Celestina with small, speckled eggs for the rest of her
days. Jammed tight under this arm was a parasol.

When she'd made her patrol of our humble streets, and sat
sipping water at Ze Lima's corner café, we watched her hoist
her long frame from the chair, picking up last her parasol.
Celestina headed for the river. Her crinoline hems sagged in the
heat; the guinea fowl scuffled in their crude cage. Out of sight,
she took off the pinching shoes, sighing, feet splaying in the
cool riverbank mud.

At the point where the water rumbles under the road to
Salvador, she set down her bundles. Where the old jackfruit tree
drops its seed bombs half in mud, half in the water, looping an
arm over the green current.

With a hoe-blade unrolled from her canvas, jammed onto the
walking stick, she cleared a patch of low white stumps. She
began pointing the straighter bits of wood for fence stakes,
mopping her brow. We heard her bitten machete ringing out

and reports from our breathless little spies: local kids stalking the woods like Indians.

With these ancient tools, Celestina spiked a fence into the ground for her two cranky birds and a makeshift shelter for herself, the carrying canvas stretched over for a roof. Later, she could see the moon through it, and a fair few stars. In the rainy months, a symphony of leaks puddled her floor, though she never cared, plashing through, with a duck's insouciance.

It was rainy season when she first came provisioning. Past the saddler's she paced, gingerly in those comfortless shoes – accustomed, by now, to staring locals. Rain pelted her head; a perpetual baptism, but she never hurried. The parasol stayed crooked under her arm. Madalena and I watched, and wondered.

The Rural Supplies Store was first to attend Bom Jesus's newest resident. She needed rope to lash a hurdle door for her shack. Next she came creaking towards us.

There was only Dona Marinete in the shop with her maid, clucking over her maize flour order, lingering, in hope of gossip.

On the threshold Celestina stopped, dripping like washed collards in a sieve. She inclined her brow towards dumbstruck Dona Marinete, whose jaw dropped.

'*Bom dia*. What weather!' I greeted her.

Celestina withdrew the parasol from its tight place and thrust it on the counter.

'A bushel of flour, I should like, please. And a good 3lb of sugar, *Senhor*.'

She looked me in the eye proudly, yet called me '*Senhor*' as a maid might. I wondered how to address her – '*Senhora*' seemed grand for a black woman in old crinolines. While I weighed sugar my other customers bewailed the downpour, eager chins tilted at Celestina. She said nothing, and set her provisions by the door. Nodding at the rain, she declared, 'I'll collect it later.' Dona Marinete opened her mouth, but

Celestina spun on her heels, and departed, picking through the terracotta wash.

Plucking at the maid's sleeve, Dona Marinete left too, hitching billowing skirts clear of the mud; Maria tottered behind, struggling to keep a sun-faded black parasol positioned over her *patroa's** bouncing curls.

Not two hours later, Celestina returned.

'Pssst! *Senhor*! I think the Good Lord's sparing us more rain. Maybe I'll take that flour now.' She smiled, less guarded.

'O! I've not had a minute to check on those clouds!'

'No matter; weather's fine.' Tutting, she forbad any fuss, arranging her sack-load. The rain had stopped, it's true, but iron-red puddles held reflections of fat clouds.

'Maybe not for long, mind.'

'I'll take it!' she shuddered impatiently.

She shouldered the load like a strapping farmhand and was off down the track. Already the first fat spots of rain were hitting her headscarf. She'd have a bushel of paste by the time she reached her place. I stood and watched her go, shaking my head slowly.

My new customer awoke with her birds next day to set a fire and cook up sweetcorn puddings, sticky pumpkin hearts and passion-fruit boilings. Late morning, she appeared in the square, setting her wares on upturned crates, a cautious two feet under the gables of the town hall. Business was slow at first – she hadn't counted on the suspicious nature of Bom Jesus people. Still, we were a people deprived of sweetmeats, save the dusty old biscuits in our store. Gradually, customers were seduced by smells, tasted her special recipes and were smitten.

In Bom Jesus, Celestina's economical conversing had whetted curiosities. When pressed she'd say she came from 'the countryside'. Quite unawares, she had driven the ladies from the big houses wild with inquisitiveness to the point of almost losing their refined ways. Dona Serena had even ridden the sugar-cane barge as far as Dores, under the guise of 'a vigil against cane pilfering', ogling, from the deck, Celestina's patch. All to verify whether she really did sit straddling a rock, 'fishing and chewing tobacco like a man', as our spying young folks had reported. The gaps in her story, like honey traps, invited us to fall in and wallow in preposterous stories. She was a witch from the forest in the north; the mother of '*Saci*' – the peg-legged rascal who soured milk and set plagues on bean crops. She was, tattled washer-girls from Cascudo's coffee plantation, an African Queen, owing to her stately rhythm of walking. (I put that down to calluses from those shoes.) The *senhoras* of the plantations, over afternoon coffee, dismissed such fairy-tales. Eyes narrowed knowingly, 'She's blacker than the grains in this coffee pot, dears', they said, spitting crumbs of corn-meal cake over dainty cups. 'Must be descended from those shipped over from Africke. A Gold Coast slave baby, ladies.' She'd run away, perhaps, or bought her freedom. It didn't matter much: they knew where she was from.

Dona Celestina stayed ahead of the gossips. Her divine wares soon brought out-of-hours callers to the riverbank. A sign appeared in childish script, 'CAKES, PIES & CONFECKSION-ERY. *Any request considered*.' Madalena said one of the boys at school painted it, with payment in pumpkin hearts. They say she'd fashioned some type of a clay oven. Soon, she'd no need to go the square any more. For the inquisitive souls of Bom Jesus, it was the perfect excuse for snooping. Always ready for them – the guinea fowl raised the alarm – she'd close the door, squeeze on shoes, and wait on the packed earth, the birds scratching around her feet. In nonchalant twos or threes, dangling empty baskets, they came. Celestina held their crumpled papers to the light filtering through jackfruit leaves, squinting at spidery ink. Her bony fingers conjured sweet steam and ingredients in the air, slyly guessing what those scribbles meant. The fingertips came to pause on her chest and raindrops gathered upon the ribs of banana leaves as she memorised recipes, considered a price.

That first year, the rains never let up. Celestina came to us regularly, carrying the furled parasol, rain or shine. Madalena asked, '*Papai*, why doesn't that *senhora* put up her parasol? She's getting all wet.' And I would pinch her for her insolence and send her scurrying to offer water, or a *cafezinho*, to our rain-mizzled client.

One ceaselessly wet day, the shop got crowded – the baker's boy, two travelling salesmen, and Dona Marinete's daughters down from the *Fazenda Fortuna*, all sheltering from the rain. I'd set Madalena making coffee: the smell made people forget the weather. Celestina, approaching through sheets of silver, faltered a little in her stride on seeing the dampened huddle.

'*Bom dia*,' she mumbled. I came out from the back shop to greet her.

'I'm wet, flesh and bone! My usual flour order, *Senhor* Joaquim,' she sighed.

Suddenly I felt my own daughter's insolent curiosity jumping in my throat – she was so utterly drenched that day – why did she never use the damned parasol? It was an old thing, she was muttering, and a little fragile. The assembled shelterers raised eyebrows at each other. In the end, I was discreet, recommending *Senhor* Alois's services,

'He mends everything, cages, baskets, wheels. A parasol could not be so different.'

Celestina thanked me rush, rush, and was gone. I watched her hobble towards Alois's place. They smiled and conversed as sun punched through the rain clouds. But later, when I'd despatched the last of my sheltering salesmen, the old man was bewildered by talk of repairs. He'd taken no commission from the sweet maker. She had paid a social call, nothing more. He shrugged, clipping the last wires on Dr Limoge's stoat cages.

Our hardy *quituteira*† was becoming a legend. Few resisted her coconut-ice pyramids, and angel *babas*. Soon, she qualified for a bulk discount: a happy arrangement; we prospered together. On occasion, she even left the parasol with us when her load was too cumbersome.

Late one afternoon, Madalena can be seen running out to a cloud of yellow butterflies, their twitching wings mirrored in a steaming puddle. We've just made coffee, and the trees drip musically. I sit sipping on my peroba-wood stool, taking Celestina's parasol on my knee. The closure is a little perished but keeps the canvas panels neatly furled. It hooks over the tiniest mother-of-pearl button. With a mahogany point it's a fine piece of craftsmanship, even if Celestina never uses it for its intended purpose. I return, then, to parcelling up cassava meal.

Madalena is going through a dancing phase. Getting her to the schoolhouse is impossible, for she is always under the mango tree, pirouetting and stamping. She takes twigs in her hands, and spins like some little dervish. I, engrossed in balancing parcels against stout brass weights, am unaware that Madalena has tired of butterflies and spied a fine parasol to embellish her dances. With the stealth of a shadow, my impetuous daughter has taken it and gone slinking outside.

Her dainty fingers stretch the perished closure over the pearly button. The canvas folds fall looser on their spokes. She feels inside for the catch. Her hand loses its way a little against raw edges of fabric. The mechanism is stiff. But with gentle force she pushes open the radial of spokes.

Dust and ancient moth wings fly in her face. She coughs, shrieks; her mischief revealed. I come running and we stand and stare as if at long-forgotten bones. Sun filters through thin ribbons of canvas. Between spokes, the fabric gives way to grotesque, fray-edged holes and green islands of mildew. Rust-stained threads flutter to earth, and the rich dust of years swirls and settles; some on Madalena's nose. The canvas remnants, carefully arranged, had concealed this decrepitude. Rain comes suddenly, battering our roof as Madalena stares in horror at me and then at the ravaged thing in her outstretched fist.

Try and try as we might, we cannot fold the parasol's ragged panels into their former order. Whichever way we close and roll, decay protrudes and dislodged motes and insect fragments pepper the canvas rags.

My look must have been terrible when Celestina reappeared. She was breathless, rain spangling her wiry hair.

'Oh, *Senhor* Jo!' She called. I came from the storeroom. 'I was delayed. I believe we are due for some sunshine.'

She stopped, her gaze falling on my hands. For a long moment, she looked at the rain rippling the puddles. The clay-clouded water mirrored her unfurled shame. Madalena came, we tried to explain, but it was all too bare. The parasol, no sun or rain guard, was but spokes and shreds, and a lot of dust and mould besides. And we knew now why she carried it always closed. It was just a symbol, like a badge or an ostrich-feather hat. I looked at her shoes, cutting wealds in her ankles, and realised she'd no way to pay Alois's repair bill.

Celestina looked at her parasol: her property, holes and all. The threads had been brighter in the days when she'd carried it, intact, over the head of a mistress – days when she herself had been property, no better than an object, a tattered sunshade. Now she carried her no-good parasol to tell the world that she was a free woman who had belongings and that she belonged to *nobody*.

There were no customers then, no need for a lie, but I said it anyway: 'Such a fine object. I would not, perhaps, entrust it to the local craftsmen.'

At last she raised her face to meet mine. She said the words, but she knew that I understood better the graven set of her jaw and her unmoving eyes. She spoke slowly, 'So you would agree, *Senhor*, that it might be better to await the right class of tradesman?' She accepted my feeble offering.

'Yes, Celestina,' I shrugged. 'It may be better to wait.' We breathed out as she turned to leave.

The rains didn't stop until late February. Celestina carried her parasol for many weeks to follow, somehow refurled to suggest ivory entirety. We tut-tutted over it without opening its folds, and she complained of how holes show up just when it rains most, as if the holes were newly appeared. The other customers shook their heads in sympathy, and we agreed that some day she would find the right person to repair it.

Later it occurred to me, with irritation, that our little charade might be bad for *Senhor* Alois's business. Between us we made quite a fuss, implying no craftsman was equal to the infamous parasol. People might think him incapable of simple repairs. But I discovered through Madalena's eavesdropping, that Celestina was his and my best advocate, singing our praises around town.

'O *Senhor* Joaquim is a true connoisseur and *Senhor* Alois so patient with me. He knows how to treat articles of quality.'

And so we settled into a comfortable conspiracy.

The horsemen from the farms now rode into town a little plumper in their saddles from Celestina's cakes. The ladies sent to Rio for exotic ingredients for Celestina's blending. There was a certain air of competition among the big houses to improve their secret teatime recipes – all Celestina's, of course. She worked until she ran out of candles, later on full-moon nights. Gradually, she bought bricks to build a bigger oven and cord with which to knot a hammock.

With the slow way of country girls, the young *senhoritas* of the plantations picked up on the fashion for the new, dainty parasols a little late. In Rio and Petropolis, Dom Pedro II was never seen without his. The royal court and the *Carioca* ladies had fallen for them like a fever the year before, strolling on Copacabana with tiered and lace-frilled models. It was perfect timing for us, behind the Rio folks or not, as Madalena was getting old enough to help *Sr* Alois in the workshop with parasol mending and remodelling, and it kept her away from the farm-boys.

18

Business thrived too for Celestina. Parasol-twirling prome-
nades were fashionably followed, in all the best houses, with
coffee and cake, which vogue ignited even greater competition
between the plantation houses. She baked endlessly, dreaming
up 'exclusive' recipes for each *Senhora*. Alois and I made a deal.
Next time she left the parasol with me, I'd send it over to him
for secret mending. It was our great pleasure to imagine her
surprise at finding the holes mysteriously gone. Until we
realised: she may never open the thing. We even bet on
how long it would take her to discover that she could open
her parasol without shame.

Our plan never came to be. Around that time, she hung up
the parasol and it never rested on our shelf again. Perhaps – who
am I to say why? – respected for her craft as she was, she forgot
the need to carry her badge of freedom.

The parasol was the only thing to disappear from Celestina's
routine. Her crinkled smile – long accustomed to the harsh
elements without benefit of canvas protection – regularly lit up
our shop. She came to sip coffee and talk about business and
how times were good. Thanks to her, we are the proud keepers
of Matilde and Adao, whose speckled eggs provide my morning
omelette and whose infernal squawk wakes me at five each day.

Celestina left no heir, though her birds grieved silently. It was
sullen Maria, gone to collect Dona Marinete's orange-flower
cake, who found her slumped peacefully over a heap of egg-
shells. Don't ask me where my girl gets her notions but
Madalena ran down there while they carried off the body
and found that damn parasol in the shack. Cradled in the
jackfruit tree, she ripped mildewed tatters from spokes and
fed them to the racing river below. The bruise-coloured map of
Celestina's life before Bom Jesus sucked away on the current.
We worked until 3.30 a.m., under Alfonso's put-puttering
lamp, recovering the frame in starchy fabric, fresh as Chantilly
cream.

In blinding January sun, we proceeded, Madalena weeping

silently. From church to river, I strained my old arm holding the parasol over the coffin. Dona Celestina, like never in her life, was laid to rest shaded by the finest parasol.

Glossary

*patroa – mistress/boss
†*quituteira* – maker and street vendor of sweets and savouries

Levitation

John Dodds

When she was four Katya brought back to life a big trout meant for family dinner. She watched the trout curl up and repeatedly slap its tail against the wooden chopping board laid across the sink to catch bloodspill and guts.

Katya had forgotten this until last night's dream, in which she relived the moment as vividly as if it were just happening. She wondered if the dream and the memory had something to do with the lunar eclipse. The night of the red moon – that's what they called it when she was a girl in Poland.

She remembered something else about last night. Warm breath on her neck and the familiar scent of almonds and freshly baked bread. She was awake, but afraid to open her eyes in case the scents would disappear.

Katya had more pressing thoughts on her mind today. Her visit to the doctor especially. But she did not want to dwell on that and so tried instead to concentrate on binding the stems of wildflowers to prepare them for drying. The clothes pulley above the kitchen table already held a dozen upended bouquets snagged on butcher's hooks. Wild roses, willow branches, furze, cornflowers, poppy pods, dandelions, hawthorn twigs and coconut-scented broom, more she could not name in English – nowadays she spoke only English and tried hard not to even think in Polish. The desiccated blooms were sold to gift shops and to regular customers through her mail-order business. The only magic she could perform these days was to re-animate flowers. And even that was just a parlour trick to imbue them with pungent scents they never had in life, distilled from her own special blends of herbs and aromatic oils.

But the door to her childhood had been left ajar by her dreams, and now she remembered that when matka wasn't looking, and only when she wasn't looking, she would levitate things. Cups and saucers. Vegetables. Balls of coloured wool, which she spun in the air like the planets in an orrery. Delight had to be contained, because if she let the joy out, if she giggled or laughed aloud, her concentration would go, and the balls of would tumble to the floor.

Matka had known about the trout all along, of course. 'You never ate fish again,' she told Katya years later. Secrets cannot be kept from mothers.

'Will he come today?' matka said. She never allowed herself to be called 'mum' or 'mother', insisting always upon 'matka'. Let her daughter anglicise herself to 'Kate' if she must. But there should always be respect for the person who pushed you into the world.

'Perhaps he will,' Katya replied but without heeding the oft-repeated refrain. 'What do you think, matka?' She held aloft the completed spray themed in russets, browns and yellows.

The old woman made a dismissive back-handed wave and gave her attention back to solitaire. Jonathan, the part-time gardener, sometimes played cards with her, the unvoiced understanding being that she must win at least half of the time. Katya added a little extra to his wages for this understanding.

Only detritus remained on the scarred oak table. Not enough to make another spray. Katya swept all of it into a plastic refuse sack. In the top of the sack filled with kitchen scraps were several empty Coca-Cola cans. Matka was addicted to Coca-Cola. She bought the stuff by the trayload and once, when Katya helped herself to one, lost her temper and accused her daughter of thieving.

'Sucrose addiction,' the doctor had suggested. 'As bad as heroin, if you ask me.'

'She gets bored.' Katya had felt an irrational need to apologise. Since the stroke, her mother had developed compulsions, of which an obsession with sweet things was one.

Doctor Howard still visited from time to time, though there was nothing more to be done. The paralysis of matka's left side had not stopped her pursuing her passions, however. Card games especially. Matka played solitaire as if she had an opponent, with as much attack and slyness as when she played poker with Jonathan. Her spreads were mounted on a specially made wooden rack, a giant version of the kind used for holding Scrabble tiles. Her mother made Katya think of the court suite: the Queen, King, and Knave who only show their best side, the side that worked. Perhaps the whole royal family had suffered a stroke. Or they might be concealing their other sides for other, more mysterious, reasons.

'No,' matka announced, triumphantly slapping down her final card, completing the game. 'He will come, I am sure of it. Knock on the trunk of the ash tree three times, raise your hands to the heavens, that was how they used to pray in the old days.' As she spoke she scornfully eyed the pair of dwarf apple trees just beyond the window.

The yuletide ritual of knocking on the ash trunk was part of matka's endless fund of myths and stories harking back to the old days. Matka, like some others of her generation, subscribed to two religions, the Christian and the pagan. And at the heart of it all was a belief in the Great Goddess who was a snake and a bee and a bird. A belief that nothing could shake.

'Coca-Cola,' matka demanded. There was no Polish equivalent.

Katya sighed and went to the refrigerator. One shelf was half-filled with the scarlet and silver cans. She popped one open and set it on the table next to her mother's good hand.

'Glass or straw?'

'Straw,' her mother said in Polish and Katya mentally translated into English. Already she was doing a one-handed shuffle of the cards in the rack ready for the next game. 'You see I am busy.'

A glass is too much trouble when you need to concentrate. It meant looking away from the cards.

She glanced up at the wallclock and realised she was twenty minutes late for her appointment. The receptionist in the surgery could be a frosty bitch if one was late for an appointment. Well, too bad.

She slid open the cutlery drawer and rummaged among the unsorted piles of knives and forks and spoons until her fingers alighted on the hard green plastic straw with the loop at the top. Plonking the straw into the Coke can she said, 'I'm going shopping now. Do you need anything while I'm out?'

Matka, not looking up, said, 'Doughnuts. The ones with jam in.'

'But you know what the doctor—' It was useless to protest. 'Okay, fine, then. Doughnuts.'

She wished today were Wednesday. Apart from Jonathan, only her painting workshop gave her some respite from taking care of her mother. While Simon was alive, at least in the first few years of their marriage, she believed love was all encompassing and had room in it for difficult times, difficult people. Now it felt like a brittle rubber band that showed cracks when stretched even a little.

She left the house without another word and climbed into her blue Volkswagen Beetle. Once a week, Katya would take her mother into town in the car, for window-shopping, or a stroll in the park on warm days. Matka was not as enthusiastic about the car as her daughter, insisting it was far too small and uncomfortable to ride in.

'Why do I need a bigger car when it's only the two of us?'

'You have money, Katyinka. Spend it, why don't you?'

Matka often tried to encourage her to squander the money

Simon had left her in his will. But, apart from buying the Beetle, the only luxury she had allowed herself, she could not bring herself to spend any of it, and the funds had lain untouched in a building society account for nearly three years.

She started up the engine. She was not sure she felt ready for what the doctor was going to tell her.

Jonathan was in the living room when she returned. He wasn't due today. Nodding hello, he indolently shuffled the pack of cards. If he must be here, she thought, why isn't he out in the garden working? Matka, across the table, dozed in her wheelchair, a fan of late-morning sunshine across her face.

She offered tea and he answered, in that perpetually amused tone of his, 'Sounds good.' Matka had awakened by the time tea was brewed, and she asked for some, too. Katya brought her a glass in a silver holder, with slices of lemon on a saucer, and a jam doughnut to go with it. Matka always drank her tea Russian-style, black, sipped through a sugar cube held between her teeth. Jonathan drank his tea the same way, and had told Katya he now preferred this tea to coffee, which he had drunk to excess in any case.

They drank in silence until matka exclaimed, 'Did I hear the door?' She turned to face her daughter. 'Answer it, why don't you!'

'There's no-one there,' Katya replied.

'Jonathan,' her mother insisted, seeking an ally, 'Jonathan, you go and answer it, there's a good boy.' She said this in English. Jonathan was the only one she addressed in English. After all, she needed English to successfully bluff at card games.

Jonathan nodded and got up. Katya followed him into the hallway.

'Must you do everything she says?' She was irritated by the way he obeyed her mother's every whim.

He smiled and drew her towards him. 'I'm not doing it for her.'

She shrugged him off.

'Hey,' he said, 'What's wrong? What are you angry about?'

She sighed. 'I saw the doctor.'

He pulled away. She felt him withdraw in a way that was more than physical.

'And?'

Matka's voice from the living room said, 'Who is it?'

'No-one, matka,' Katya said. 'No-one.' And to Jonathan, 'Later.'

The afternoon was interminable, Jonathan playing game after game of cards with matka until she grew tired and asked to be helped to bed for her nap.

She and Jonathan often used this time to make love.

Sometimes, in her room, on her bed in the house her mother owned, she welcomed his dry, warm lips on hers, or pressing into her throat. If she closed her eyes she imagined that his body smelled of almonds, his breath warm and yeasty like freshly baked bread. But if she opened them he smelled only of himself, a smell she could not quite describe, subdued as it often was by cologne. Matka sleeping in the room below them imposed its own limitations, yet made their secretive fucking all the sweeter.

Once matka was asleep, they tiptoed upstairs. Jonathan pushed her backwards onto the bed. Hurriedly, he unbuttoned her blouse, put a hand inside her brassière and cupped her breast and squeezed. She could respond if she wished, but it was not what she wanted.

Once again she resisted the advance, and pushed against his chest. 'No. Not now. I need you to listen now.'

He drew back as if he had been burned. She sensed the germ of ill-temper as he leaned his back against the headboard. He reached out for the pack of cigarettes Katyka kept on the bedside table, lit one and puffed at it a couple of times.

She looked into his eyes. And as she looked she saw how little warmth they contained. Strange how she had never seen that before. It was a look she had first seen years ago, in the eyes of her father when she was a girl. Expressionless. Cold. And if there was an emotion in her father's eyes at all there was only one it could be: rapaciousness.

Her throat tightened. She had to speak. But she was afraid. 'What? What is it, my love?'

'Don't call me that. You know you don't love me.'

He shrugged. This had been a mannerism of her father's, too. Why hadn't she seen it before?

Father had devoured her with his greed and robbed her of childhood.

She felt in those times like Golden Curl, a fairy-tale that matka used to tell her. Of all the tales, the stories of fox women, werewolves and the rest, the story of Golden Curl was the one she never forgot. It was the tale of the little girl who could not speak the secret of what she had seen in the hundredth room, cursed by the wood witch, even when her silence caused the death of her baby brother and her husband.

Jonathan said, 'Aren't you going to tell me what's on your mind?' He paused. Then, rather reluctantly she thought, added, 'What did the doctor say?'

She nodded. 'I'm not pregnant after all.'

She looked into his face then. Hoping for a change in him. Hoping that he would see how wrong he had been, and see that everything could change for the better. But in the end she saw no more than she had expected. Relief. She saw relief.

Jonathan's kinship with her father now gelled in her mind. Instead of feeling hurt, she was oddly reassured by this. It was familiar. Something she knew how to survive. She looked away from his face and down at his hands and saw the traces of dark soil beneath his gardener's fingernails, imagined the loamy earth curled in his very fingerprints. She wondered why she had ever let those hands touch her.

Rebuttoning her blouse, she stood up and said, 'You'd better go.'

Jonathan knew better than to argue. In the hallway he tried to kiss her goodbye, but she turned her head aside.

She felt good about one thing, though. Lying about the baby.

As she closed the door a wave of tiredness enveloped her. She needed to rest and so decided to go to bed. The staircase rising above her wavered, as if she had been crouching and had tried to stand too quickly. The stairs seemed to rush away from her to a far horizon. Her head felt gigantic, the top of the stairs tiny, too small even for a human foot. It was a form of migraine, she knew, but it always took her back to the half-wakenings she'd had as a child, sitting up in bed with a start, the perspectives of her bedroom distorted as though viewed through the wrong end of a telescope. She would cry for her matka and matka would always come to rescue her. The tiny door of her bedroom would open and her tiny matka would enter, looming larger as she drew closer and closer to the bed. Matka would give her a glass of water to drink. The water always dissolved the vision. Her fear took longer to dissolve. She would always imagine that, without the glass of water her matka gave her, the world would stay the way it was, horribly distorted like the reflection in a convex mirror.

Once she had closed the bedroom door behind her, she lay down on the bed and tried to slow her breathing. She closed her eyes to subdue the onset of panic. If she saw nothing the fear was less. Arpeggios of blackbird song drifted through the window and she rolled onto her side, cradling her belly with her hands.

After a time she must have slept. A touch on her back awakened her. The flat of a hand, its shape and texture and temperature as familiar as her own voice. And there was something else, too. The scent of almonds and freshly baked bread.

If she turned around she would break the spell, but it no longer mattered that she could not see him. All she cared about was that he was there.

'I betrayed you,' she said, fighting tears.

'No,' he said. 'You could never do that.'

'Are you really here? Have your really come back to me?' Perhaps she spoke. Perhaps she only thought the words.

'For today,' he said.

And she realised that it did not matter if it was only for a day. Or only for an hour.

Will be come today? Is this what matka had meant? Katya had grown so accustomed to her mother's eccentricities that she had stopped questioning what she meant when she said certain things over and over.

He kissed her softly on the back of the neck. He said, 'Your mother knows things. Things you forgot.'

'I didn't forget,' she said. 'I just . . . My father stole them from me. The possibilities. The magic.'

'These things can't be stolen. Unless they are forgotten completely, they never really disappear.'

'I'm carrying your child,' she said, but no answer came other than a soft kiss on the back of her neck. And presently her eyes grew heavy and a long, deep sigh drew her down and down into a profound sleep.

A voice wakened her. Matka's voice, calling from her room.

'I'm hungry, girl,' matka said, as she helped her into the wheelchair. 'Pasta, I think. And how about some wine?'

Katya said, 'Do you really think wine is a good idea?'

'Pah! What else would I have with pasta? Lemonade?'

At least she hasn't asked for Coca-Cola, Katya thought, as her mother set the wheelchair in motion and steered a course for the table.

Katya removed the card rack so that she could lay a tablecloth and set the table for dinner. Picking up the pack of cards, she paused and, handing them to her mother, said, 'Show me a trick, like you used to. In the old days.' The words were out of her mouth before she realised she had asked this in Polish.

Matka looked solemn. It was a sign that she was trying not to smile.

Deftly, she began to shuffle the cards one-handed, fingers and thumb weaving the deck into a new configuration. Then she placed the deck face-down on the tabletop and fanned them out.

'Now,' she said in a challenging tone, 'pick a card.'

Peaches

Lorn Macintyre

B ecause of the cliffs, the harbour at the end of the mile-long headland could only be reached from the sea. The Vikings had used it as a raiding base, cutting slipways into the rock for their galleys and leaving behind a harsh name. A thousand years later these slipways were still in use by the MacKinnons, who inhabited the solitary house. No-one knew on the island how long the family had lived there, but it was certainly well outwith living memory.

There was no possibility of bringing an electric cable along the headland. The house was lit by paraffin lamps, and the fire was peat, which the twin brothers cut on a moor further north. They brought the fuel supply round by boat, tossing the black sods to their sister, Flora, who stacked them against the side of the house. She was dressed the same as her two brothers, in blue dungarees and wellingtons, and her hair was tied back with a piece of rope. Despite her appearance, she was a good-looking woman, with high cheekbones and a determined mouth.

Duncan and Alasdair shot their nets most days. They laid their glittering catches in boxes which they nailed up and took round in the launch to the town, to send south. When the cheques came back in payment they took them round to the bank in the town, where they went once a month for their provisions.

The three of them stride along Main Street in their dark oilskins and souwesters, the sister in the middle. They never buy any meat, because they butcher their own sheep. They never buy the bread that comes from the mainland in oily wrapping, already sliced, because she bakes their own. They buy a sack of flour, a special order, which Alasdair lifts onto his back to take down to the boat.

Flora is looking at the shelves. She would love to ask for a small tin of peaches, because she tasted them years before, at a school treat. She remembers their rosy yellowness, and how she spooned up the syrup. But her brothers wouldn't allow her to buy peaches because they never have sweet things. If she wants biscuits, she can bake them in the temperamental oven that is cool on days when the wind is from the sea.

The month's supply of pipe tobacco is stacked in tins on the counter. They buy a bottle of whisky, but this is strictly for medicinal purposes, for a toddy if one of them has a cold. The boxes of provisions are carried down to the boat, and they go back along for a barrel of paraffin, which they kick along the street, bouncing it down the steps to the boat, where it's roped to a seat.

The provisions were unloaded and she returned to her chores, using the oven when the wind wasn't against her. They returned to casting their nets, sitting at their supper in their seaboots hanging from their waists, talking incessantly in Gaelic about the sea, as if it was a temperamental woman. They had many Gaelic words for its treachery, for the blows it could deal you when your back was turned to it.

They nailed their catches in dripping boxes, amassing in the bank a sum of money that they would never spend, because their only extravagance was the boat and the nets. They would never exchange the boat, and the three of them mended the nets carefully, sitting on the shore, working their faultless Gaelic into the membrane under the towering volcanic terraces.

She was sick of the sound of the sea, sick to death of eating salmon and mutton. Sick, too, of Gaelic. She was planning this other life, waiting for her opportunity. One afternoon two men came ashore in a rubber runabout.

'Where are you going?' she asked in uncertain English as they filled the blue container at the outside tap that also served the house.

They told her that they had been cruising among the Western Isles for a fortnight and were now returning to the mainland.

'Can you give me a lift?' she asked.

They waited until she emerged with the brown suitcase with metal at the corners that Alasdair had bought when he had had to go to hospital for an essential operation thirty years before.

She sat on the deck of the boat, the breeze filling the sails above her. The man at the helm had a chart spread out before him as he negotiated the treacherous reefs her brothers knew so well. She had never been to the mainland before and was surprised at the size of the town.

She had taken a hundred pounds from the tin on the mantelpiece. The first night of her freedom she stayed in a bed and breakfast on the seafront, with a woman who spoke Gaelic and who questioned her closely on where she came from.

'I don't recognise the dialect.'

Flora had always been taught never to give anything away at school about her home circumstances, though girls in the playground had called after her that her family were squatters. So she avoided the question and told the woman that she was looking for work.

'What kind of work?'

'As a waitress.'

'Well, the Esplanade Hotel is always looking for staff. Mind you, they work you very hard. If you're going for an interview I would advise you to wear something more suitable.'

Next morning Flora went and bought the cheapest dress, with a subdued print.

'What experience have you had of dining-room service?' the smartly dressed manager of the Esplanade asked this dowdy creature in the ill-fitting dress, with shoes that seemed to belong on a much older woman.

'I worked in an hotel before,' Flora lied, desperate for a job.

'Silver service?'

She nodded, though she didn't know what the phrase meant. She was taken up to a room under the slates she would share with three other maids. When she tied the apron round her hips and went downstairs to the dining room she was lost. The only table she had set at home was a basic one, a knife and fork at each place. She stood watching as the other girls laid out the sweet knife and fork alongside.

The bus tour were in their seats even before the reverberations of the gong had ceased. Flora laid before them the lukewarm plates of packet soup, and brought the extra slices of bread that they demanded. The head waitress gave her a ticking off, telling her that they were only allowed one slice of bread per person.

The heat in the plates didn't bother Flora, because she had been used to lifting out tins of bread from the temperamental oven at home. But while she was serving the steak pie and vegetables she tripped and tipped the meal into a lap. The stout woman was on her feet, raging that it was the only clean dress she had with her. The head waitress had to come across, to apologise and promise that the hotel would get it cleaned, express, at their expense.

The dinner was even more complicated, because some of them ordered wine, and Flora poured it over the cloth instead of into the glass.

'You haven't done any waitressing before,' the head waitress confronted her when the guests had departed to watch a Highland show in the lounge.

'I need the job,' Flora pleaded.

The head waitress took pity on her and gave her a lesson on laying out cutlery and serving wine. Flora began to feel more confident. In the evening, after she had finished work, she would walk up the hill and sit on a bench, looking across to the mountains of her island. In the first few days she felt homesick for the harbour with its incisions in the rock, and for her dour brothers, but now there was a sense of liberation, of joy. One night she went out with the girls to a dance, and found that she had a sense of rhythm.

The wine waiter from another hotel asked to walk her home. His name was Aldo and he told her that he came from an island called Sicily, where the heat was intense.

She let him kiss her in a doorway. It was a tender moment and they arranged to go to the cinema.

She had her hair styled and bought new clothes from her first month's wages. If they were both off on Friday evening, she and Aldo went to the dancing. He taught her to waltz, his hand on her spine.

He was teaching her some words of Italian, and in return she taught him how to say good morning and good night in Gaelic, and also to say, 'It's raining,' because he was always complaining about the weather.

'How you say my love in Gaelic?' he asked.

She hesitated. '*Mo ghaol.*'

She had to pronounce it several times before he got it right.

'I take you to Sicily with me,' he promised.

'*Mo gul,*' he repeated, looking into her eyes.

One evening, a man from the tour was flirting with her as she put the salmon salad in front of him. She was bringing him the horseradish sauce when she felt a strong pair of arms encircling her from behind. She was screaming and kicking as her brother in his seaboots carried her out of the dining room, among the stunned tables, down the steps and across the esplanade to the slipway where the other twin was waiting with the launch. The people from the tour were crowding the windows to watch as the launch roared away with the struggling woman in the bottom.

She was watched every minute of the day by the brothers in case she absconded again. They wouldn't leave her alone at the house while they were out fishing, so they took her with them in the launch. She was expected to help with hauling in the net, and when they got back home, while they boxed the salmon for despatch on the boat, she prepared the supper.

When they went to town for provisions she walked between them and was never let out of their sight. One of them went into the chemist's with her when she bought her supply of sanitary towels. They made her sleep between them and took turns in having sex with her. There was no tenderness, and she didn't resist because then they would have used force. She thought of Aldo, holding her so carefully on the dance floor. She thought of the heat and brightness of Sicily, where he was returning to at the end of the season.

A year after she had been brought back home Alasdair was eating his supper when he suddenly stood up, the cutlery still in his fists, staring at the door as if a ghost had just come in.

'What's wrong?' his twin shouted.

He pitched forward across the table, his face cut by the broken plate. When they laid him on the floor and opened his shirt there was no heartbeat. She turned towards the stove with a smile while Duncan was weeping over the corpse. That afternoon they took the launch round to the town. She had the feet, the other brother the head as they carried it up the slipway to the undertaker's store, where Dr Murdoch wrote the death certificate. The coffin came off that evening's ferry, and they took it back with them in the launch to their habitation, carrying it like a fishbox into the house, where it lay between two chairs. Flora went about her work, cooking and cleaning, as if it wasn't in the room.

But when she set down a cup of tea for her surviving brother on the coffin he swept it to the floor, where it smashed round her feet.

'Have some respect,' he told her savagely.

'How can I have respect for him, the way he treated me?' she answered with equal anger. 'I'm glad the bastard's in there.'

The next blow sent her across the room, and she almost staggered into the fire.

'Don't think you'll get away,' he told her.

'Oh I'll get away. One way or another, I'll get away,' she vowed, her Gaelic magnificent in her vehemence.

Murchison, the minister, said that it was the bleakest funeral he had ever been asked to officiate at, with only the brother and sister at the grave in the remote cemetery by the sea, the inscriptions on the stones eroded by the weather.

When Duncan went out fishing he took her with him, and would never turn his back on her in case she pushed him into the sea. He knew by the hatred in her expression that she was capable of anything.

She was his slave. He continued to use her in bed, and sat at the table, waiting for the plate of mutton or fish to be put in front of him. When they went round the headland to the town for provisions he wouldn't let her out of his sight for a second.

He was twelve years her senior and he was getting slower. The biting chill of the ocean had got into a hip. He walked with pain, but wouldn't consider going round to see Dr Murdoch. It got so bad that he could no longer get on top of her. When he tied up the launch at its moorings for the night he took a vital part out of the engine, because he knew that he wouldn't be able to catch her if she ran out.

The arthritis was in his hands now, and they began to look like the barnacles he and his brother used to scrape from the bottom of the launch when they beached it every few years, to paint the bottom with anti-fouling. During the night he cried out in pain.

'You'll need to nail up the boxes now,' he told her because he couldn't hold the hammer.

'If I do that you're putting the bank account into my name as well.'

'So that you can run away?' he confronted her.

'So that I have something to live on when you're gone.'

'I'll outlive you,' he told her.

The next time they were round in the town, he put the bank account in her name as well.

Then he couldn't manage to shave, but knew that he daren't put his cut-throat razor in her hands, so he grew a grey beard, which made him look even more stern and biblical.

'Here's your supper,' she said one night, putting the plate on the floor.

'Why are you doing this?' he moaned.

'Because of the way you and that bastard treated me over the years. An animal wouldn't use its own kind the way you've both used me. I had a chance of happiness on the mainland and you took me back to this hellish place. I could have been in a place called Sicily by now, in the sunshine, instead of this godforsaken place, in the rain. Come and get it,' she told him, pushing the plate with her foot as if he was a dog.

'I'm sorry,' he whined.

'I put a curse on both of you. I prayed that he would die, and that you would suffer,' she told him, pushing the plate again.

He came across the flagstones on his ruined knees and crouched, tearing the fish with his hands because he could no longer hold a knife and fork.

'And your tea,' she said, pouring it into a bowl beside the plate.

He tried to lift it between his ruined hands, but it smashed on the flagstones. He cried out in pain during the night, and one morning he couldn't get out of bed.

'I'm not taking the nets out,' she told him. 'You're going to have to go into the home in the town.'

'Please keep me here,' he pleaded. 'I'm sorry the way I treated you. I'll make it up to you, Flora.'

'You make it up to me? Look at the state of you. If we had a dog like that we would put it out of its misery.'

'Then put me out of my misery,' he pleaded, pointing to the cupboard where they kept the gun for shooting the seals that interfered with the nets.

'You're not getting out of it so easily, like that other bastard. You're going into the home in the town.'

'Please keep me here, Flora. I want to die here, in my own bed.'

'You'll die in the home, knowing nobody,' she told him. 'You'll never hear Gaelic again and never see the sea again.'

When the launch swept into the town he was lying in the bottom. She phoned the doctor from the kiosk, and the ambulance came and took him up to the home. Then she walked in her flapping oilskins to the bank and asked to see the manager.

'How much is in the account?' she asked.

'Ninety thousand.'

'I want to withdraw a thousand.'

She went along to the shop and bought a big tin of peaches and a tin opener. She stood at the railing, eating the rosy yellow fruit with her fingers, then drinking the rich syrup.

Before first light next morning the passing trawler saw the fire at the house on the headland. An hour later, the launch came into the harbour. She was wearing a dress in the blowy day. She carried the old suitcase to the bus. The bank manager knew that she was somewhere in Glasgow, because that was where she was drawing money from the account. Within a year there was very little left in it. When her brother died in the home they tried to contact her, but the letter came back. 'Gone abroad.'

The Carntyne Elephant

Frances Sessford

Train carriages are rank with the smell of early mornings and cigarettes. Or the old ones are, the ones on this neglected line. It's a comfortable smell. It lifts me back in an instant. As if I were to bang my heels together and say, *There's no place like home.* It's jigging on my mum's bony knee to the rhythm; it's the hurl to primary school and the sun on warm desks; it's going to my aunt's house and looking but not touching; these familiar journeys before the new school, and buses and fights and doubts. It's sunlight filtering through the smoke above an old man's head, and me trying to catch it.

This night the train hums patiently at the platform. I select an empty carriage, but as I turn to sit it trembles. Two neds swagger through like drunken wooden puppets, arms dangling in the sleeves of outsize baseball jackets, feet dragging in scuffed trainers. They begin a game, rushing from one seat to another then another, giggling with no humour when they touch each one with their skinny, hyperactive arses. They smell unwashed.

'Haw big man, 've ye got a fag, haw big man, whit's the time, haw big man, is this the right train fur Queen Street, haw big man, haw big man, HAW Jinky. BEAT IT, ya fanny . . .'

They roll off the seat and start fighting on the floor until the train heaves free of the station and rocks them apart. The bigger one rolls to my feet. I see his skeletal ankle poking out from under the frayed hem of his jeans. Blue veins spider through his

41

white skin; I can't stop myself seeing the downy hair. I can never not see.

They go away. I'm tired after the game. I need to be awake for the third stop from here, but I trust that I'll wake up at the right place. He'll be difficult to spot in the dark, but I know that solemn shape so well, I'll make him out all right. What will I ask for tonight? I lean my head back, stretch out my aching legs. I drowse. Memories roll like old cine film. I'm peeking around the door of a room bursting with women. In the heat, the smell of tired, unshod feet mingles with perfume. Beads clack along with nods of sympathy and disapproval. Clothes in all shapes and colours are being pulled and fitted and smoothed. I creep into fond laughter and pull at something soft and glittery in my mother's lap. *Me too, Mummy, me too.* She drapes it around my shoulders. I begin to sing. They all laugh, some of them have their hands clasped at their throats. They think I'm being wee Jimmy Osmond. *He's only seven, isn't he good?* I fling my head back to strike a pose, but I crack it off the sideboard and start howling instead.

But I was being her. When I was wee we had a picture of Diana Ross in our room. We'd got her out of one of our mother's papers. My brother had stuck her up on his side, but I was sure she would rather have been on mine. Sometimes I would sneak over to his side and speak to her. As we got older we stopped seeing her and the space for her grew less and less. But we could never take her *down.* And, years later, when the room was mine and at nights the dark squeezed me till I panicked, she was there with me.

One day I came back to help my mother decorate our old room. Diana had been ripped to the floor, lying with the old *Beanos,* the jigsaws with pieces missing and the board games with lost instructions. It was all bagged up in black plastic and thrown away. I did it myself. After all, it was only paper.

I jolt back to the carriage. My head has bounced off the seat rail and it snaps up. I cringe, wondering if I've cried aloud. But the noise is only the train screeching to a halt at Shettleston. The sky has cleared after rain and the clouds scud low, dragging their orange underbellies over the high flats. My eyes want to close again, but they're flicked by the glimmer of gold between the window and the carriage door. Then they pull wide open when she steps on from nowhere.

She wasn't on the platform as the train came in, I'm sure. She must have twirled out of the wind, just as the door opened. The wind has died, all its strength spent on blowing her here from the past. Massive crusts of gold barb her ears, the slicked lips gleam even in the carriage's weak light. It is Diana of the picture. She stalks through the hush to my seat. Has she come for me? Why didn't I save her, why do I prefer boys to girls? Panic flips my heart, its reluctant thump matching the stride of her heels. I cringe under her shadow and close my eyes. The train sways off again into Glasgow's darkness.

When I open my eyes again there is a guy in drag sitting across from me. He considers me with eyes like black moons.

I don't want to stare but he is everywhere. When I look at the floor, ten vicious red toenails snigger up at me; when I look out of the window black tendrils of his hair snake into the corner of my eye; and when I try to gaze into the distance without seeing, some cheap scent eddies to me with every lurch of the train.

I give up avoiding him and take on the toes. They are delicate and hairless, not like mine, bound tight against the high-heeled soles by shiny black straps. The very tips of the soles are scuffed and tatty, as if tiny mice have nibbled them.

'D'you like that colour?'

He raises one feathered eyebrow. I just shrug and look back to the window. He balances a cigarette between two long, red-ended fingers, poised in mid-air. His foot traces a lazy rhythm.

'D'you mind if I smoke?'

'No.'

'Thanks. I know you're not supposed to here, but it's late. Who's going to know?'

'I suppose.'

'I'm Marilyn. What's your name?'

Marilyn. Not Diana.

'Martin.'

'Sounds a bit the same, doesn't it?'

'I suppose.'

'You suppose? What else do you suppose?'

I'm floundering. He is practised.

I've forgotten about the other two. Their pointed faces appear, pressed to the glass between the compartments. They begin to call out.

'Heh you, ur you a man ur a lassie?'

'Heh you, you're wearin' lipstick 'n' stuff. Ur you a poof?'

I stare at the toenails again. I watch them oscillate through the smoke, the foot jerking like a bad-tempered cat's tail.

'Haw, big man, is that yur fancy wummin wi' ye?'

'Haw, ma mate fancies you by the way.'

They are getting brave. The smaller one strikes out right into the gangway and comes up to us.

'Heh you, ur you a poof?'

Marilyn glares into his face.

'Naw. I'm Charles Bronson. Now beat it, ya wee shite.'

The ned runs back. There are whispers.

'Cheeky wee bastards, it's their beds they should be in.' He sighs it, as if he is commenting on the colour of the sky. He is nonchalant like a model, twirling a strand of black hair over and over through his fingers. Then suddenly the lock unravels and flies through the air with the rest.

'Haw! Gie's that back, ya wee bastard.'

They toss the wig to each other, dodging up and down the carriage with it. Marilyn is on his feet, charging back and forward between them. The small one ducks out from under his flailing arms and runs down the length of the carriage with the wig trailing from his head like Medusa. Pins dangle and rattle round his chin.

44

Marilyn tanks down the carriage towards him.

'Ah said, GIE'S IT!!'

But just then the train squeals at another stop and the doors bounce open. The pair jump down from separate doors. They are gone. Their glottal cackles echo back as they scurry up the banking opposite the train. Marilyn's glory bobs once, silhouetted against the sodium-lit night sky, and disappears.

The train doors close. He flings himself into his seat and huffs.

'That bloody syrup cost me a fortune, so it did.'

I try to look sympathetic in a non-committal way. I glance down at the red toenails again. They seem to have lost a bit of their bravado.

'You might get it back,' I offer.

'Are you kidding? I won't get so much as the pins back.'

'It might get handed in.'

'Handed in where?'

'I don't know. To a police station . . .'

He snorted. 'It'll end up on the dump.'

'Maybe someone will find it and put it on him.'

'Who?'

'Him.'

I nod out of the window to our left. The train has stopped while some points crunch into position. We have come level with the Elephant. I've passed him hundreds of times, but the train has never stopped. I've never been this close.

'What in God's name is that?'

I'm silent for a moment. I've never actually told anyone.

'It's the Carntyne Elephant.'

My voice is coming from miles away.

'The what?'

Did he not hear me or do I just sound like a prick? I say it a bit louder.

'The Carntyne Elephant.'

'The CARNTYNE Elephant. Oh, right. Is it official?'

I revert to a shrug. But then I think, *No, there's more to say.*

'He's been there for as long as I can remember. He used to be pink but they painted him back to grey. He's always there. Have you never noticed him before?'

'No. I've never been on this train before.'

'You can wish on him if you like.' I try to fling the words away, turning to look at the Elephant. He stands in a mesh compound, next to a Portakabin, with only broken concrete slabs and pipes for company. He looks solemn, but not abandoned. He's had me for company all these years, and who knows how many others? All those wishes. He peers in at us like an Indian god, benign, enigmatic, a keeper of all the secrets of the universe.

'He's cute,' says Marilyn. 'Do you think I could wish for my wig back?'

He says it so flippantly that I glance to the Elephant, almost in apology. The Elephant's expression doesn't change. He looks straight through the wire mesh, contemplating us. His little golden eyes are wise and knowing, twinkling through their veil of rain. He does not judge. He does not care. You'll get your wish if you really want it.

'You're wishing, aren't you?' says Marilyn. 'Tell me what you're wishing for.'

I mean to deny. But the train lurches, making it blurt up from my belly and through my mouth. 'I've asked him to make me more like you.'

He flings back his head and laughs. I am mortified. Even the Elephant, who knows it all anyway, even he must think I'm daft. I glance out to him again, but he is gone. Marilyn's Adam's apple shakes as he laughs but the movement looks more like the tremble of small, dry sobs.

His head falls forward.

'Do you know what my other names are?' he drawls. 'Paki Madge. The Trash Mahal. Back Passage to India.' He says them with deliberation. Nothing I haven't heard at football, in the pub. There, I switch off. Here, it is too close and I flinch.

'Do you think that's funny?' he asks.

His voice is like cats' claws on silk. I can't look him in the eye. My own voice is hoarse.

'Who calls you that?' Like I have to ask.

He shrugs. 'Guys in the street, neds, the other trannies, anyone that likes. Sometimes I think it's funny.'

He lets out a long breath and sits forward in his seat. I lift my eyes. There are fine webs of lines around his eyes and open pores under the heavy make-up.

'So, why do you want to be like me?'

I look out to the dark. 'Because I'm sick of being me.'

'That's not much of a reason.'

'I'm a fraud.'

'Who isn't?'

'You.'

He laughs again, another bitter deluge.

'No? I dress up as something I'm not.'

'It's not the same thing,' I protest.

'It is. It's exactly the same. What you want is courage, Martin. And belief.'

'Is that all?'

'It's not a lot when you think of the alternatives. Round the bend. Or in the jail.'

I sit, seeing nothing for a long time. The train is slowing in the Queen Street tunnel. The carriage emerges into the bright station interior. I gather my bag to me. I look to the door, then to him, then back to the door.

'I need to go. This is my stop.'

He sits back and smiles.

'Okay.'

There is nothing I can think of to say. So I step from the musty warmth to the cold hard shine of the platform. I move with the rest of the late-night travellers, trudging to the ends of their days.

I hear a voice behind me. He is leaning from the carriage

window. The train has started to move and he draws level with me. He waves and smiles into my face.

He is passing. He is past. He shouts back: 'Compared to living in someone else's skin, it's a piece of piss, Martin.'

He is gone. The tunnel is black.

I wave.

I will wish on the Elephant for him.

Unrestricted

Carol McKay

He wis like a wean playin the Playstation. Ah wis gettin flung aw ower the place every time he turned a coarner. Ye could even hear the motor screamin. *Stoap it, William,* Ah wis squealin, bit he wisnae listnin, jist birlin his hauns roon wi the steerin wheel an stampin his feet fae wan fit-pedal tae the other. Ah'd never seen him that excited. His nostrils wis flarin like a horse at the racin an he kept lickin his lips.

Then he stretched out his leg when we were out ae the traffic an soon we were powerin through the country, like in a tunnel ae hedges. Ah didnae really pay attention – Ah wis mair interested in William.

Ah'd never seen him that excited.

'Here's yer jaiket.'

Ah held out the blazer his ma had bought him fae the heart shop. It was black wi shiny buttons, bit the middle wan wis missin, so Ah'd cut aff the other two an sewn oan three black yins Ah'd took fae ma ain. Ah'd no be needin it fur a coupla weeks, an Ah could sew them back oan when there wis mair chance ae it fittin me again. Ah left the gold wans oan the sleeves fur him. Like cufflinks they were. Like James Bond or the Saint, somebody swanky or – suave, that wis it.

He didnae take it, or take his eyes aff the screen.

'Are ye takin it or whit?'

'Aye, right,' he said finally, an reached out his hand, feelin blind fur the jaiket. He tucked it beside him oan the bed.

'Ah jist ironed that!'

Ah hud tae judder the ironin board forward so's Ah could get by. The room wis that cramped an every week Ah wis crampin it mair wi ma belly. Ah lifted the blazer an hung it oan a hanger ower the wardrobe door.

'Ah want ye tae look smart the morra.'

William snorted, an kept his eyes oan the Playstation.

'How?' he says. 'It's no as if Ah'm gettin married.'

'Ha, ha.' Ah carried oan wi the ironin. The room reverberated wi the sounds ae cars revvin on a startin grid. 'Maybe they'll no be too hard on ye if ye turn up smart.'

Three big thuds interrupted me. Ah felt them vibratin under ma feet. It wis her doonstairs.

William swore an paused his game. The room wis that quiet ye could hear the slap an hiss ae the steam as Ah ironed his shirt. He jist sat, watchin me.

'Kerry, it's no gonnie make any difference how Ah turn up. They're gonnie pit me away – get used tae it.'

Then fae doonstairs we heard the sound ae that baby cryin. It made me think ae mines.

'Don't say that.'

Ah went back ower tae the wardrobe an hung his pale-green shirt ower his jaiket so's it wouldnae get creased.

'Get us that while ye're up, hen, will ye?'

He wis pointin at the Playstation box. Ah squatted doon tae get it: openin ma legs so's the wean wouldnae get too compressed. Ah handed him the box an he pulled out the instructions, lettin his lips finger the words as he wis readin. Back at the ironin board, Ah started packin a wee case wi a clean nightie, ma grey trackie bottoms an two wee white an lavender baby-gros.

'Look,' Ah says tae him, haudin up a wee lemon-coloured teddy.

He glanced up. 'Cool.' He looked back doon at the paper, an up at me. 'What's that?'

Ah checked where his finger wis pointin. 'Unrestricted.'

The teddy wis soft tae the touch, an wore a dead cute wee ribbon. 'Ma da sent it fur the wean comin.'

Ah fished out ma scissors an cut aff the tag. Ah held it fur a minit, anen Ah drapped it in the bin. Ah packed the wee teddy back in its poke an pit it in the middle ae my trackie stuff tae keep it good. There wis another thump fae doonstairs; the sound ae the man shoutin, an the baby cryin louder.

It goat on William's nerves: that's why Ah hated it. He wriggled tae the edge ae the bed. 'See that fuckin wean!' he says tae me. Directin his voice towards the flair as if the wean could hear him, he shouts, 'Shut up!' anen shakes his heed.

Ah wis foldin a knitted shawl. It was white, an there wis sworly patterns, an Ah could feel an smell the fabric softener the wummin in the heart shop said she'd used tae freshen it. Good as new, she'd said. Good as new for a new wee baby. Ah looked at William an spoke tae him quietly.

'Maybe they'll gie you wan ae they tags.'

Ah couldnae believe the wey he looked it me.

'Tags? That'll be fuckin right.'

Ah felt ma heart stound, aw caged up somewhere inside ma ribs above the baby.

William's eyes were fierce when he wis angry an his lips grew thin. 'Only time anybiddy'll get a tag on me'll be roon ma big toe. When Ah'm deed!'

Ah hated the heartburn; Ah swalleyed it doon hard. An ma hauns shook: Ah wisnae brave like he wis.

'Whit aboot me?' Ah says tae him.

He glared at me. 'Whit aboot you? You're no goin inside.' He slung the game box an aw the papers tae the bottom ae the bed.

Ah knew it wisnae fair. Bit Ah didnae know how tae tell him that.

'Ah'm nine months pregnant, William. Whit aboot the wean?'

He shook his heed an looked at me. His nose wis aw sneered up. 'Ah don't get it,' he said.

'Whit aboot me an the wean?'

The room wis that quiet noo. We were frozen, like the characters in wan ae his games.

'Ye kin stey here. Ma ma'll no throw ye oot.'

Ah slammed doon the ironin board. 'That's no the point.'

'Well what is the point then, cause you've fuckin lost me,' he says.

Ah jist felt totally miserable. Ah wis that big, an ma belly wis that tight, an Ah looked roon the wee room we were in, wi his tatty pictures ae that skinny cunt Kylie an the telly oan the chair an the muck aw roon the skirtin board. Anen Ah heard the wean doonstairs greetin again.

'Ah'm stuck wi it fur life, amn't Ah?' Ah says.

Anen his face went aw soft like a wee boy's, an he patted his knee fur me. 'Come here, hen,' he says.

Ah sat oan his knee an he kissed me, wrappin his haun in ma long hair an haudin it tight.

'Ah'll no git mair than six month,' he says, dead gentle. 'Ah'll be oot in three or four.' His eyelashes curl up at the edges. Sometimes he gies me a kiss wi them, like we used tae cry a butterfly. His breath tickles ma cheek. 'It'll no be any problem.'

Ah bit he's no gettin roon me that easy. Ah broke away fae him. Ah folded up mair claes an pit them in the case fur the hospital.

'If you get put inside Ah'm goin doon tae ma da's,' Ah tellt him.

'England? Whit fur?'

Ma hauns were shakin when Ah tried tae dae up the zip. 'A fresh start,' Ah says. 'Better than bein stuck here on yer ain wi a wean in some cooncil scheme.'

Bastard wis laughin at me. 'Huv they no goat cooncil schemes doon there, like? D'you think their life's jist wan big holiday park?'

He leaned up fae where he wis sittin an rooted in his pocket fur his fags. That wean doonstairs wis still greetin.

'See that fuckin wean – if it wis mines it'd soon shut it up,' he said. He shivered, an he rubbed his erms as if he wis cauld. 'Gie me wan ae yer fags, hen, will ye?'

Ah tossed him ma pack. He took oot two an lit them, an passed us wan. It jist seemed tae make everythin calm doon again, an Ah sat beside him at the heed ae the bed, smokin.

'You should gie them up, if ye're that concerned aboot the wean.'

'Aye, Ah know,' Ah said.

He picked up the two controllers. 'Ye want a race?'

'Ah'm no very good,' Ah says.

'Ach, go on.'

Ah took it an held it up above ma belly. 'Awright, bit don't laugh if Ah'm rubbish.'

Ah kin never tell which wey up the cars are goin. Ah wis pressin the squares an the circles an aw Ah could hear wis the cars howlin. Dead loud: Ah hate they sound effects. Ah jist gied up an let him win it. It's easier than staunin up tae him.

'Easy!' he shouts, an he throws the controller doon.

'Tellt ye Ah wis rubbish,' Ah said. Ah gave him ower ma controller, an he reset the game an started playin by hisself. Ah goat up an went back tae ma packin, bit it wis nearly done. Ah sat oan the edge ae the bed watchin him, an fiddlin wi the label ae the case.

'D'ye mind when we went tae the caravan?'

'Aye.' He wis too absorbed in the game tae be listnin.

'It wis good, wisn't it?' Ah sighed. That wis probably when Ah goat pregnant. Ah went ower tae the windae an looked out at the street lights comin oan. It wis jist the time Ah liked, when the birds were on the taps ae the roofs singin out their last wee bit ae chirpin.

'How could ye prefer tae get put inside, William?'

'It's only fur a couple ae months.'

'Bit ye'd be able tae get oot.' Ah wis speakin tae the back ae his heed noo. 'We could go tae the park. Take the wean tae the sea-side . . .'

He flicked his head round. 'Naebiddy's taggin me like a dug.'

Ah went ower an sat oan the bed between him an the TV screen.

'Dae ye mind when we went oan the dodgems?'

We baith squashed intae the wan caur. Ma feet slipped oan the metal flair an Ah thumped in beside him.

'Are ye awright, hen?' he said tae me, pittin his erm roon me.

'Aye, William.' Ah cooried in against him, cause Ah loved the smell ae him, an the hardness ae his erm muscles. Ah loved the wey he spread his legs out in the wee caur, squashin me up, cooried in beside him. A guy in another caur had his eye on me an William noticed it.

'Did that arsehole wink at you?' he asked me.

'Aye, William.' Ah could hardly keep masel fae smilin.

'Prick,' he says.

The man took wur money an got aff the circuit before the big power surge. William pit his foot doon.

'Stupit English bastard,' he said tae me. 'Ah'll show him.'

'Get oot the wey!' he says, bringin me back tae the bedroom. Ah dodge fae side tae side tae annoy him so's he cannae see his Playstation. Then he pits his fit on ma erse an shoves it. 'Move!' His voice is like the guy doonstairs wi the baby.

Ah get up, huffin an puffin, an no jist because ae the baby. Ah hate this room. Ah hate fuckin prick-tease Kylie lookin at me fae every angle. Ah look at masel in the wardrobe mirror.

'Ah hate lookin like this.'

Ah looked at masel in the mirror in ma da's caravan.

'Ah cannae believe this, William. Can you?'

We were aw smiles then. He came up behind me an we looked at wurselves, jist grinnin, in the caravan mirror. Seein the room, wi the lilac quilt, an the shower an the cooker, an the gold velour couches. It wis brand new, an that wis how we felt tae.

'C'mere, hen,' he said, an he pit his hauns oan ma tits, lookin in the mirror, massagin them roon an roon. Ah felt the passion burstin right through me, an Ah wis desperate tae have him aw hard an firm aw oan me an in me.

Ah wis a lot skinnier then, bit he said Ah wis jist as sexy in a wey as Kylie.

Ah looked at masel in the mirror oan the wardrobe.

'Ah hate lookin like this.'

'Ye're gorgeous,' he said, an he made a grab at ma bum, but Ah wouldnae let him.

'Ye'll get nain ae that inside either.'

He scowled. 'Ah get fuck all now.'

He got up an stamped his fit oan the flair because ae the wean howlin.

Ah tried again. 'How kin ye no let them pit a tag oan ye?' Ah pit ma erms roon his neck. Ma tits are massive noo, but then, so's ma belly. Ah jist tried tae ignore it. Ah'll no be like this furever. 'When the wean's born we kin spend aw day in bed thegither, jist like in the caravan—'

He wis startin tae pull away fae me. Ah reached up an whispered everythin Ah would dae tae him, assumin the wean slept, that is. He wis gettin twitchy wi the sounds ae that wean doonstairs greetin.

'Jist you an me,' Ah tellt him. 'Jist you an me.'

His fingers were hard diggin intae ma erms tae shove me aff.

'Aye,' he says. 'Jist you an me an a load ae weans screamin!'

He went tae the windae. He opened it an shouted, 'Will you shut that fuckin thing up!'

Ah fiddled wi the handles ae ma case, thinkin aboot the wey

he wis on holiday. William didnae care that there wis a wean in the front seat ae the car. He jist saw that the wummin hid gone intae the petrol shop an left her keys in it. He'd seen the English guy that winked at me drivin away in a car, an he didnae like tae think ae him gettin wan ower oan him.

He wis like a wean wi a Playstation. Ah wis in the back, gettin flung aw ower the place every time he turned a coarner. Ye could even hear the motor screamin. *Stoap it, William,* Ah wis squealin, bit he wisnae listnin. Ah'd never seen him that excitin. His nostrils wis flarin an he kept lickin his lips.

Soon we were powerin through the country wi the wean still sleepin in the seat beside him.

'Stoap it, William!' Ah shouted again, an he pit his fit oan the brake an pulled up sharp at a gate jist aff the road. He slammed the door an came in the back beside me. He wis aw sweaty, bit that made it excitin. Ah laughed: Ah thought he wis gonnie kiss me, bit he jist grabbed ma hips an dragged me flat oan the back seat, flippin out ma tits an bitin at them, then pullin doon ma pants an thumpin his dick up. Ah felt masel aw rip. That's when the wean gret.

Ah'd never seen him that excited. He's gonnie get mair than six months fur that fur definite.

It wis totally dark noo. Ootside. He'd left the windae open, an his ma's curtains were flutterin in the wind. It wis quite cauld, bit Ah didnae want tae shut it. Ah wanted jist some wee bit ae freedom by me.

Ah looked roon at him. He wis back at that bloody game again. The wean doonstairs wis greetin; greetin an greetin.

'You don't know whit it's like tae be in prison,' Ah finally says tae him.

He whirled roon. 'An you dae?'

Ah took a step towards him. 'Aye! Ah dae!' Ah wis shakin. Ah nodded tae the room aw roon me. 'Look at me! Ah feel as if Ah'm in a fuckin prison right now!'

'Whit are you sayin?' he says. 'Is ma mither's hoose no good enough fur you?'

Ah felt it aw surge up in me. 'No, it's no that. It's no that, William!'

'Stupid cow! What is it then?'

He stood up, an Ah battered ma fists on his ribcage as if Ah could breck through.

'Ah feel trapped. Ah feel trapped,' Ah said. 'Dae ye hear me?'

He's that fast, ma William. He grabbed ma wrists in wan haun an took oot his flick knife. He held it tae ma throat. His voice wis aw hoarse.

'Dae ye want me tae cut ye free then?'

Ah shook ma heed.

Dead slow he moved the knife tae ma belly.

'Dae ye want me tae cut yer tag aff fur ye?'

Ah couldnae speak.

Efter a minute he let me go, an folded his flick knife up again. Ah fell tae the bed, bit then Ah got up an finished packin ma suitcase. Locked it. Ah hud tae stoap ma hauns fae shakin. Ah hud tae.

William rooted in the cigarette packet but there wis nain left. He crushed it an threw it oan the flair.

'There's nae fags,' he said. 'Away up the shop an get us some.'

Ah pit oan ma jaiket. Ah thought aboot the buttons, but Ah wouldnae have been able tae fasten them.

He'd picked up the Playstation controller again.

'Ah've got nae money.'

He took oot a five-poun note an threw it at me. Then he realised what Ah wis haudin.

'Whit ye takin yer case fur?'

Ah felt dead still inside; there wisnae a single bit ae me flutterin.

'Ma ma says Ah kin leave it up at her bit till Ah go tae the hospital. Her man'll bring it up fur me in the car.'

'Right,' he says, an unpresses the pause button. Ah looked at him, jist the wance, ower ma shouder as Ah wis walkin past Kylie oot the bedroom. His face wis that excited. Then Ah saw him frownin. Doonstair's wean wis greetin again. He turned up the sound ae the cars racin, tryin tae droon it aw oot.

Help

Kath Murphy

'So what do you want, love?'

'What do you want,' she says, like a parrot, her hair sticking out like she's seen a ghost, crinkly like chips. Used to be smart, it did, shampoo and set or whatever, like if you threw a brick at her head it would bounce right off.

'You shouted me, love.' I was out on the pavement, skidding along the frost towards the shop, wondering if I could get a big fuck-off jar of coffee in my coat and then run. And razors. I need razors. Face stinging from the blunt blade and taking the head off that spot. Splat on the mirror.

'Yes.' She looks around. It's tidy, just the pot on the table with a quilted tea-cosy and a bottle of milk with the cream sticking to the sides. And her purse. Her hand reaches slowly across the table, as if she thinks I won't notice, then suddenly she grabs it. Little smile from her.

'Butter,' she says. 'I'm out of butter.'

'I'll get you some,' I say, reaching to take the purse from her but she snatches it away. She pulls out a ten-pound note. That should do.

The front door's rubbish. One kick and it would be in. She hasn't even got a chain on it.

I run to the shop. The woman behind the till watches me all the way round the aisles. They got robbed two months ago; she was on her own. Didn't think she'd be back to work but she was in the next week. Lad what did it, Jamie they call him, stupid bastard only lives round the corner, been coming in here all his life, and it was on camera. Said he didn't mean to hurt no-one, he'd never have used the knife, it was just the drugs. She said she saw the look in his eyes. He liked it. Said he rubbed the blade up and down her cheek, like it was his – She stopped speaking when she saw I was listening. Said she reckoned he'd been thinking about it a long time.

There's not much in the fridge. Sweaty cheese. Pink bacon. One kind of butter wrapped in foil, one lot of marge in a yellow tub. She said butter. I yank it out past the dusty plastic strips that catch your skin. S'posed to keep the cold in, they are. Cold enough in here.

She's still watching as I walk to the till. Her eyes are grey like the metal shutters on the windows. She says she's no fivers as she counts out the pound coins. I shove them in one coat pocket, put the butter in the other. I can feel the coins bashing against my leg.

I knock on the door and the old woman opens it straight away.

'What do you want?' she asks.

'Come to read the meter, love.'

She frowns.

'You gonna let me in or what?'

She opens the door and I follow her in. It's neat, with the pink paint on the walls, the matching tiles. Smells a bit lardy, but that's okay. I pick up the tea-cosy and stick it on my head. It makes me laugh, but she just stands there.

'Here,' I say, 'you'd better have this.'

I stick the butter and the change on the table. She picks up a pound coin and looks at it slowly.

'This – isn't – right,' she says.

'Course it is. Price of stuff these days, it's a disgrace.'

She looks at me again, so I count it for her. 'Look, it's not Kwik Save round there. Butter was one pound nine, you gave me a tenner, that's eight pounds and ninety-one pence change.'

She's lost interest in the money. She's looking at me.

'I remember you,' she says.

'Yeah. Rich.'

'Your mam's that poor crippled lass.'

'She in't crippled. She's just got MS.'

'And you.'

'What?'

She's smiling like we're old friends.

'Sit down if you're stopping,' she says.

'Okay.' I pull out a chair.

We used to play out on the rec at the back of her place. It wasn't much. It was a dump. Grass growing through burnt-out cars. Bags of rubbish. Porno mags.

She played hell about the noise, so we used to take the piss out of her big white keks hanging on the line. The more she went on at us, the worse it got. Some kids threw stones at her.

In the end she got her son to put trees up all round her back garden. At first they looked like little Christmas trees, but as they grew he trimmed and trimmed them till they made a big fat hedge. Now they look straggly and tall as the house. Perhaps he's had enough of her as well.

'I used to be scared of you,' I say, putting my feet up on the spare chair. She looks at them. There's probably dog shit on my boots, but she doesn't say anything. I wait to see what she does next. I'm in no hurry.

Mam's got Leanne with her for another hour. She played hell with Social Services before, said she didn't want some old cow coming round interfering. Didn't want to have to hide her stash like a criminal. She said I was all the help she needed. They said it was for my sake, I'd missed too much school. In the end we had no choice. I'm not going to school, though. I'm past that now.

Leanne's cool. Nineteen, blonde ponytail, comes round mornings and evenings with a Tommy Hilfiger jacket on top of her overall. Mam's happier since she's been around. We both are. When Leanne comes in smiling, Mam asks if she had a good one last night. She asks her if she ever gets stoned, and Leanne says course not, but Mam says she does really, as if it was a big deal.

'I'm under the doctor—'

'Lucky you, love.'

'You always were a dirty bastard!'

And she was a bitch!

'What do you want?' she says. 'Money?'

'Yeah, about ten thousand quid.' That's what it costs for a year's beta-interferon. It was in the paper, one man mortgaged his house to pay for his daughter's treatment. We haven't got a house. When Mam was working she was gonna buy our flat off the council, then the area went downhill, so she looked for somewhere else, but then she got ill –

She's thinking about it. In the papers they always say they keep their money at home, under the mattress or whatever. That's why they get robbed.

'I've a son about your age,' she says.

That in't right. He must be fifty if he's a day.

We used to watch her from the rec. We hated her. Always had, don't know why. Used to play knock and run. One time, we bunked off school, when I still used to go. They dared me to wait, to knock and not run. They knocked, they ran, but I was still there. The door opened. She opened it.

Mam was seeing someone then. Peter, his name was. I was just starting to think he was all right. Then she got ill. When he saw the way it was going he was on his toes. She hardly spoke for weeks. I didn't know what to do.

One time, before Leanne started coming, I went to help Mam out of the bath, and she closed her eyes, said she didn't want to look down on the unemployed, said it was an old joke. I'd never heard it before. Then she started crying, said who'd want her now, it'd be like fucking a sack of spuds, then said there were some men who preferred it that way, and started to laugh again. I've heard her saying that to Leanne, about the sack of spuds, but she doesn't cry then. Maybe it's better now that she can talk to Leanne.

'Potatoes.'

That makes me jump. 'What?'

'You said you'd fetch them. After school. I can't make your tea without potatoes.'

Bottom lip going. She reaches for a cup. It's empty but she puts it to her mouth anyway, like they do in the soaps.

I look out of the kitchen window but I can't see beyond the hedge. They're building on the rec now. The site's all fenced off. At night there's a gadge with an Alsatian walks around, but he's not much use on his own. A lad broke in and tried to jumpstart a JCB the other night. What's the point in that? He couldn't go anywhere.

Flats, they're building. I thought there might be a ground floor one we could have, but they're private.

Mam likes me to rub her feet of a night. I carry on like they smell but I don't mean it. It's alright with the weed and her candles burning and some crap on the TV or maybe one of her CDs. Some of them aren't too bad, like Fatboy Slim or the old Oasis stuff and Mam says it's better like this, isn't it? If you were out there with your mates you'd only be getting into thieving or smack but you don't need to cos I let you do just what you want here, and are you sure you locked the door?

Her eyes are scanning the room. When she looks at me she almost jumps out her chair.

'What are you doing here?'

'Same as you. Growing a beard.'

'I know you. Your mam's the—'

'Don't you talk about my mam!'

'Toast.' She gets up and switches on the gas under the grill then just stands there. I jump to my feet and run towards her.

'Spark it!' I say, as I hit the ignition. 'You'll blow the place up!'

She has a box of matches in her hand. 'I know. Don't think you're so clever, all of a sudden.'

She presses the end of a match to my wrist, with this spiteful little grin like a kid, but it doesn't burn, because she never lit it. She gets a loaf out, opens it and takes out two slices, turns, slumps back onto the chair. Her face is like a face I've seen before, it says, I can't try any more, can't laugh it off any more. Sometimes I want to say to Mam that she doesn't need to joke about it.

'You could do with a smoke,' I tell her. 'Chill you out a bit.'

Could drop some in her tea. She'd be even more out of it then. I go to take the slices out of her hand, but it's clenched tight, the bread going doughy and mashed up. She scratches me with her other hand.

'Get your own!' she says.

I take some from the pack and stick it under the grill. Shame there's no toaster. I look in the drawers for a knife, find one, think about how white bread's so much nicer, especially toasted, crisp on the outside, doughy in the middle, flick the toast over. I find a plate in a cupboard then wait some more. We have wholemeal now, better for Mam. It's done.

'I was young when I started making this,' I laugh.

'Making this,' she says.

I put some butter on the toast, spread it thin and even, neat to the corners, the way Mam likes it. Put it on the table in front of her.

'It'll take more than that to get round me.'

'Yes, love.'

'I'm under the doctor,' she says, in a feeble voice, 'for my memory.'

'No – I thought it was for piles.'

She laughs. Then she natters at her hand. She takes off her wedding ring. It looks dull next to the wrapper on the butter.

'This should get you summat,' she says.

She's been on her own as long as I've known her. Can't imagine her married. Not in those keks.

She holds the ring up at me, says in a croaky whisper, 'Just don't leave me, will you? Promise you won't leave me.'

'You've got your toast,' I say.

She picks it up then frowns, as if she doesn't know what to do next She puts it down. She reaches out and grabs my arm really tight, so I can feel each finger through my coat, and I'm thinking, if you've left greasy prints on my sleeve I'll –

I shake her arm off and stand back. The ring is on the table; the knife is still in my hand. It's old-fashioned with a rounded blade. The handle is yellow like her cheek. Bone, I think they call it. I hold it tight.

Her face has changed again. She looks scared, suddenly. 'Who are you?'

I lower my face near to hers. I can see toast crumbs in the grey hairs around her lips.

She's afraid. She's looking round. Eye on the kitchen door, but there's no way out, what with the hedge and the flats being built and scaffolding and oily puddles where there used to be hot sun and Mam at work all day not worrying where I was.

It was sunny that day, the day they knocked and ran. I stood there. Heavy footsteps took forever to come. The door opened. Her hair was like a helmet made of steel wool, so grey it was blue and she had these cold, staring eyes and this evil grin.

She didn't say anything but I could see in those eyes she knew all about me. She knew I was scared, and she knew I was over the rec with the others, looking at those magazines. Dreaming of a blonde bird on a beach somewhere far away. Her, with her big bosom and belly and the dress that always looks like it's the same one, whatever colour it is.

I turned and ran and behind I could hear her laughing and she shouted after me, 'Don't you want to come in?'

As I bend over I can smell my own sweat, not dirty sweat but the clean hot smell you get from running as fast as you can go. And the aftershave I nicked from the shop. Leanne saw it in the bathroom. She said it was her favourite. She poured a little bit onto her wrist and sniffed it.

Big eyes like saucers. She don't know nothing now, but I do. I know about Jamie and the sad cold eyes of the woman in the shop, him just wanting something, anything and Mam sobbing in the night when she thinks I'm asleep.

I'm out of here. I throw the knife on the table with a clatter. She frowns, mumbles, fingers reaching for the blade. I'm gonna ask Leanne out soon, I've decided. Mam won't mind.

The Last Day of the Year

Alan Bissett

The fire made short whiplash sounds. Thomas watched its motion carefully, the flames prancing behind the bars of the hearth like ballerinas forced to perform. Linda's mother was fussing back and forth with the Hoover. There were the dull, removed sounds of a fight over a dress from upstairs. Children pattered on all fours in a thick pile throwing toys, voices.

Christ!

'Tho-mas?' one of them said. 'See, at the bells, will you come up and wish us Happy New Year?'

'Nng?' he said, through a wall of teeth.

'Will you bring us up a dri-ink?'

The peat burning made a thin whine like a kettle whistling far in the distance.

'And will you put whisky in it and not tell Mum and maybe play the Plaaaystation with us?'

Thomas shifted in his seat, restlessly, then stood and left the room.

In the hallway two kids leapt out and attacked him. He pretended to be wounded, falling, and they charged him with raised bayonets, making him cry, 'Help! Help!' with each fresh stab until they tore away and he buttoned up his jacket over the wounds. Sighing.

'Where are you going?' said Linda, coming downstairs. She held the dress across her forearms like a body pulled from a blaze.

'Out. This place is doing my head in.'

'Hang on, I'll come. There's nobody arriving for hours yet.'

He hesitated.

'Yes. Yes, of course. Come.'

The decision felt weighted, like plumbline, momentous. He passed her a coat and some gloves, and suddenly wanted to say absolutely nothing to anyone ever again.

They walked uphill arm in arm. Linda was speaking about her father. The frost crunched beneath their feet and her breath plumed out like silver flowers and the words were held between its fragile petals. Thomas watched her talk – watched not listened. He couldn't work out if he was bored or not. He inhaled, and the winter air tore through his throat as though it had fins.

'It's one of my favourite places,' Linda was saying, dreamy. 'I used to come here even before Dad was buried. So peaceful. Do you have any places like that?'

Thomas looked at her and thought: *you.*

'When I go I want to be cremated though,' she said. 'Just to make sure I'm dead. Slam me into an oven at gas mark ten and—'

'Don't talk like that,' he snapped.

The cemetery could be sensed before it was seen: a flattening-out of the air and sound, as if life had been hammered into quiet on an anvil. He looked back the way they'd come and saw a world ridged with frost, delineated, sparkling.

'Isn't it beautiful up here?' Linda said.

He agreed that it was.

She snuggled into him, the way she did late at night watching TV. He wanted to push her away. Like a match burnt to the quick, it flashed, his teeth clenched, his fingers spasmed round her wrist.

Then it passed.

His breath shook.

In the distance, high-tension towers marched out of an H. G. Wells book, all skeletal steel and death-rays. Thomas remembered the old public-service ads that were on when he was young: a little boy would always fly his frisbee close to high-voltage wires, it would land on a pylon, and he'd eagerly run to retrieve it. *Don't!* Thomas wanted to shout at the boy. *I know what's going to happen!* But it was inevitable. The boy never decided to leave it where it was and jog home; he always climbed after it. Thomas had to hide his eyes, but he could never stop the boy, never prevent him running cheerfully towards death, every time.

He hated the echoing, bare, room-without-carpets sound that 'once is all it takes' made, but there it was. You could live inside a cliché, he'd realised. You could make a cramped, cold home for yourself in the amount of times it had been said, and it was habitable, the way arctic tundras are habitable to survivor-types.

This world had a sick sense of a good night-out.

Gogsie's stag do, the lot of them, the lads, charged, buzzing, tequila, *boom*. When they'd strode up the Grassmarket – him, Gogsie, Mark, and the rest – the night seemed to clear before them. The banter crackled, fizzed at their core. He'd felt eight feet tall. Sculpted from bronze. *Come ahead then* provocative.

Gogsie was playing it coy: he didn't want to go to a strip bar, he was getting married the next week, it's not on boys, blahblah. It was a pose, Thomas knew – moral little Gogsie, itemising himself away from the knuckle-draggers. His own stag night! They'd dragged him into the warm dry-ice groove of the Fantasy Bar, and while the rest of them had sauntered through curtains, led by some half-bare teenage girl and trailed by jeers, Gogsie had *called his fiancée*. It was a joke, the whole gig: a stag night where the stag phones his woman. Three times Thomas had come out of that room of mirrors and angle-poise stares and sinuously turning tricks with his body locked rock hard to see wee Gogsie staring away from flesh into innocent space, like the messiah. It got on Thomas's nerves. Gnawed at them. Sweat lanked his face. One of the boys – Andy or Mark – wrapped a meaty arm round his neck and Thomas punched the air, suddenly euphoric. Gogsie was a gay-boy, they agreed on this. It confirmed something. Tightened it. *Christ*, he wanted to nail one of those strippers. Show Gogs how it was done. And when clarity bit insistently through the drunkenness, he drank more, *slammed* more, insulated himself from it and called over another girl through the lensing wall of his vision with a beckoning digit and a gin grin and gradually the blonde fringes brushing his face, the hair-fine touch of thigh in the crook of his denim, the fingertips lightly trailing his chest flensed away all reason.

Wisps of grief were blown in the breeze. The headstone was plain. Sadly missed. Fondly remembered by.

The date of death.

Thomas stood beside Linda as she patted flowers onto the grass. 'I hope Mum's alright. She always gets weepy at the bells because of Dad. Although there's something nice about him going out on the last day of the year, don't you think?' She didn't wait for a reply, and he was glad. 'Dad loved New Year. He used to always get the accordion out and play "The Rose of Allandale".' She started singing.

'*Wherever I wandered to the east and west, and fate began to lower . . .*'

Thomas had been there when Linda's Dad had passed away: her mother at one side of the bed, she and her sister at the other, clasping hands.

'*A solace still was she to me, in sorrow's lonely hour . . .*'

The cancer had cleaned his insides out. Scraped his mind and guts and fight and slapped them into a pan.

'*By far the sweetest flower there was, was the Rose of Allandale . . .*'

By the end he was a papery shell, useless as the husk of wasp stirring on a windowsill.

Her singing dropped. The wind carried it off.

'Happy New Year, Dad,' Linda waved, dabbing her eyes. 'When it comes.'

Thomas almost yanked her away.

As they walked between the rows, he noticed for the first time the design of the place. Its simplicity. There really wasn't anything creepy about graveyards at all. There was, in fact, something sterile about them. Regimented. All intersecting lines and neatness, as if attempting to strap death down. They didn't want tears spilling beyond this place, burning everything through with a searing, acidic grief. That would not do. We must endure. Death is a statistic, an insurance claim, it can be built into your forward-planning. Let us shape death as a grid to prove this.

It made him sick.

Gogsie had phoned a couple of stops along the track of morning-afters. Thomas and Linda were lying in a pool of sheets and languid minutes, feeling the love-making tingle and fade like glitter. He got up and made eggs and toast, whistling, then he carried it into the room like a French chef. They fed them to each other, spluttering, gagging on albumen.

'Don't force it!'

'Not hungry? I'll eat yours.'

'*Ah, you peeg! You Breetesh peeg!*'

When Gogsie called they were nearing the end of a TV film about a lecherous boss being sued by his secretary. They'd both cackled uncontrollably when the boss admitted, 'I enjoy wo-men,' and the prosecutor asked, 'Like a good steak?'

The phone rang and Linda mewled.

'Two minutes,' he said.

'Do you think they'll find him guilty?' Linda shouted after him.

'Nah,' he said. 'They always get away with it.'

'Not this time, I bet.'

'This time too!'

On the line, Gogsie pottered around with wedding arrangements like an old man tending plants. Thomas yawned. He mumbled *yeah, yeah* when he was expected to and only woke when Gogsie said, 'So that girl you were with . . .'

'When?'

'The stag night.'

Images flashed: red hair, fingernails, a tattoo.

'The . . . one who worked in Asda?'

'No, the other one.'

He flicked through some more mental Polaroids.

'That Irish girl?'

'God, you *must* have been pissed. Can't you even remember?'

He recalled skin rough like dungeon walls. Fingers at his belt-buckle.

'Oh Christ . . .'

'*Yeah,*' Gogsie pressed, 'and do you remember where you picked her up?'

'I dunno . . . Revolution? The Three Sisters? It doesn't matter, just make sure Linda doesn't—'

'Calton Hill,' Gogsie said.

Thomas froze. He could hear the sound of the telly upstairs, a judge asking a jury if they'd come to a verdict. Gogsie said slowly, as if speaking to a child.

'I think you'd better go to a doctor.'

'What do you mean?'

'Did you use a condom?'

'Course I did,' he said, cold settling on his skin. 'Probably.'

The sky stretched away in front of them, then stopped. Thomas couldn't quite come to terms with how it stopped, how the horizon just seemed to tuck it in like bedsheets. Where did it go?

'You're very quiet today,' Linda said.

'Sorry.'

'Are you saving yourself for tonight?' she bumped her hip against him. Her voice curled, girlish. 'For kissing?'

'Mm.'

'Or dancing?'

'Mm.'

'Well, I don't like you quiet. It makes me think something's wrong.'

'I'm just enjoying the walk, that's all.'

'Oh, come over here, this is a nice bit!'

She dragged him over the hill, to the oldest part of the graveyard, which was worn down, neglected, the headstones sinking into the ground. Some had collapsed entirely, fallen like angels tired from fighting the good fight. They lay on their backs, staring up at the darkening sky, dreaming.

'Me and my sister used to come to this part when we were wee,' Linda grinned. 'We'd find the oldest graves and put flowers on them.'

'Why?'

'Because it's a shame,' she shrugged. 'Nobody mourns them any more.'

Thomas pictured Linda and her sister as girls, strewing the worn stones with daffodils. They were nurses, tending the sick. It made him happy.

'Actually,' she said, 'this whole cemetery's nearly full up. My mum's terrified she's not going to get in.'

'She's dying to get in?'

'Yeah. Because it's where my dad's buried.'

He instantly felt ashamed of the joke. It spilled down the front of his jacket like egg yolk. Linda hadn't noticed it, but others had. He sensed them. They worried him all the way down the path, between cellophane-wrapped flowers hissing the afterlife. He shrank, bundled his hands into his pockets.

Tell her.

She knows.

How can she?
He hasn't told her.
He hasn't told her so she can't know.
How can she know if he hasn't told her?
Messages buzzed. He wanted to clamp his hands to his ears. They buzzed louder. Perhaps he wouldn't have to tell her. Perhaps the air would tell her. He begged it. He stared at the world, willing it to unfreeze and nudge her arm and sit her down while he stood whistling to himself nonchalantly. He pleaded for help from the nude straplings, from frost rubbing at the hard grass, from a cluster of homes that had been built at the edge of the cemetery. Families planning holidays. Fixed mortgage repayments. He thought about the results that had come back and looked at the gleaming cars, their newness, and the newer the car, the more of an affront on humanity it seemed. How dare they, was all he could think. How dare they. How dare they. *How dare they!*

'Linda?'

'Hmm?'

He stopped. He took her hands and rubbed their gloved slimness. Her fingers danced. Her skin shone with cold. He didn't think he'd felt more love in his life than he did for her at that moment. The words reared behind his teeth like little horses.

i am so very scared

but when he opened his mouth the wind scattered them, lifted them, into drifting motes of the deceased.

'It's lovely up here, isn't it?' he said.

'Yeah.' Linda looked. 'Sometimes there are really beautiful sunsets. The light hits that cross on top of the church and it seems to catch fire. You can see it for miles.'

They both stared up at the cross.

There was silence for a while. And sky. A band of light had

settled on her eyes, preserving her. *Let's not go*, Thomas thought, *let's stay locked in this sunlight forever*. But she leaned over, kissed him, and the spell was broken. A soft warm fear moved again in his blood.

'C'mon,' Linda smiled, tugging his arm. 'I'd better help Mum get things ready for the bells.'

He nodded.

The sun was setting. It disappeared behind the earth for what seemed like the last time. There were bottles and laughs to be cracked open, drams to be poured, friends to be welcomed in from the cold. He pulled her towards him, the way he did at night before they drifted off to sleep.

'Happy New Year, love,' he shivered. 'When it comes.'

The Strechle

Iain Bahlaj

L isa had only asked about the picture to say something; now she had to listen to the old woman's story. This auld wife, whose skin was like crinkly Christmas paper, whose bones and veins were wires and cables under the surface. But – and it was funny, this, the way the old woman looked in the near-dark – Lisa felt safe. Her heart was back to a steady beat, her mouth wet again with slavers.

She had grown up in a small fishing village, the old woman was saying, croaking. *Just a wee place on the coast. It wis a hard life. Nane ih yon VDDs n Satellite TVs.*

Lisa had perched herself awkwardly on the end of a three-quarter-sized couch, the dish the old woman had used for the rhubarb crumble still cradled in her lap. Her mum had told her to hand it back in. That should have been it, end of 'chore', like the Simpsons would say, but then she'd noticed the painting . . . and she had been curious.

Noo, this story ah'm tellin yi. A loatay folk widnae believe it, bit it's true, ah'll vouch fir it – her whole body staying still, hardly moving. *Ah'll vouch fir it*, she repeated, then stopped.

For a start, was it a painting, or what was called an engraving? How old was it? What was the thing in the water, the thing on the end of that long spindly arm, the thing using its weight and leverage to try and tip the small fishing boat.

An octopus? Nah. The legs were solid, and had joins, like . . . cra –

Strechle, the old woman croaked out. The word sounded like a throat-clearing and Lisa wondered whether she had heard properly.

A bony finger pointed towards the picture.

That hing . . . *is what yi call a strechle.*

The old woman started her story.

About a girl – a girl around Lisa's age. She lived with her parents in a small village by the sea, her father fishing, her mother cooking, cleaning. The girl had had a little brother, but, in a tragic accident, he had died. Collecting shells, he'd wandered too far into the white water. He'd been dragged out and drowned.

Or:

The strechles goat um, as other villagers would say.

The girl would hear them, as they warned their bairns about the sea and the dangers it held. She'd hear the story they told:

Noo, mind, dinnae go too near the watir. Thir wis a wee boy wance, who went too near the watir, n nivir came back.

Where is ih noo? a bairn would ask.

The strechles goat um.

The strechles . . . The girl knew all the strechle stories – she'd been brought up with them. Her brother had been told similar stories, and now he was part of them. A warning.

Strechles were like lobsters, folk said, but bigger, much bigger. And their backs curved, so they appeared more round than oblong – more like a flea than a lobster – when seen side-on. They had the same shell, though, the same basic crustacean armour. This armour started a mustardy yellow, before turning black in patches as the creature aged.

Fishermen told tales of fully grown strechles, their antennae the size and thickness of a man's arm, wrecking boats and throwing men into the cold sea. Other times a strechle would be scooped up with the fish, only to escape – the torn, withered remnants of the net testament to its size and vicious nature.

The village women, meanwhile, were full of stories concerning baby or adolescent strechles, wandering into shallow waters, ready to steal a bairn.

And, occasionally, the women would add, they would even invade people's houses to snatch babies from their cots. These raids tended to occur in certain weather:

Whenivir a haar would drap, the women would tell their children, *whenever yi cannae see yir haunt fir grey. That's when thi'll come.*

That's when ti might hear it, the sound thi make: like shells crackin.

N the smell . . . that's when yi might smell it . . .

Salt watir . . .

The old woman's fingers, tapping relentlessly – the cowboy song – seemed like the only bit of her with any life left. They stopped.

Di you believe in the tooth fairy?

What? the girl said, trying to sound as surprised as she was; really. *Ah yist ti when ah wis like . . . five.*

Yi'll ken the truth noo, ih? Thit it wis yir mum n dad?

Ma mum, the girl said.

Well, a lotay people think thit aw the stories ir like the tooth fairy – jist somehin yir mum n dad tell ye.

Jist like thi tell yi the tooth-fairy story, so yi'll stoap greetin aboot yir tooth, n the blood, thi'll tell yi anither story jist ti scare yi. Ti stoap yi daein somehin.

Like the old changing rooms, the girl thought, and the jaggers. It wasn't her mum and dad who'd told her, it was the first and second years, and Jamie. The stories about how they'd cut your face, where your top lip met your bottom, both sides, then kick you or burn you with their lighters so that, when you screamed, your mouth burst right back.

Chelsea smile, they said.

Well, the old woman found her thread, *this lassie thought thit the strechle stories were the same thing. Jist stories. Jist daft tales, ti keep the weans away fae deep watir. But then . . .*

She heard it in the middle of the night. Her mum and dad were out visiting friends, she was alone, and it was dark. The sound, crunching, it was probably footprints; she closed her eyes.

She'd just started to get cosy again when she heard the creak of the door, and the crunching, louder this time. Exactly like shells. Maybe her mum and dad had a bag of shells for some reason. Her mum liked shells, like the colour of them. Before her son died, she would collect shells with him. That's what it would be.

The girl closed her eyes, shut them tight, until all she could see was a bright-red blanket, then black blotches.

Then the smell hit her, wafted up her nostrils: seaweed, a touch of rotten fish and crustaceans, but mostly salt water.

She squeezed her eyes tighter, and felt the shadows in the room swallow her body. Her eyes would never be opened again, she told herself. They could stay shut.

So why did she open her eyes? She changed her mind. Because if she didn't it could be there, ready to kill her, and it didn't feel right, for some reason, to be killed with your eyes shut, without seeing what was doing the killing.

It was in the corner of the room, parts of its body illuminated by the moonlight, parts still shrouded in darkness. It was the size of a man bent over, touching his toes, and the girl could make out a shell, and two or three long, spindly legs.

The antennae cast their shadows on the wall, uneven, ragged, and the noise started again, suddenly. The sound of somebody standing on shells, standing on hundreds of shells like women in foreign countries stood on grapes to make wine.

The girl – like everybody then – believed in God, and religion, and she started saying her own prayers, mumbling under her breath. And underneath the fear she started to wonder. Whether God would reveal Himself to her as soon as she had died, or whether she would have to wait.

Whether she would meet John, her dead brother.

She kept her eyes closed and listened. The sounds were getting louder, the strechle was getting nearer. She hoped her death be quick, that it would break her neck before it carried her back, or suffocate her fast.

Yi wantin anither cup ih tea?
What?
Anither cup ih tea? The old woman shook an invisible teacup with her bony hand. *Yi like wan?*
Nah.
It's gittin dark ootside. Ir yi awright walkin hame?
Aye.

Time was ticking. The girl wished she'd hurry up and get to the end. She considered asking the old woman about the jaggers – had there been any noises in the night, or needles in her garden?

The old woman might look at her differently, though. Like a bairn. They could be like that . . . one minute old folk were telling you that young ones grew up too fast, next minute they were saying how they'd had a full-time job when they were, like, six.

Yi sure. Yi're no wantin a cup ih tea, then?
Aye.
Sure?

She wanted to know how the story ended, too. How, she wondered, would a strechle kill a human being?

Em . . . ah take it the lassie wis killed?
The crinkly skin creased at the corners of the pale lips.
Killed? She laughed. *No, shi wis nivir killed . . .*

She was waiting for it, though, as the creature inched closer. Her eyes were closed, she had seen everything she needed to see. She could feel the aura it was doomed to carry around with it – cold and sad – and then its icy breath. The girl was crying. She bit her lip and tried to take what was coming calmly.

After building up her courage for a few long moments she opened her eyes again. The strechle was there, looking at her, but now the girl was unafraid. Something had come over here, some calmness, and now she could look at the creature without flinching.

The creature itself seemed more peaceful than before. Its jaws moved to a slower beat, the shell-shattering sound slowing down. Its mustard-coloured antennae moved awkwardly through the air, like a blind man's stick.

It seemed to be searching for something. An old, worn cabinet by the side of the girl's bed took up most of its attention. The girl's prayer book was pushed off, then an unlit candle followed – the sounds they made as they fell making the girl's bones shudder inside her skin. Finally, the antennae settled on a shell that lay there. The girl had kept this shell next to her bed for years, that was its place. The shell was important.

It was then it came to her. It came to her – why the strechle had scuttled into a house with no babies. Why it hadn't simply stayed outside and eaten the bits of leftover fish. Why it hadn't attacked her.

Jo, the girl started to say, but her dry mouth wouldn't let her finish. She summoned some saliva and said:

John . . . is that you?

Then, just as the shell-cracking sound grew more violent, and excited, the strechle trying to form words its mouth simply couldn't manage, the girl's parents rushed into the room, followed by the friends they'd been visiting, followed by more villagers.

The strechle turned and let out a horrible, piercing scream.

It made for the door and the crowd, including the girl's mother and father, parted in fright. As soon as they'd recovered from the shock, they ran after the strechle.

Wi seen the tracks up, yi awright? somebody shouted.

Leave it, the girl screamed at them, but they paid no attention.

They ran with knives, sticks, stones and boulders, oars – anything they could find. They ran and the girl followed, screaming in vain, cutting her bare feet on stones and nettles so that she left a trail of blood.

As the crowd reached the beach they gradually slowed down. The girl heard blows, some more of the strechle's screams – partans being boiled alive – and then a man's triumphant voice, announcing:

Goat it.

The girl only caught a glimpse of the strechle. It lay on its side, dead in the sand. Its blood was thinner than human blood, being mostly salt water.

So that was the end of it.

The girl looked around the room. At the photographs on the woman's fireplace – so old they looked as though they'd been scrunched up and dipped in tea. The people in them looked serious, solemn, as though they'd been snapped at a family funeral.

One picture – of a hard-faced woman, her hair slapped to the side, staring at the camera – would be the old woman, the girl supposed.

But it was the other picture which drew most of the girl's attention. It was in a plain wooden frame, old and dark. The photograph was of a wee boy. He looked like any other boy, really. Only his eyes stood out; they'd been painted blue.

And in front of the photograph was a shell.

That's John, the old woman wheezed. *That's the only picture oh him . . . that's the wan thit wis oan the cabinet, the wan thit wis knocked oan the flair. N that shell . . .*

Wis the shell thit it pointed ti, the girl finished for her.

Aye . . . n what age ir you?

Nine.

Well, ah wis ten when it happened. Jist a year aulder.

The old woman's head tilted to the side. Something inhuman

gurgled inside her mouth, then stopped. She wheezed, jerked forward, and her skin turned a shade towards purple.

Finally, she opened her mouth and spat out set of false teeth.

Ver-near choked . . .

Every tree cast a shadow on the walls of the garages, and every shadow looked like a long, worn, old hand. Lisa tried to keep her head down. The wind was in her ears. She thought of the old woman; she was obviously mental. Her head was full of wee shops, Lisa had heard her mum say once, and they were all shut. Shame for the brother, though, if he really did drown.

She kept her head down, looking at her feet, trying to think of what she would do when she got in – her homework on the Black Death, maybe she'd finally finish it.

She'd passed the changing rooms now, and it must have been deserted, because she heard nothing. But still, she couldn't look back.

The jaggers would creep up on you, she suspected. All you'd smell would be the fags on their breath, and all you'd see just a glint of a blade or a needle.

The wind behind her; when it hit her neck it was like somebody breathing on her.

Then the voice came, and it was like it started inside her head then went outside. She started to run.

Lisa, it was saying.

She kept running, listening to her own breathing. The voice was deep, male, and it sounded familiar.

Lisa.

She kept running. At her own house she'd slow down. By the back gate, with only a few feet to the sanctuary of the back lobby.

Lisa.

Until she could see the light through the glass and net curtains.

Lisa, where ir yi gaun?

The Sheep

Linda Saunders

The sheep had been dead for some time. It lay on its side, head thrown back, throat exposed, neck arched, dying in the search for one final gasp of air. The crows had pecked out its eyes, leaving a blank, hollow stare. Its belly was swollen, distended by gases. Emerging bracken, breaking through the ground like the tops of miniature green shepherds' crooks encircled the body and the large stones surrounding it. Soon, it would all be hidden.

The two boys, scrambling down the rough, craggy hillside past coconut-scented gorse, over grey, tired, ankle-catching heather and preceded by a black shaggy dog on a long lead, had not noticed it, their peripheral vision registering it as another white rock. But the dog, scent-sensitive, detecting decay, pulled in the direction of the sheep. Before they actually realised it, they were almost on top of the body.

Yuk! A dead sheep.

How did it die?

Dunno, p'raps a fox.

Or a dog?

Maybe an eagle!

It could have fallen, I s'pose.

The dog sniffed. He grabbed a section of fleece and tugged. It became stuck in his teeth. The younger boy, sandy hair, freckles and a touch of sunburn on his cheeks, pulled it out. It stretched, a thick strand of dental floss.

The elder boy, taller, growth-accelerated and gangly, gingerly pushed the body with his foot, which shifted inside his slightly-over-large wellingtons. In the area where the sheep had lain was a patch of maggots. Sudden exposure to sunlight made them wriggle.

Gross!

They're only maggots. Like you use for fishing.

Touch them then.

No way!

I dare you.

You touch them. They might cure your eczema.

Don't be daft, how could they do that?

They might have a secret ingredient or something. Go on, if it makes it better, you could be famous. You said you wanted to be a scientist.

I've changed my mind.

Sissy!

D'you think Gran got maggots when she died?

Dunno.

Does everything that dies get maggots?

I told you, I don't know. Let's leave it.

The elder boy pulled the reluctant dog away from the body and they moved along the grass at the edge of the soft valley floor. In the peat bog, the heavy spring rains had formed streams, silver serpents coiled around tussocks of dark green reeds and mounds of red-gold sphagnum moss.

Fresh air, the mother had said. A lack of pollution. Freedom to roam. No crime. Let's have the perfect spring holiday. A renovated crofter's cottage is just the thing. Enthusiasm from the parents; less from the children. We'll get bored, they said. What will we do? Explore. Do things on your own. Learn how to entertain yourselves. You'll enjoy it honestly, you will. We'll take the dog, too. It's a family holiday. He must be under control – on a lead – because of the sheep. It'll be fun. The sun might even shine.

The front of the croft led down to a tumbling river. To the rear, the open hill. Common grazing. Don't get too close to the river, she had said, so they had gone the opposite way: over the top of the hill and down the other side. Exploring, as instructed, while the parents unpacked supermarket-purchased groceries, a more-than-adequate supply of alcohol (who knows where you can get a decent bottle of wine in such a remote place?) and vast quantities of snacks. Take some crisps with you, she had told them. But don't leave any litter: bring it back with you.

The boys skirted the edge of the hill. The wet ground intruded into the grass and their wellingtons squelched in the muddy patches. They used rocks as stepping stones, the dog leading, straining on his leash, causing the elder boy to walk faster, synchronising balance and speed with the decision of where to tread. The hill became steeper, vertical slabs of grey-white crumbly rock interspersed with small ledges of grass from which spindly trees clung for survival and delicate primroses nestled. Now the firm ground ran out, the bog meeting the foot of the hill in a bold territorial claim. Pulling the dog to a halt, the boy stopped. He sat on a rock, waiting for the younger one, who looked to his brother for serious decisions, to catch up.

Now what do we do?

We could go back.

Boring!

We can't get over the hill now, it's too steep.

We could go on until we can climb up it –

What, through this boggy stuff?

It looks okay if we jump the streams and things. We've got wellies.

Well, if Jet goes first, we can see how deep it is.

It was quite firm, they decided, setting off in single file. The dog's paws got a bit mucky, and the black oily mud, with its extraordinary adhesive qualities, only came halfway up their boots, causing a loud *splorroch* as they walked. The younger boy, bringing up the rear, discovered that his jeans were becoming splattered from the mud thrown up by his brother's boots, so he dropped back and fumbled in his pockets for his packet of crisps. The light began to fade, rain clouds taking possession of the sky.

The rustling of the packet alerted the elder boy to the presence of his own snack. Looping the dog's lead around his wrist to free up both hands, he pulled out the crisps and opened the packet. But the dog was pulling hard, making it difficult to co-ordinate properly. They should have left it behind. He turned round.

Have you finished your crisps?

Nearly.

Can you take the dog for a minute while I eat mine?

Okay.

The younger boy put the remains of his crisps into his pocket and took the dog from his brother. They wandered on in contented, companionable silence. The elder boy finished his crisps, and as he poked around in the bottom of the packet for the remaining crumbs, he dropped it. As he bent to clasp it, a gust of wind caught the open packet like a little spinnaker and sent it further into the bog. It lodged itself in a snowy drift of small white flowers.

They didn't know about the cotton grass, the white rabbit-tail heads bobbing in the stiffening breeze. They didn't know that it betrays the quagmire's presence. White: nature's danger signal. As he moved confidently over the ground to retrieve the packet, his weight shifting heavily onto his right foot, the black, evil water crept furtively over the top of his boot. He had to move his left foot to take the change in weight, but when he put it down, that began to sink too. The elusive waste paper was only a couple of metres away. The mud reached his knees. He twisted his upper body to look behind at his brother, who was delving into the depths of his crisp packet in search of the last elusive morsel.

Help me! I'm stuck!

What?

I'm stuck in the mud! Come and pull me out.

The combination of authority and genetic bond caused the young boy to react with instinct and make his way towards his brother, initially mindless of the mud's danger. The dog pulled on the lead towards the stuck boy, panting, anxious to join in the game. The younger one realised neither he, nor the dog, were sinking – it must just be a particular spot that was dangerous – but when he was almost within an arm's length of him, he felt the ground cling to his boots.

I think I'm sinking too.

You only need to get a bit closer – can you stretch?

No, not any more. Can you grab Jet?

But Jet suddenly didn't like this game and pulled hard at an angle, causing the young boy to lose his balance and his footing. He put his hands out to save his fall. But he held onto the dog.

I know! Let Jet off the lead and throw me the end, then you can pull me out.

I can't let him off! I'm not allowed. Mum said.

He's not going to get into any trouble. What else can we do?

I could go and get help.

We don't have time. You've got to get me out. Do you want me to die? Do you want the maggots to get me? Get me out of here, you idiot!

The sky turned into a huge grey-green bruise and the rain started to fall in large drops. The young boy, struggling with conflicting instructions, finally released the dog. He threw the loop end to his brother, who reached to grab it, missed, and fell on his front.

Can you crawl out?

No, have another go.

This time, the loop landed close, and the boy was able to slide it over his wrist and hold on with the other hand.

Now pull!

I'm trying.

Harder.

I can't get a grip. I'll have to go back a bit to stop sinking.

A few steps back the land provided better leverage, and slowly the two boys moved in the same direction, the younger one heaving hard in a tug-of-war with the mud. When he reached firmer ground, the elder one used his elbows to inch himself forward until he felt safe. His brother gave him a final tug with his hand. They both sat on lumps of reed, soaked from the rain, muddy, scratched by the low branches of bog myrtle, tired with relief. The crisp packet sat out in the bog, shining like a large jewel against the dark ground and the heavy sky.

I've lost my wellies. They were loose to start with.

Then it'll take us a long time to get back.

We'll get into terrible trouble.

We'll have to say we had fun. Enjoyed ourselves – y'know, played games.

You mean pretend it wasn't dangerous? I was scared.

Yeah, so was I.

You weren't the one who was stuck.

I was still scared.

Are you ready to go?

Yeah.

They got to their feet. The elder boy looked down at the lead, then his eyes scanned the bog.

Where's Jet?

He was here just a minute ago.

I can't see him anywhere.

I knew I shouldn't've let him off! I knew it! It's your fault!

He can't be far. He never goes far.

The young boy put two fingers in his mouth and emitted a high, shrill whistle. Again. Shouted: *Jet! Here, boy!* Another whistle. Nothing. Then, as they walked carefully back towards the hill, they heard an excited bark. A sudden sense of relief. Losing the dog would be even more serious. More barking. They looked up and saw Jet standing high up on the ledge of a craggy outcrop, his silhouette framed against the skyline, blurred slightly in the rain. He was barking at something below. And then they saw it. The sheep, at first running rapidly down the almost vertical slope, all black-stockinged legs and fleecy petticoats. Then, as its back legs lost control, it somersaulted, over and over, bouncing on rocks and stunted trees. At the bottom, it lay quite still. By the time the boys reached it, the crows had already begun to circle.

Scrimshaw

Angus Dunn

It isn't easy, conjuring a bone up out of the ground. But I have done it, with only three young people, a dog and a small landslide.

There we are, on a spring day in an old graveyard, surrounded by old trees. The dog is gambolling around the bushes, hoping for rabbits. One girl is picking daffodils, one is swinging on the curved branch of a cedar. I am watching them all, the mad energy of the dog, the quietness of Anna, picking flowers. My younger sister, Margaret, in the tree, swinging and singing to herself.

'I'm going in there,' I declared, and I head off down an earthen ramp between brick walls. It leads along a passage to the vault of the local laird's family. As I move along the passage, the light grows less, until I can barely make out the empty sandstone doorway that leads into the vault. The doors have fallen in long ago.

Behind me, the girls have come to watch, holding arms for comfort.

I step into the vault and the soft hummocky sand underfoot feels just like the darkness pressing against my face, undefined and threatening.

Two steps I go, then another. Then I turn around, and I cannot see the doorway. I can't see anything. In a moment of panic, I lose my sense of where I am and where the door might be. My heart is pounding.

Then I hear the girls whispering in the passageway. I still

can't see the doorway, but I know roughly where it is. I close my eyes and that is better. Now I don't expect to see anything, so the dark is easier to cope with.

My heartbeat slows, though it is still fast.

'Come out, Alan.' It is Margaret.

'Please.' Anna.

'Nay,' I boom back, 'Never shall I leave this dire and dreadful place!'

The sound of my own voice frightens me again and I shuffle forwards, arms out, towards the door. My fingers touch sandstone, then I find a gap. I step forwards again and there is a scent of daffodils, then Anna's hand is on my arm and I feel instant relief.

The girls stay close, reaching out to pat me now and then as we walk up the ramp and into the bright, green graveyard, where light touches everything. There is sound too. Birds are calling; the dog is scrambling around the undergrowth outside the fence. Where the hillside has crumbled, several metal posts are hanging free, and Merlin has scrambled underneath and is rooting about in the gully beyond.

'Merlin! Here, boy!'

There is a brief pause before the dog's head pokes under the fence. In his grinning jaws there is a stick.

'Here, boy! Good dog!'

The dog struggles through and gallops up to us.

'It's a bone! That's not a stick, it's a bone!'

It's true. Though it looks like a thumb-thick stick, it has two unmistakable bulges, one at each end to fit into a shoulder or an elbow joint.

Anna steps back, hugging her bunch of daffodils. Her eyes are wide.

Margaret laughs. 'Where did you get that, you stupid dog?'

'Get it off him!' Anna's voice is high.

'Drop it. Drop it!'

I hold the dog by the collar and Margaret prises the bone from his jaws.

'Got it!' She holds it up high and Merlin leaps. Birds are calling in the ivy, up in the trees. Wind is whispering through the bare branches of elm, through the evergreen cedar.

Margaret holds the bone high and Merlin leaps for it. Margaret is laughing; Anna is fearful.

I am watching.

Margaret looked after the bone for the next few years. It usually stayed in her room, but it was often found in other parts of the house.

In the living room, my father would pick it up and idly tap it on his glass ashtray, keeping time to the music for *Going for a Song* or *The Beiderbecke Tapes*.

I believe, though I have no proof, that for Margaret it was the prime agent in a ritual designed to make various young men of the village fall in love with her. It seemed to work. Possibly she also used it to put a hex on her rivals – but there was less direct evidence of that.

For my part, I used to stand on one leg and point the bone backwards over my shoulder, aiming its influence at imaginary enemies. Sometimes I did this in the garden, where everyone could see. It didn't work.

Anna never really took to the bone, or said she didn't. But I think she really rather enjoyed the frisson of the macabre that surrounded the bone – or the idea of having it in the house.

Mum looked at it from time to time and frowned, wondering why she didn't find this strange object an unpleasant intruder, why she didn't insist on its being removed from the house. Then she'd turn back to the TV with a little shrug, and the bone would stay.

If the bone had any energy clinging to it, it was not malevolent. I liked to think that the bone was enjoying this little excursion, before it got back to its job of mouldering away.

The bone is in the house now, though it took some ingenuity to get it there. My grandfather, on the other hand, is no problem.

There he sits, where he always sits, in his small house near the beach. His tools are laid out on a cloth on the coffee table, and he works away for hour after hour, absorbed in his work.

We only had one bone, but my grandfather had plenty. He carved them into small sculptures. Scrimshaw, he called it.

'It was a pastime in the whaling ships,' he said. 'Sailors with time on their hands.'

When I was four or five years old, I used to think that he used Granny's bones. It was a good logical conclusion for someone so young. I could see the sequence clearly:

He carved bone, but not very much.

Granny died.

He began to carve lots of bone.

So he'd obviously found a new source.

I didn't like to ask, of course. He was not an easy man to approach. He wasn't unfriendly, it was just that he didn't go out of his way to make you feel at ease. He didn't try to explain things. Just said what he had to say.

I liked to visit him. There was something very satisfying about being there in his house. In the heart of the family, somehow. Just him and me and Granny's bones being turned into curious carvings.

And they were curious. On the medicine chest, a serpent lay, bone white. On the TV, a squid wrestled with a tree. A hunched raven stood by the front door, outside in the weather, slowly turning green.

Some of them were more obviously pretty – a fawn lying on a hillock with a flower or two picked out beside its fore-hoof. A lily flower. A decorative Celtic knot.

Sometimes he would turn and look at me sharply, watching me watching him, wondering if I was interested in the craft. But I wasn't. I just liked the idea of Granny's bones turning into something else. Then the scraps and leftovers got thrown in the bin, and that was all right too.

I eventually realised that, however satisfying the idea, the bones most likely just came from the butcher. Some of them were obviously too big to come from Granny. I still enjoyed visiting him and seeing him working away with his knives and scrapers. Years passed. The house filled up with carvings.

There's a hiatus then, while I go away and spend time elsewhere: university, North Africa, several jobs. When I came back, he was still carving. Though his hands were thinner and slower, he was more skilful. I asked him where the fawn was, the sleeping fawn.

'Threw it away. I went back and looked at it one day and I didn't think much of it. I did another one. It's . . .' He stopped and thought. 'It's on the windowsill at the top of the stairs. Where it catches the sun.'

'You know,' I said, 'I used to think you were carving Granny's bones.' I laughed, but he didn't. He turned his sharp look on me.

'What made you think that?'

'Just a notion I took. After Granny died you did a lot more carving.' I shrugged. 'I was young. It was a silly idea.'

'Well, well, well. That was very perceptive of you.'

'What? Come on, they're not really Granny's bones! She didn't have enough for all this.' I gestured round the room.

'No, that's true. But if they're not from her, they're all for her.'

'Ah.' We seemed to be talking our way into a delicate area. I coughed and asked if I should make a cup of tea. He ignored me.

'She wasn't easy to live with, you know. A strong woman.'

'Oh? Are you sure you don't want a cup of tea?'

He shook his head. 'We had the most terrible arguments.' He smiled. 'She won most of them, I think.' I just waited for him to go on. 'But when she was dead, I missed her – and I even missed the arguments. Strange, eh?'

He was looking at the carving in his fist, not at me.

'After she died, I picked up my tools one day, and all I could think about was that damned smug look on her face when she knew she was in the right. Even though I knew it would do no good, I couldn't help getting angry at her. And that's when a strange thing happened. I put all my anger into the bone. I used the carving to answer her.' He looked up at me then, and smiled again. 'And she couldn't answer back!'

I laughed. He looked like a mischievous boy. I gestured around the room at all the white carvings. 'You must have had a lot of arguments.'

'Yes, we did. And as I remembered all the arguments we had, I started new conversations – and new arguments. All these things I've made, they're all the things I never had a chance to say to her. Partly because she never gave me the chance, and partly because there's things that you just can't say in words.'

He bent over his work and after a while I went for a walk round the house, looking at the bone figures in a different way. Some of them were recognisable, now that I knew who they were. Here was Granny's stern and solid hand lying on a windowsill, clenched. That hen scurrying away – she must have just shouted at it. I wondered if Granddad was the hen. The serpent still lay on the medicine chest, and I wondered what that meant. And that was what the house was like: some parts were so clearly my granny that I could almost hear her voice, but most of them were pictures of someone much more complex than I had ever known.

'I'll take that tea now,' he said when I came back into the living room.

I brought through tea and biscuits and put them out on the table, brushing aside the dust and shards of bone.

'Have a look at this,' he said, and he handed me his latest piece.

It was a hooded figure in a robe, beautifully finished. Even the folds in the cloth were burnished. The robe covered the entire body, but the feet poked out from beneath the hem. The toes were precisely detailed, each toenail distinct, even on the little toe.

He leant forward, holding out his hand. There was a scrap of wire wool in it. 'I used this for the toes,' he whispered. 'I know they didn't have wire wool on the whaling ships, but, hell, it's the best way to finish the little details.'

I turned it round to look at the face. It was hidden deep in the cowl, and it was rough, unpolished and distinctly malevolent.

I looked up at him.

He looked back at me. 'Well?'

'Well, it's. I don't know. It's not her, is it?'

'Oh, aye. That's her all right. Smooth and beautiful on the outside, strong as an axe on the inside.'

I shuddered.

'Her blood runs in your veins, you know. And all the better for it.'

'But she looks dreadful.'

'Aye. But that's the way she was. That's the way people are.'

I looked him over and tried to imagine him like this, dark and fierce inside. He nodded.

'I had a whole life before you came along. I wasn't a grandfather all my days.' Then his eyes settled on my face and I looked back, and we didn't say anything for a long time.

'I'd better be going,' I said.

'You haven't finished your tea.'

It had grown cold. I picked it up and swallowed it at a gulp, then walked to the door. He struggled out of his chair and came with me. Strangely, he shook my hand as I left. He'd never done that before and I'm sure he meant something by it.

Granddad died, as is the way. I was sad, for a while, but he had left me with such a conundrum that it almost felt as if he was still there, looking me in the eye and telling me about Granny and him.

So I went back for the funeral and, afterwards, at his house, I took a couple of his sculptures: the fawn asleep and the cowled figure with the savage face. I took his tools too, the homemade scrapers and the knives with wooden handles. 'Made from an old saw,' he told me once. 'Best steel you can get.'

And before I left, I went to see my mum and dad, and I climbed up to Margaret's room at the top of the house. She was working in Glasgow now, but her room was as she'd left it. It didn't take much searching to find the bone, and I took it away with me.

Looking out of my own window, I can see the lights of the city spreading out to left and right as far as I can see, but, directly in front, the lights reach an edge, and stop. The sea. One or two small lights move out there – boats, far out and going further.

On the windowsill sit the two carvings I took from Grand-dad's house: one to remember him and one to remember Granny. Because, no matter whom he made them for, each one is a picture of him too.

And that's where I work on the bone, carving one head out of each end. One for him and one for her. I'm not very good at carving, but they will do. They'll say what they need to say. Two people completely separate, but joined together.

When the carving is done, it's time for the melodrama. A long train journey back home, then into the graveyard at dead of night, with a spade. I find their gravestone and carefully cut out a turf and dig a trench. I drop the bone in and cover it over. By the time I've stamped the turf back into place, no-one would know it had been disturbed. The sky is overcast and a small rain is falling. I put out my torch and let the dark come back.

It is black as midnight; the night has its paws on my eyes, but I am not afraid.

Unravelling

Angus Dunn

'I show you only the best!'

The shopkeeper beckoned us through to the back room. Jake and I sat down on a pile of rugs and looked around. The shopkeeper stuffed hashish into the bowl of a water pipe and passed it to me. I sucked hard on it until the smoke came through, then passed it to Jake. The merchant pulled carpet after carpet from a pile, letting us see each one before going on to the next. I reached for one of them and stroked the wool. It felt good.

'How much for this one?'

'You have dollars?'

'Some.'

'Only three hundred dollars.'

Jake laughed, coughing out a cloud of smoke. He turned over the corner of the carpet and shook his head. 'This is a shop carpet.'

The shopkeeper was outraged. 'No, effendi! This is antique!'

Jake held up the carpet, showing me the reverse side of the weave and some indecipherable marks in Persian script. 'Look,' he said, 'it is a new carpet. It's been on the shop floor for a few months to make it look older.'

The carpet was about seven feet by four, with an abstract pattern marked out by lines of deep green. Within these lines, oranges and yellows glowed. When the shopkeeper gave us a pipe to smoke, he was probably hoping for just this kind of effect.

I touched the orange, to see if I could feel the warmth of the colour. 'I like it anyway.'

'You see? This man, he knows a good carpet!'

Jake snorted and bent to the pipe again. The water gurgled as he drew in a good lungful of smoke.

'I'll give you fifty,' I said.

'Fifty! Is not possible!'

The baby crawled towards the carpet and you picked him up. 'That carpet can't stay there,' you said.

'Why not?'

'Well, look at it. Brian can't crawl on that – it's not exactly clean, is it?'

I tried to look at the small carpet dispassionately. 'You're right. I'll Hoover it.'

'It needs more than that.' You grimaced. 'You don't know where it's been.'

I laughed. 'Oh, yes I do. I certainly do!'

'Well, it needs cleaned.'

'All right, all right.'

It seemed a little disrespectful to put the carpet into the washing machine, but I could think of no other way to clean it thoroughly. Not knowing how the carpet would take it, I stuffed it in and turned the washing machine on: lowest temperature, gentlest wash. When it came out, I carried the heavy damp bundle to the washing line, hoping that it hadn't shrunk.

Jake was too stoned to travel with. I left him with some road-hippies in Kabul and headed back. It was a bad time of year to be travelling. The snow was still thick in northern Turkey, and the bus was old and cold. Every few miles we passed the wreck of a bus or an articulated lorry. Walls of snow edged the road. The constant attrition of grit and slush had carved the snow into baroque sculptures, white towers edged with black residue from diesel exhaust. I drowsed, dreaming that these random snow-sculptures had a meaning and I could almost decipher them. Every now and then I woke, thinking – this is delirium brought on by hypothermia. The man sitting beside me looked like a Turkish bandit. He had a savage nose and a wild moustache. I sat close to the window, giving him as much space as I could.

At the next stop, I got the driver to open the luggage compartment and I untied the carpet from my rucksack. I climbed back onto the bus. Thirty or forty Turks watched me curiously – and me without a word of Turkish, apart from '*ekmek*', bread. When we started again, I laid the carpet on my legs to keep warm.

The bandit looked at me, then away. He probably carries a knife, I thought. I tucked the carpet snug. It was still six hours to Istanbul. My eyelids were beginning to droop when I caught the eye of the Turkish bandit. He scowled and nodded sharply. I turned away. He tapped me on the shoulder. I kept looking out of the window, desperately wondering what to do. The fierce Turk took my shoulder and shook it and I had to turn round to face him.

'What? What do you want?'

He scowled and nodded once more, then he jabbered something and poked my knee with his finger.

I held up my hands. 'Listen, man, I don't know what's wrong, but whatever it is, it's not my fault, right?'

He sighed, picked up my carpet and carefully draped it over both my lap and his.

'Oh!' I started laughing. 'Yes, Okay. No problem.'

He patted my knee, patted his own. 'Okay?' he asked, his eyebrows raised.

'Yes, yes. Very okay.'

I sat there, grinning to myself. After a while I sensed movement from the Turkish bandit and he nudged me again. '*Ekmek?*' He tore a chunk off his loaf and passed it to me.

I smiled and nodded and used the entirety of our shared vocabulary: 'Ekmek okay.'

When I got home from work, I saw it hanging there, blowing in the wind. The pattern was clear once again, almost like it had been when I first saw it in the shop: the curlicues and the almost-flower shapes, the lines that might be Arabic calligraphy or might just be decoration. The oranges and the yellows were bright – but not quite as bright as I remembered. The dark-green lines had faded to a blue. It showed no signs of shrinkage. I was glad that it had been washed.

I unpegged it. It felt lighter. Was that possible? I held it up in the sunlight and pinpricks of light came through. It had become worn.

I folded it carefully, carried it to the house and replaced it in front of the fire. You came through then.

'The carpet's clean.' I said.

'Good.'

'It's a bit worn, but look at the colours. That orange there, that's what I liked, when I first saw it. It looked warm, friendly.' I laughed at myself. 'Friendly? Well, it did.'

'Cup of coffee? I'm just having one. Brian's still asleep, thank God.'

'Yes, coffee, thanks.' I straightened the carpet before following her through to the kitchen.

I was hitching north through Spain. It was July, and very hot. I got a lift with four penniless French students. At nightfall, we pulled off the road. The ground was stony, with scattered bushes. The sky was clear and the night was warm. I rolled the carpet around me and slept on the ground.

Finally finding work, I needed a place to stay. I found a room in a shared house. It was a grim room. Bare boards for a floor, bare walls and a bare bulb. The furniture was a shoogly bed with two thin blankets and two coarse sheets. I laid the carpet on the floor and I was home.

At a conference in Salzburg, we all stayed in a hostel run by nuns. It was a bit of a surprise, but it didn't seem to inhibit anyone, so I joined in the drinking and dancing until late at night.

Next morning, I felt awful. Not hungover, but shattered. I couldn't face the idea of travelling. The place was stirring, people heading for breakfast. I needed quiet. In an annexe, there was a meditation room – I'd seen the sign on the wall, in three languages. I slipped downstairs, left my rucksack in the corridor and entered the room. It had high windows and a blond wooden floor, and it was wonderfully quiet. I did a few simple exercises. Two other people came in and did likewise, silently. Then another person, and a few more. Soon there were a dozen of us, all silently stretching and bending.

Enter the Master. No question about that. Built like a tank, with a shaven head and an Oriental face. The silence became even more silent. He pulled a small bell from his robe and rang it. Everyone arranged themselves on the floor cross-legged. I sat down too. He frowned, pointed to the others, then back at me, saying something in German. I looked around. Everyone else had brought a mat.

I smiled and held up one finger. I slipped out of the door and returned with the carpet. I rolled it out and sat again. The Master grunted, rang his bell and began chanting strange syllables, not in German. We all closed our eyes. Afterwards I had breakfast and left, and I still have no idea who he was.

I pushed the last spoonful of mush towards Emily's face and she turned sideways. I wiped the food off her ear and let her out of the high chair. Brian came screaming into the living room, arms spread, being a jet plane. He stopped beside Grace, who was building a city and had Lego all around her.

'There's been a crash landing,' he told her. 'Everyone has just been wiped out in a giant fireball!'

'Can you please go outside if you're going to crash land,' I said.

Emily was crawling over to the fireguard. I wiped the tray with her bib.

'It was a power dive. I had to wipe out an alien invasion.'

Emily was pulling herself upright, the wires of the fireguard squashing into her little plump fingers.

'Fine, but can't they invade the garden?'

Brian was quiet for a moment while I folded the high chair. 'They're descended from cockroaches,' he said. 'They don't like the sunlight.'

'You're too clever by half. But no more screaming in the house.'

Emily saw Grace, playing with the Lego, head bent, long hair falling straight down. She loved Grace's hair. It was golden and shiny and her favourite thing in the world was to get one hand in among it and rub it against her own ear. She looked down at the carpet and her knees began to bend. Then she stood upright again and let go of the fireguard, lurching towards Grace.

'Jean,' I called, as loudly as I could without distracting Emily. 'Jean, she's walking!'

I heard your feet clattering down the stairs and the door opened. You stood there and I sat still, watching. Even Brian was motionless for a moment. Emily took another step, caught her foot in the carpet and fell onto her knees among the Lego.

'That carpet has to go,' you said, while Emily was being cuddled and comforted.

'It's just a little frayed . . .'

'Yes. And it's dangerous. Emily fell today, but it could be Grace tomorrow, or anyone.'

I sighed. 'Okay. I'll move it.' I folded it and took it upstairs. It wasn't really that bad, just a little looseness in the weave at one end. But it really ought to be out of the way, at least until Emily could walk properly. I went into our bedroom and laid it down at the foot of the bed and it was instantly at home.

'Look,' I said, later. 'Isn't that a good place for it?'

'Oh,' you said.

'It looks good there.'

'I suppose so.'

The Intercontinental Hotel, Amman. I was overwhelmed by the opulence of it, the subservient staff, the immense and wonderful buffet breakfast table.

Coming back after a day's work, the lobby was cool enough to make me shiver. I went to my room and sat there. The expenses didn't extend to visiting the Starlight Night Club up on the roof. There was nothing to do and underneath the excessive comfort, it was just another anonymous hotel. But this was my lodging for the next few weeks. I took the carpet from my luggage and laid it out on the soft flooring.

When I got home from work, the cleaners had carefully folded it and put it away on the slatted luggage rack in the wardrobe. I took it out again. Each day, they put it away. Each evening, I took it out again.

The only Jordanian I ever spoke to was my driver, Jamil. He thought I was beautiful. He said so. Then he winked and stroked my shoulder. I dissuaded him, forcefully, but we were still friends. He started teaching me Arabic words and phrases. It was something to do on the long drive out to the site. He taught me Muslim affirmations, and was delighted when I picked it up. He was half-laughing at me, I'm sure, but I joined in the game.

La illaha il allahu! We shouted the phrases in the car as we sped recklessly along the road. Alhamdulillah!

In the hotel, after eating, I took a penny whistle from my bags and tweetled to myself. I couldn't hold a tune, but there was no-one to hear – and the resonance of the room made it sound better. I put the whistle down and tried out the phrases Jamil had taught me. Alhamdulillah! Bismillah! They rang out in a very satisfying way.

In the morning, I always ran through a checklist before I left. Wallet in the pocket, plans in the shoulder bag, passport in the bag strung around my neck. All okay. I turned the door handle and quickly scanned the room. Hardly a sign of human habitation, except the untidy bed and, on the floor, the carpet, which would be neatly tidied away when I returned. Before I left the room, I called out loudly. La illaha il allahu!

It sounded great.

I turned from locking the door, and the cleaners were in the hall, a few yards away. They watched me intently. They must have heard me shouting in my room. I could feel myself blushing as I walked past them.

When I got back that evening, the carpet was where I had left it, though the rest of the room had been tidied.

When I got back from Amman, I needed a place to stay, and for the first time in my life, I didn't want to rent. I wanted something more permanent. When you came up to my flat for coffee, the first time, that carpet was on the floor, in front of the fireplace, where an electric fire stood on the tiled hearth. We turned off all the lights, but left the fire on, so that the room was warm and dim. The glow fell on you and me, and it fell on the carpet. There was nowhere to sit, nowhere to sleep, there was nothing else in the flat.

'This bedroom needs redecorated.'

'Does it?'

'Of course it does. Look at the handprints on the wall. The felt-tip pen. The . . . What is that?'

'Don't know.'

'Well, it was fine while the kids were young, but now it needs redone.'

'Mhm.'

'Blue? Or peach. What do you think?'

'Whatever you like.'

'No, tell me what you'd like.'

'Blue.'

'Not peach?'

'Blue.'

You redecorated it one weekend while I was away with the girls, climbing Arkle. We stayed in the bothy and came back late on Sunday. You must have been working non-stop. The bedroom was bright and fresh and new.

'Wow! What a job you've done. It looks great.'

You simpered theatrically. 'Oh, it was nothing. Just a lick of paint, a new carpet and an inspired sense of style.'

I looked around. 'Where's the carpet?'

'On the floor, silly.'

'No, the little one, my carpet.'

'Oh, it really doesn't go with the peach. I put it in the utility room. It's a bit shabby. I hadn't realised how bad . . .'

'It's all right.'

You shrugged. 'I think it's about time we got rid of it.'

'Time we got rid of it?'

'Yes, you know. Time we replaced it.'

'We replaced it? We?'

'What do you mean?'

'*We* shan't replace it, because it's not *ours*. It's mine.'

Your lips tightened. 'It's frayed at the edges, it's threadbare and it's faded. It's time it was thrown out.'

You said it flat, in the tone of an ultimatum. My heart thudded loudly and my chest felt too tight to breathe. I couldn't think of anything to say, while you looked at me, and I didn't even know where to start. Because I could see that it was not an accident, this little argument. It was the latest move in a long campaign. You wanted rid of that carpet.

Half a lifetime ago, I bought a carpet in Kandahar. It warmed my legs and those of a Turkish bandit, it has given me shade in the heat. It has been a prayer rug and an exercise mat. It has been my blanket and my bed in railway stations, in buses, on ferries and on the hard ground. Wherever I was, I only had to lay it out and I knew that I was home. There have been times when it was all I owned, apart from my clothes. I didn't try to hang onto it, it just happened. One day, suddenly, it's twenty-five years later and the carpet is still here, and nothing else is still here.

But while the words filled my head, they wouldn't come out of my mouth. You can tell when someone is not ready to listen, you can tell when a mind is made up.

'This carpet has been with me for half my life,' I said. 'It's been to places you can't imagine.'

'A pity,' you said, 'that you didn't leave it in one of those places.'

With a leaden thump, an insight fell into place. You were jealous of my carpet. And the amazing thing was, you were right to feel jealous. I love that carpet, though I hadn't realised it until that moment.

As the words came out, I knew they were going to cause trouble. 'I've known that carpet longer than I've known you,' I said. 'It belongs here.'

What an odd way, I thought, for our life to fall apart.

How She Came to Write a Poem Called 'Apostrophe'

Dorothy Alexander

*H**er friend died and she was heartbroken.*
That was in February.

In December when the chill had really taken hold there were a few days of spectacular hoar frost, and it was on one of those days that the first image of the poem hooked itself in.

On the edge of a field in the middle distance, a line of bush-like trees formed a sparkling horizon. There was something about them, held in the powdery air of frost that elicited the first words: trees, cold-powdered, whispered, static. She repeated them as she walked. She wrote them down when she got home.

Her friend died and she was heartbroken because it was as if she had come to know some wild but gentle creature that had emerged from the edge of a dark wood; its timidity, its watchful calm bringing out in her a stillness, a desire to be near.

Isn't it the case when you love something that you never tire of looking at it? Each viewing notes a minute difference, there to be appreciated. She felt this way about the hills of the Tweed valley. It was an easy, accessible feeling. She was driving along the valley south of Innerleithen, wondering how she might feel if she didn't live here, when this line appeared in her head,

'In exile I would write the colours of the hills in winter.'

And further along the same road, at a certain bend where it comes very close to the river, the water looked almost still, and that day it had taken on a peculiar colour because of the snow, the shaded position, the trees. She pulled into a layby and scribbled in her notebook, 'the river, eau de Nil, in snow, quiet'. She put brackets around 'in snow'.

And she had gained its trust, this vulnerable, shy creature.

One day in January, as she crossed the Lowood bridge near Melrose, she noticed how the low sun shone through an artless, jagged mix of bare deciduous wood and Scots pine. The sky had thickened in the frosty air, fogging the sun:
    orb, glowing in black trees.
She wrestled with the image, trying to make it exact; it was more an effusion of white mist.

Her friend died and she was heartbroken because she would miss the way her long fingers described the beauty of a thing, the way her limbs moved like a river over stones that would run through her fingers should she try to hold it.
    Because from the minute she knew that it was to be death at the end of winter, it was as if the blown light of February had been absorbed, locked into naked trees, as if there could be no synthesis of spring.

And then it was February again. Sitting on the couch in her upstairs room, she looked out at the sky framed by skeletons of ash and birch, at the undulations of the nearest hills. She sketched the words:

(winter sky),   shades and tones   very bright
low light fissured cloud grey sage quiet
whispering   still
openings of blue, of cream,

the trees don't move, the hills don't move,
trees black and still.

At the bottom of the page she later scribbled an assortment of words that had appealed to her from the dictionary: undersurface, linen-fold, stiffness, apostrophe, mediaeval, and a little reminder of something from the Tao, 'in the Tao there are no separate objects, just differentiations of form within the universe'.

She tried putting together all the fragments and little notes she had made.

As her first line she would take, 'in exile I would write the colours of the hills in winter'. She thought that she might carry on, name the trees, describe the fields, count out the names of farms, villages, towns along the roads of home, a litany of remembrance, poignant. But she was not in exile, therefore she would write of each minute change, each daily, seasonal difference, and the underlying emotion would be quiet joy, something intensely alive and real; the river would flow, she would feel the air, touch and smell the earth.

Because she had held her as she sank forward in bed with her face in her hands and said that she was scared.

But then another voice took over. It began,

'as now in winter the sun appears as an effusion of white'
(she scored out white)
'mist through black trees,
a litany of rivers
exiled in snow
smooth their patterns to eau de Nil
the sky has written the colours of the hills
its undersurface of clouds
shades and tones of bright and low light
fissured, remembering
trees hold haze and powder

113

whispered static
earth, stiffness of linen-folds'.

It was February, the month she died. It was going to be about grief, remembrance, and how time puts distance between.

And since then there had been the doctor's visit. The doctor had told her three weeks at most. She should get her affairs in order.

This knowledge hung between them now. Her friend was sitting in an armchair. She was wearing a light dressing gown and a pale-blue woollen hat because her hair had never grown back after chemotherapy. She was so thin and pale that her face seemed to be disappearing. But she smiled as always . . . so pleased to see her. Her voice was as warm as ever, just the dry edge of it a bit drier, a bit weaker. Conversation was by the way, she smiled and laughed, and when it came time to leave she said that she was welcome any time.

That this might not be the final farewell was the only thing keeping it all sane. She said her name as they embraced. A last look from the door, then out to the car. She felt as if she had left all colour behind, that from now on she would see the world in monochrome. Climbing the steps to her house, she noticed a small group of unopened snowdrops. There was something about their helmet-like heads that was so like hers. Later she wrote a poem with too many adjectives in it.

> *Ghosted drifts of sleet,*
> *your face with the certainty of death in it;*
> *an unopened snowdrop filled with ironic laughter,*
> *breaking through cold pity to pure white compassion.*

She wrote 'lucidity' at the top of the page.

Underneath the last line, she wrote:

'(hills, fields), engraved, cradled, ghosted, unopened snow-drops, stoic'.

The word 'exile' was expanded to give what she knew would

be the final line, 'in exile from a time with you in it'. A column of words started to form in the right-hand side of the page, 'irony, remembrance, laughter, memory, compassion'. 'Mediaeval' moved into place beneath 'effusion' and 'mist'. 'Apostrophe' moved to the top of the page.

Apostrophe: a mark of elision, denoting something missing.

Because she remembered when they cycled to Gott Bay. It was a day of wind and sun, the air a brisk colour-wash of remembered blues. Dried marram rasped through their wheels but fell silent when they stopped and saw the bay for the first time. 'This is heaven,' her friend had shouted to the wind, and to her. Sand lay like a strip of torn vellum. Great waves rolled and pushed their huge energies. They had stood and stood; all their looking rhythmed, scoured by wild water. Terns, close above them, shared the unruly wind, held them in their eye. And when she thought about that day it was hard not to see, even in that moment, that fate already had her cast: genre, film noir; soundtrack, waves tearing.

She scored out 'the colours of the hills' and wrote 'compassion' above. 'On' was added to the beginning of the next line. 'Ironic' replaced 'exiled' in the line about snow, and two new lines emerged,

> 'remembering earth; stiff as linen-folds
> fissured, engraved with unopened snowdrops'.

In the meantime she picked up a Nonesuch Library edition of Donne's poems (she was in the mood for something mournful). She searched for 'A Nocturnall upon St Lucie's Day'. She sought the grief-laden texture of its cadences. The songs and sonnets were followed by the epigrams and then by the elegies. Elegies; elegy, the word went round and round. She was writing one.

'Elegy', a mourning song, a lament, a serious, pensive poem.

'Elegiac quatrain', four line stanzas, written in iambic

115

pentameter, rhyming abab, classic example Gray's 'Elegy Written in a Country Churchyard'.

She visited her friend three days before she died. She took some rice pudding . . . something soft, that she might be tempted to eat. She took a big cashmere scarf that her grandmother had knitted. She took a card that had a painting of frilled cream-coloured tulips against a pale-blue ground on the front. Inside the card she wrote how much she appreciated her as a friend and that she loved her. Opposite this she inscribed a short poem by Raymond Carver, written when he was dying of cancer. It was called 'Late Fragment'.

> *And did you get what you*
> *wanted from this life even so,*
> *Yes I did.*
> *And what did you want?*
> *To call myself beloved,*
> *To feel myself beloved on the earth.*

She took a fresh piece of paper. Apostrophe, title. Elegy written in the top right-hand corner.

She counted out the syllables of the pentameter. They looked like this:

> As now in winter the sun appears through
> black boughs, effusion, mist, mediaeval.
> A litany of rivers, ironic
> in snow, smooth their patterns to eau de Nil.

She was amazed.

> The sky writes compassion on the underside
> of clouds, in shades of bright—light,
> remembering earth stiff as linen-folds,
> fissured, engraved with unopened snowdrops.

116

This would need some work, and the last stanza would have only two lines.

Trees held in haze and powder; whispered static,
in exile from a time with you in it.

But they scanned. They half-rhymed.

She was so pleased. It looked as if it would work as a form of elegy. She deliberately did not want to force it into the classic form. She wanted to be aware of it, acknowledge the rules but break them to give a lighter, more modern feel. In the second stanza she changed the third line to 'remembering earth's stiffness as linen-folds', 'remembering' now given only three syllables. Another small column of words began to appear in the bottom right-hand margin: 'former, previous, ancient, old, golden, lapse, something missing, absent, predecessors, lineage, forbears'. A circle was whirled around 'lapse'. Sounding 'ps', it took its place at the end of the line. Then, as if from nowhere, the word 'oblivious' arrived and the second line was rewritten thus: 'of clouds, oblivious to bright or lapse'. And that was it. She checked it over: syllables, rhyme and half-rhyme, the chiming of the short a's, the long o's, the short i's, the incidental rhyming of first and third line end words in the first two stanzas with other words in the second and fourth lines of each; not too many adjectives, and those that were there were working hard.

Her husband read it. 'Fissured is a favourite word of yours.'

She stared and stared at the offending word. She pencilled in 'fractured', although 'fissured' was not scored out. Two days later 'fractured' was inserted. It gave another short 'a', it kept the sense, enhanced it even, gave it a harder feel, and chimed with the hard c's of 'ironic', 'compassion', 'static'. She scribbled out 'the' before 'underside' and changed it to 'undersides'. Her husband didn't like this. That was his favourite line, just the way it was: elided.

*And when she wrote in a poem that she wore her grief as a shroud
of spilt colours, she could hear her friend reminding her that the
pigment of their lives was as indeterminate as the blue of the sky.*

Apostrophe

As now in winter the sun appears through
black boughs, effusion, mist, mediaeval;
a litany of rivers, ironic
in snow, smooth their patterns to eau de Nil.

The sky writes compassion on the underside
of clouds, oblivious to bright or lapse,
remembering earth's stiffness as linen-folds,
fractured, engraved with unopened snowdrops.

Trees hold haze and powder; whispered; static;
in exile from a time with you in it.

A Tasmanian Tiger in London

Rachael McGill

raised by numbats

No-one was answering the phone in the accommodation office and the weather predicted on the radio was sleetsnowrainwet-cold. Shelly had tried unsuccessfully for an hour to fantasise about the neighbour she was hoping to cultivate a sexual obsession for. Also she was being visited by an uninvited tiger. Previously there had been no tigers in her life but over the last few days there had been sightings.

On Tuesday evening she had been reading the paper to fill the hours between the end of work and the reasonable time to go to the bar. She was not feeling strong so she had started with the science pages as the least likely to contain things which might remind her of other things which might be sad. But the science pages contained a story about the resurrection from the dead through genetic engineering of the extinct Tasmanian tiger, or thylacine. The thylacine was a wolf-like animal with black stripes. The last one had died in a zoo in 1936 and now they were going to piece together its DNA and grow an embryo using the egg of a numbat, its nearest living relative. The numbat looked like a tiny kangaroo. The writer of the article had some worries about the psychological effects on the new thylacine:

> *Would thylacines embryonically hybridised with num-*
> *bats, gestated inside numbats, and raised by numbats*
> *(presumably as little numbats) know how to be thylacines?*

119

I'm not part of a family, I'm just a child my mother had, Shelly thought. The reading of the article had set her progress back approximately two weeks.

I might as well have been raised by a numbat, presumably as a little numbat.

And what was more worrying than the issue of identity was the whole question of whether the thylacine would want to come back.

I am numb like a numbat, she thought.

I love him, I'm wearing his socks.

A second tiger thing had happened the next morning when she went into the tube station. A bearded man was shaking a tin and holding up a placard asking people to help save the last two hundred Siberian tigers. The brand-new Tasmanian tiger Shelly had inadvertently allowed into her head was angry. 'Leave them alone,' it growled. 'They're going to die, let them die. What makes you think they have any desire to remain on this planet as it is?'

The violence of the Tasmanian tiger's reactions to things that Shelly had become numbatted to was unsettling. It noticed in someone's newspaper that a Malaysian tanker had been spilling the corrosive chemical phenol into the South China Sea since Friday, wiping out fish. It became outraged and upset. Shelly sympathised because the new tiger didn't yet understand that the world was just like this, but all the same it was tiring.

The next day she put on his dirty blue socks and incanted as she battled home from work through the rain, 'I love him, I'm wearing his socks, I love him, I'm wearing his socks.'

The tiger found her incantation pitiful and her weakness repellent and wondered why she would want to go to work in dirty socks that didn't fit. The tiger was not a positive development. She was disgusted enough with herself for reverting to the socks thing without having someone around drawing attention to it.

pebble-like moments

The bar that night put the tiger on edge. People came in relaxed then started growling at each other. Others came in walking a few feet apart and later nestled together like sleeping pups, noses against cheeks.

Shelly's friend Adele talked about a man she had met in a club. 'We just clocked eyes and it was like "yeah, how are you, mate?" '

Shelly couldn't remember what she'd felt the first time she'd met Owen. She knew she'd been in the Crown at lunchtime with her mother and he'd come in and sat down opposite. She didn't remember what he'd been wearing, what she'd been wearing, what she'd thought. All her brain had recorded was the swinging of the long yellow earrings of a woman she'd passed on the way to the bar.

The Tasmanian tiger wondered why the people in the bar invaded each other's territory and ate from the same packet of crisps.

Shelly had realised that Owen was the only man she would ever love two weeks later, while handing him a ticket from the machine to stick on the car windscreen.

'He said do you want to see me again and I said no, mate, let's just leave it in the moment,' said Adele.

Leaving it in the moment was not something Shelly had a talent for. She had pebble-like moments rattling in all her pockets. They were nothing special, they should have been left on the beach, but she liked to touch them when she was nervous.

different kinds and different colours of felt-tipped pens

No-one was answering the phone in the accommodation office so Shelly walked up the hill to the college, encouraged by the dream she had had the night before. She had dreamt she had lots of different kinds and different colours of felt-tipped pens.

The course wasn't till September but Shelly had already thrown herself into the appreciation of stationery. Clear box files, wallets with plastic zippy bits, folders with boingy rubber bits at the corners. The college students didn't carry bags: they walked about with folders clasped across their chests.

Shelly was aware that the world was full of a million things but she could only ever concentrate on one or two of them at a time. When tired, sad parts of her spoke and said, 'But surely all anyone really wants is to be madly in love with the same person forever?', she no longer told herself that the world was full of a million things and love was only one. She got quicker results by telling herself that the world was full of stationery.

The tiger agreed that stationery might serve as some sort of protection. Its camouflage had so far felt effective only against the upholstery on the Northern Line.

In the accommodation office no-one had torn the strips with her phone number off the bottom of her advert and there had been no enquiries.

In the café the woman with the wavy grey hair leaned across her apricot tart to the man who scratched and asked sadly: 'But how does Derrida expect us to escape logocentrism?'

Shelly was going to be studying social work, which she didn't think contained Derrida, but she knew that after having been a student it would be acceptable for her to use it as the name of her first cat.

'Or,' said Wavygrey, 'is it logocentricity?'

Like eccentricity and electricity. Shelly felt hopeful because she wanted to be wrapped up in conversations like that almost as desperately as she had wanted to be wrapped up in a double duvet on the sofa of her mother's lover.

The girl with the orange hair was there. Shelly could never stop staring at her: there was more to look at on her than on other people. Five students were floating around the orange woman waiting to say something. The orange woman was drinking an espresso and working on a laptop. 'In a second, Julie,' she called, 'I'm just sending Noam Chomsky an email.'

'Educated fools,' Amanda would have said.

I love him inside out.
Shelly went home on the bus and halfway down the hill Sexual
Obsession got on. Shelly stayed very still and looked out of the
window. The tiger piped up: is he a student too? Is an email
good or bad?
Shelly ignored it and recklessly read the science pages.

*A US geoscientist predicts that the earth has reached the final 10%
of its lifespan.*

Is this a coincidence or is he following you? Will he know what
we can do about the fish?

*Within half a billion years the oceans are expected to dry up and
low carbon-dioxide levels will destroy plant life.*

Why don't you talk to him? Should we look for some food soon?
    What had happened to the science pages? They used to be
about why garlic was good for you.
    Just before the library Sexual Obsession stood up. Shelly was
relieved until she remembered she was obsessed with him. She
shoved the newspaper down the side of the seat so it could upset
a wider audience, gathered up her mutinous box files and
followed him off the bus.
    Love, Owen said, was like waiting for a bus. Did you wait for
your ideal bus or did you get on the first one that came along even
if it only went some of the way? That, Shelly had replied,
depended on whether it was raining. It's a mental attitude said
Owen. Some people don't let a few spots of rain put them off.
    Was Shelly frightened of males, the tiger wondered, and if so,
why did she think about them all the time?
    Sexual Obsession went into the library and Shelly hovered
outside under a tree. Go in, said the tiger. A library's the perfect
place to bump into your sexual obsession. It was learning
quickly. But was it learning the right things? If only the poor
animal had managed to get inside a more edifying head.
    Owen was worried because the word from her mother was that

Shelly would get on any old bus, a 242, even a 55. When Shelly said that the trouble was that often when it wasn't raining she was convinced it was, he put his hand lightly on her shoulder. He knew this was a serious admission but at the same time he appreciated the fact that she was keeping up his metaphor about the buses.

Shelly had hesitated for too long and was now unwilling to go into the library in case he was only dropping books off and came back out at the wrong time and confused things. But she didn't want him to come out and see her standing under a tree either. She could feel panicky yelps preparing themselves so she concentrated on reading things written on signs.

Her shoulder had been singing a song all of its own where Owen's hand was and inside her things had detached themselves and were whizzing about. She'd thought I love him inside and out, I love him inside out. She had wanted to say, 'But you're my 38 bus. You're the bus that goes all the way to Victoria, which is usually even further than you want to go.'

Authorised Clamping Unit.

Love is like waiting for a bus.

Bicycles chained to this railing will be removed.

You're my bus, you're my bus.

No parking, entrance in constant use.

You're my 38 bus.

'Shelly! Hey, Shelly!'

He had come out of the library. She looked at her watch as if she had been waiting for someone and had decided to give up. She turned and walked away, trying to look like someone distracted who might not have heard someone calling them. After the corner she started to run.

Felt-tip pens with thin tips, with thick tips, with flexible brush like tips.

The tiger roared to make itself heard: he wants to be with you, he is an ideal mate for you, all you had to do was stand still!

Felt-tip pens with italic tips that make beautiful effects but only if you hold them the right way round.

a terrible, wild little place

The Tasmanian tiger was finding Shelly increasingly indecipherable. Later that evening, the male from outside the library visited, presumably eager to mate. Shelly hid at the bottom of her wardrobe instead of answering the door.

Things were happening at Shelly and the world was expecting her to live through them. Stationery was just stationery and she had resorted to turning and turning her pebble-moments around in her pockets.

The tiger thought it might be time for dinner, but Shelly packed a small blue suitcase with an impractical collection of things and they walked in the dark past pubs with shouting, swaying people outside them to a railway station which smelled of urine.

Twice Shelly and the tiger started to make a phone call from a payphone and then stopped. At last they went to a kiosk and bought a bacon roll.

Shelly didn't eat bacon anymore: she had become vegetarian as part of her new life. She had last eaten a bacon roll in a late grubby café with Owen the night she had told him she loved him. The half-hour they had spent on the bus going to the café was her favourite pebble.

They paid 20p to go into a toilet where a woman was washing different coloured pairs of tights in the sink. She was speaking to the tights, saying, 'You want to go in don't you? No, you don't want to go in.' They sat in a toilet booth and read all the graffiti on the door. Then they left the station and waited for a bus back home.

On the bus to the bacon roll Shelly had pretended that Owen's arm around her meant everything it could mean instead of some of it. She had pretended that when she told him he would have an answer that meant everyone would be happy. It was the last time she could pretend anything before she spoiled it, scattering her emotions around like silly stripy skittles.

125

The tiger was beginning to understand that sometimes people wrote on doors or talked to their clothing rather than explaining themselves to each other.

Owen had squeezed her hand. He was himself and not the blond man in *A Room with a View*.

At home Shelly unpacked the blue suitcase.

This world, thought the tiger, is a terrible, wild little place.

sweet and sour emotional dips

Shelly was putting all of her hope into the red and purple border she was drawing around her notice. She wouldn't be able to stop herself going home if she didn't get a room at the university soon. She needed to find a student who might want to give up their room early.

Someone was crying at the table behind. There was usually someone crying in the café, but Shelly listened in case it was a misfit yearning to drop out.

The unhappiness of people was contemptible to the tiger. Combined with their desperation to trust, it made them easier to fool than a baby gazelle.

'I feel terrible. Nobody ever told me you feel so terrible so soon.'

'I feel terrible,' Shelly had said. 'Nobody ever told me you feel so terrible so soon.'

Amanda had never told her although she had told her that she had never wanted children but had run out of things she might be good at, and that it was a myth that all mothers loved their babies.

'I don't want to tell Adrian but I'm scared.'

The orange hair was scared.

It had been like flu but worse. Shelly wanted to sleep until it went away.

'I can't wait six weeks!' cried orange hair.

'I can't wait four weeks!' Shelly had said. Her life was on hold: she could concentrate on nothing but the uninvited

126

processes that were taking possession of the body she had thought was hers.

Her moods were unpredictable. 'Don't go out now,' she had wailed. 'I'm having an emotional dip.'

'I can't go to Literary Theory, Julie. Will you stay here with me?'

Owen had taken a week off work and had left her only to go to the shop.

'I'll get you tortilla chips and sweet and sour emotional dips,' he said.

'It's OK Marina. I'll come with you to the . . . the . . .' Julie said.

When she came out he had been waiting on a small grey sofa and looking worried. He had driven her back to his house and she had slept for two days.

'It's thousands, private, isn't it?'

And he had put it on his Visa card.

'Must be,' Julie said, 'must be thousands.'

It was the factual inaccuracy that made Shelly turn round. She never spoke to strangers, particularly not to beautiful young women in pairs, but all three of them were crying, so it was different.

'Please, please!' came out of Shelly.

She put both her hands on their table because they were shaking.

'It's a charity,' she said. 'I kept the leaflets.'

When it left Shelly, the tiger was planning to cover long distances using the Northern Line, where the darkness was pleasing, though not the noise.

my bed is my sugar
The room was on the top floor with a view down the hill to where she used to live. So perhaps she could still keep an eye on Sexual Obsession, Shelly joked to the tiger. But the tiger was hiding. Somewhere under a chair.

Practically one whole wall was window. How could she be unhappy when she had a file that closed with yellow boingy bits and a whole wall that was window?

She was so high up that yesterday looked a long way away. They were even further away, the family who were too close to her bones.

Shelly had felt odd, considering the circumstances of their meeting, that she was taking over Marina's boyfriend's room. But Marina said that he needed to go. He was going to work in bars in Greece and his family were livid.

With her old blue duvet cover on it, Shelly's new bed looked inviting.

'Maybe you need sugar,' Owen had said.

All she had wanted was to stay there with him.

Up here she would gather her thoughts and rest her bones, shelter from their emotions
and her own.

'My bed is my sugar,' she had said.

She emptied her pockets of pebbles and got into bed.

The Tramway

Alex Hetherington

persuasion objects

(i)   Come out and live with us in a beautiful place in the country.

(ii)   Let go the materials that provide you with no illusions of your worth.

(iii)   I can see forever, with you by my side, our new life will be a zoetrope.

(iv)   We shall make home movies without a camera.

(v)   Install this software onto your hard drive; it will provide your computer with a personality like your own, and shall know you like you know yourself.

(vi)   Take votes for an anthem in recognition of your own town; you may choose any song.

(vii)   Put this special coin into a photobooth, when your photographs are developed they will show you a cartoon animation version of yourself.

(viii) This is your invitation to the Love Parade, you will have your own float, made from orchids and tulips.

(ix)   This is a plane ticket that will return you to your first summer holiday, travelling with Nostalgia Airlines.

(x)   This is a perfumed smokescreen; it will aid your escape, leaving others with an aroma of anticipation.

(xi)   Come out and live with us in a beautiful place in the country.

(xii)   This is the libretto for an opera about crushing flowers into the pages of gardening books.

(xiii)   This is a freckle calculator, with no subtraction function.

(xiv)   This is the telephone number for the Mission: Impossible team. Call them, they work for you now.

(xv)   This is a chart that we have written in your earliest handwriting; it describes the way colours look. Colours, perhaps, that you cannot see now.

(xvi)   This is a way to make a whole city stop for a moment and form into a fabulous dance routine. This method can be used only once.

(xvii)   This is the badge we wear, it says 'I am Popular.' Other badges we have worn have said 'Winner of a Shopping Spree Competition', 'Television Presenter' and 'I've been on Television, And Therefore Can Prove I Exist.'

(xviii)   This is 1978, which has now been turned into a patchwork umbrella. A lace balloon.

(xix)   These are all the opportunities that you missed by mistake, also included are personal ads which you should have responded to and men and women you should have talked to, but were looking the other way.

(xx)   Come out and live with us in a beautiful place in the country.

merchandising objects

Thinking I'm Falling In Love Biscuit Assortments.

Figurines, to star in the play that you will write called 'the council house of universal delight'.

Collect and Swap Shame & Humiliation/Benevolence & Adoration Cards.

Will You Marry Me? Post-it Notes.

Poetic Injustice Quotes Temporary Tattoos (12 Pack).

Inconsequential Party Dress Set (dress, shoes, handbag, shawl, sold separately).

Pack of miserable telephone call earpiece/mouthpiece cleansers.

Pack of 'You Are Very Special' Pencils, plus limited edition 'This is Your Miracle Self' Novelty Pencil Sharpeners.

Shapes of Disgrace Ice-Cube Holder.

Superhero Hair Dye (various colours, permanent and impermanent).

Dawn Chorus Anytime Compact Disc.

The Reassurance Chronometre.

Great, influential and culturally significant artist, be-an-artist-instantly wigs.

The River Of Promise, Now Flooded Cosmetic Set.

The sing-along karaoke tape of 50 favourite love songs. All backwards.

'A Measure of Courage' Novelty Ruler, guaranteed unbreakable.

The 'Saving up for Your Escape' Piggy Bank.

Car Bumper Stickers, that say things like 'My Other Car is an Intergalactic Space Rocket, I am Merely Biding My Time.'

The 'I've Got Rhythm, I've Got Music' charm bracelet.

The charm bracelet of Personal Deliverance, new charms to add to your collection, available every month.

The stone chips of everlasting vitality to cover the exterior walls of your home.

The How-To-Create-A-Commune-Of-Peace-and-Concord Cigarette Lighter.

The Verbalise Disposal Camera, which renders your photographs as written descriptions instead of images.

visual/aural objects

This is the credit card, without expiry date, cash limit and interest rate, which allows you to buy back regrets. The card comes with a number of different illustrations from which to choose.

This is a drawing in chlorophyll on a special paper, which will photosynthesise. The drawing itself is of a rodeo in a beautiful place out in the country.

This is a video recording of the fabled tiara of limitless fertility. (Currently featuring in a touring exhibition.)

This is a tape we found; it is a recording of the sound of your actual birth.

These are mynah birds; they have been taught to say expressions like: A Wall of Flowers Can Only Be Climbed After Dark. A Wall of Sound Can Only Be Climbed By The Deaf.

This is a tranquillity tone sound generator, which replaces hesitant expressions like 'um' and 'erm'.

This is a plaque, etched in marble, which says: 'Why create any new characters, all the best ones have been written anyway.'

This is a machine that creates beauty; it has your eyes.

This is a collection of photographs of you as a little boy, running away from your home with your family, running away to join a commune. Being that this is perhaps a fabrication these photographs are slightly out of focus, sepia tinted, the colour of American photographs from a warm summer's bleaching. Photographs of friends on lawns, pastures or beaches, with long hair, sitting around chatting, smiling, gazing up at the sky. You can see that some of these people are in love, and that some of them are lost and have been found. Some of these people attract you.

There's a girl with a pale, yellow T-shirt on and denim flares, she has long latches of hair covering parts of her face, she has her hand resting on the shoulder of another girl; this girl is talking with someone else, just aware of this small gesture of affection, yet held by its relaxed generosity. This girl, meanwhile, has two butterfly clasps in her hair. Or maybe they are real and have momentarily landed. The camera capturing a brilliant, enchanting, rare moment. There's a young man with his shirt off; he sits away from the group, but just close enough to be a part of it. Within questioning length, within reach, within touching length. His body is olive and strong; he's the sports jock who has dropped out to be the highwayman, the love-on-the-run, the day in bed. Love's future farmer.

There's another young man, propping up his head, propped up with his elbow, he has the hairstyle of a girl, and a fresh, sprinkle moustache, the boy of the old term, the man who returns to school. His eyes say: Loving You is Wonderful. He sits close to two other men. One has his shirt open to the waist, an indication of the temperature, both outside and inside. The other man wears a hat and sunglasses; he knows that this photograph will be seen, passed on, he doesn't want to be recognised. He's The Only Living Boy in New York.

Way at the back is a younger man, someone you recognise, or reminds you of a friend, or yourself. Caught mid-laugh, he holds his forehead in his hand, a sign he is now worn out with laughing too much, that everything has become funny, an ice-cream headache of exhilaration.

The girl with the butterflies has been talking to a red-faced girl, with large, heart-shaped glasses. The sunshine, today, has been less kind to her paler skin, which is now like a summer's day sunlight recorder, from mid-morning to late afternoon. But still she smiles, surrendered already to another night of heat rashes and cold creams. Nearer still, another girl, smiles directly at the camera, she lies on her belly, one hand says: Let's Marry Tonight. And overhead, just in sight, an aircraft flies over: it's probably a honeymoon charter.

And beside her another boy, and it looks like he's talking to somewhere/someone out of frame; holding a conversation about drinks and food later. Or about travels and leaving.

There's a child, in an oversized dress with her back to the photograph, but what you don't see, but can perhaps anticipate, is that she's about to fall over and rolly-polly down the hill. Where she will end up is anyone's guess. She may just keep rolling.

'tell me what the most beautiful thing is?'

'and do you think that if you asked everyone you knew the same question, and you compiled all the answers together, lots of answers together, like a depository, or report, you'd create the most beautiful place anywhere, ever?'

'would you need a photographic memory to remember all of this? how can you collect all this data and then make it available so that people can have a look at it, or say "that was my suggestion", among a thousand other suggestions. and people might make the same suggestion, over and over again. or how you would edit it so that it was true and concise, and that you agreed to what people were suggesting. you had to agree that what people had suggested was in keeping, was proper. it would be like curating an exhibition.'

'this is a beauty machine; it has your eyes. it has a lens, and a mirror and mechanism that opens and closes to let light through to a surface that can capture that light. the lens can be turned, or manipulated, so that you can generate beauty close-to or far away. the mechanism can also be changed and you can control the amount of light that is captured, you may over or under expose beauty, whatever. you may play with the focus so that your eyes are blurred or fixed, and then frighteningly precise. the beauty machine can be used at night or during the day, but you must be aware of the light, otherwise the light will not be captured and the machine will not work. the machine also has a trigger which you release or pull or press and you may repeat the process.'

'there is much debate as to whether or not the Renaissance painters had access to their own beauty machines, that they too captured light in the same way I have described earlier. that they too manipulated a similar machine, which, like you, would allow them to capture light, to generate beauty. that they also had a mechanism, that when taken up to their eyes would allow the beauty machine to work.'

'this is a man called Daguerre, who captured his own light and fixed it into glass and silver. these are members of his family and of buildings and parks and trees and flowers and butterflies, and scenes of other people. the people you see here are dead now, but if you look closely the you will see people that are just like you, and friends of yours.'

'this is a man called Alphonse Giroux, he had his eyes open, open to the possibility, that like you he would be able to capture and hold the things he thought were beautiful.'

'this is a man called Muybridge, who put a number of beauty machines together and captured his own light, second by second, over the times it takes for a person to walk, or a horse to trot or the time it takes one man to topple another to the floor. these are people he asked to descend stairs, or run, or to turn in place, look up and look down.'

'this is a woman called Cindy Sherman; she uses the machine to make herself into a thousand other people, but never herself, and they look just like you, or friends of yours.'

'this is a woman called Nan Goldin; she has used the machine to record her friends and their relationships, and their fantasies and desires, nightclubs and dance routines, love lives and telephone lines, love parades and taxi rides. some of the people you see here are dead now, but.'

'this is a man called Jack Pierson, his eyes see things not in focus, like he is always away or arrived too late. his machine has captured the light of hot Californian nights, and the light that transmits from happy girls and happy boys, and the things he sees are beautiful. he sees roads that go on for miles, and motels and hotels with large glittery, effervescent signs and beaches, with hot sand and sailboats, and where the sea and the sky are so similar it looks upside down and places where flowers are more red, more yellow, more orange than you can ever know.'

'this is a man called John Coplans, who uses the beauty machine to understand the beauty of his increasing age. you may see here how tired the skin round his arms and hands is now, or the way the skin on his feet and legs are a memento of his walks, his running for the train or bus, or the walking the stairs. you can see that his face and eyes and cheeks are creviced, deep conduits of speaking, laughing, talking, crying. you can see that the backs of his hands are a hundred thousand signatures later – from the learning, earliest handwriting to an automatic response, a reflex action.'

'this is Richard Prince, the things you see here are taken from somewhere else, of someone else, of objects that you may have used, these are cropped and details focused on. and these people here, they look like they live in a shopping mall or read the news on television. in this image you will see people all looking in the same direction, have you looked in their direction?'

'this is Wolfgang Tillmans and he uses the machine everywhere, taking it everywhere he goes. this is a photograph from high above the earth taken inside an airplane looking across the wing into the orange sunset, way, way beyond the plane.'

'this is a woman called Sally Mann; she sits with her freckled, sunrise children while they play. the machine she uses has made your remember sisters you never had, houses you never lived in, rivers you never swam, hot soups and coffee at the end of the day you never drank. she has made you remember that childhood is like milk.'

'OK, so what you do now is take the lens cap off and and look through the eyepiece, through the lens.'

It could be that you were there and had agreed to be in this photograph and that you were away just at the moment the shutter opened. Or perhaps it was you that took this photograph all along, a shy eyewitness. Or perhaps you were in the next frame, but this was the frame that catches up with the end of the film and you are lost somewhere in an undeveloped negative half-image half-orange and white colour field. Perhaps you can tell us who these people were and how you became their friend. How you became part of their photograph.

Or perhaps there was a movie camera rolling capturing this scene; a hand-held camera filming this day, shaking, wobbly smiling as another guest. Rapping in and out of focus, smiling, then looking up at the sky. And perhaps you were the cameraman, surveying your friends, their community, their summer love. And what we will share are the 24 frames per second and you will guide us through each of those frames, moment by moment and tell us what was happening, incrementally, shifts and adjustments: breathing in and out, a hand held up to screen the sun to look up at a plane, the rubbing of an eyebrow, the rubbing of dirt off fingers, a reflection in a pair of sunglasses, another button undone, a ring circled again and again, the slow ageing, a man running, an over-exposed orange flower, the spilt milk, the tiny changes, the tiniest changes.

We had had our imaginations caught on film, on photograph. In a beautiful place out in the country. This was a tracing of us as disciples, an outline, then filled, shaded and enhanced, with people we think are beautiful.

'No one really wants beauty after all. They just want to photograph it.'

Leaving Dan

Frances Sessford

M y house is like a Sunday house. I've got broth on, and its
thick, occasional gloops break the silence. There are no
kids running up and down the street. They've been told by their
mothers not to go past the windows, not to sneak a look. It's
too soon for them. The TV is off, of course. And now the
sudden thump of car doors shakes the dust motes in the air, and
it feels like Sundays used to feel, all holy and solemn and guilty.
I've been breathing in the soft, thick quiet and it's stuck on the
back of my throat. I wonder if my voice will come out.

We are ready. You look smart, as ever. Still no grey in your
hair, although the way your head is makes you look as though
you've got a double chin. You wouldn't have liked that.

They're forming up on the pavement. There's Peg at the
head, scowling and fixing the handbag. And Sarah, greeting
already and she's not even in yet. Well, they've got reason
today, I suppose. Funerals are only fun when you're a bystan-
der. Like at weddings – the pressure is off when you're only a
guest.

The second the door is off the latch the wind pushes to get in.
Peg's got her mink on! I tell her she looks lovely. Can you
believe it? But then, when could I ever say the right thing? She
lifts her chin to the side and presses against me. The fur is
freezing cold, bearing air from outside that seeps through my
dress and onto my breasts. It feels wet under my hands; they

slide down and away from it without sound or friction. The pressing over, Peg turns her back on me, the mink's sheen flung back in my face as she hovers at the living-room door. She has one hand on it and pushes it open, several-little-hesitant pushes, as if you're asleep and she's going to peep in at you. And then I see an old, frail mother, struggling under the weight of a fur she once filled, a ridiculous old felt hat wobbling on her head. She bought it when the town still had an emporium. Her hanky is pressed to her mouth.

Sarah's hands are so cold that I jump. The rings on her wedding finger are loose, spinning and clinking round the old swollen knuckle. They sound cheap, tinny, full of nickel. There was a war on, you know! It was all they could get. She makes her way up the hall like some slow, arthritic she-ape, the old red knuckles pressing into things for support, the banister, the walls. The door is wide open now, and I see them both in the frame, Sarah close, Peg in the distance leaning over you, sister-copies: wrinkled 40-denier American Tan, old daft hats, hankies, handbags with stiff gold clasps, never opened, jammed in the crook of their elbows.

I don't know how they can look. I mean, I had to. Seeing as it was me that found you I couldn't avoid it. But I can't again, not now that you're 'ready'. I caught a glimpse of you through that white gauze cloth that was resting on your face; your lips were shining through it. You had make-up on! If the boys could see you now. Peg says to Sarah, 'They've made him look lovely.' It's enough to give you nightmares.

The doorbell goes, and now there are so many of them pouring through my hallway. I can't remember who is who, but I know I should. They all seem vaguely familiar, so I'm guessing they were all at our wedding. Or maybe it's because they all share your genes. Honey! Yes, I remember her, the one whose mother is a hippy and gave her a ridiculous name. Well, I didn't think it was ridiculous, I liked it, but I remember Peg scowling and saying that was what came of marrying 'outside'. To which

I remember replying, at least they were married, to which she had said, it was one of those 'office things' so they weren't really. And that was that. Honey's mum always sends Christmas cards she makes herself. But she's at a yoga retreat this weekend, apparently, so Honey is here instead. Well, it'll be someone for Amanda to talk at. I'm hugged by someone, a sonsy old woman, should I know her? She is wearing L'Aimant and now it's all down my front and I'll stink of it all day.

I clamber to the door for air and to escape the fug of scent. Here comes the priest. Father Devine strides, almost runs, up the path. He is eager, so that I think he must have bounded over the gate rather than come through it. He's rubbing his right fist against his open left palm to warm his hands, or for the sake of something to do, or in anticipation, I can't tell which. His jacket is a thin shade of black, and shiny, no shield at all against the wind and rain. His young red cheeks shine from the cold. He looks excited. He is a happy man. Death, like size, doesn't matter. It all comes right in the end. If you've been on the right side. Of what? The fence? I envy him his faith. His big hands surround both of mine; his eyes are full of professional reassurance, brightening to a twinkle as he looks past me. The wind has blown the kitchen door open and the purvey is on full display. Priests – always on the lookout for an opportunity, a free meal, a soul to bring in. They are hungry dogs.

There are no more people. I'll have to go in. I look up and down the street, just in case, but there is only the rain, and a streetful of smug ex-councils.

We're all in the living room now, tall, short, fat, thin, living, dead. I lean on the door to close it. The room is a ballet of teacups and nodding hats that wobble on white heads and shield furtive whispers. I glimpse you between arms and hats and thick winter skirts. I hear the word 'sad' spoken a lot. It sibilates around the room and prickles me. Sad. But not devastated, not numb, not grief-stricken and so overcome with shock that I had to be sedated. Just sad. People keep saying it to me with 'You must be very' at the beginning, and to each other with 'isn't it?' at the end. 'Shock' is another one. Not really, with your genes and that forty-a-day habit. The shock was when I tried to hold Amanda and she pushed me away.

Honey is scrutinising my magazine, with Amanda leaning over to point out the trousers she wants. The priest is standing by you, just by your feet. He's laughing loud and long. Other people are laughing too; how can they laugh? They're all laughing together, the believers and the saved. When I was small I once saw a New Orleans funeral on the telly and I asked someone why there was so much dancing and singing. Shouldn't they be sad? And they said that death should be a happy time because the person was going to be with God. I wonder if you're with God. What about Minnie and Joe and Dad and Alexander and Boadicea and Beethoven and Mr Lewis our chemistry teacher that poisoned himself by mistake that time and the boy in our class who jumped under a train and your dad and Einstein and Kenneth Williams and Sid James? Are they all with you? God help them.

It makes me think about when my grandmother buried her husband. Not about the funeral or before the funeral, but after it, hours after, when Pops was gone, finally gone, and we felt light for the first time in days. Minnie sat erect and proud on one of the old picnic chairs that she kept in the press for when people came. She was in the middle of the other windows, all gathered to initiate the new member. They were all her age with their hats on but no coats, and spinning nickel-gold rings on their lined, thin old fingers. Anyway, she told a story about Pops and she laughed loud like she was a young girl again. She held her hand up to her face because she was laughing so hard and I remember thinking, how can she laugh so soon when Pops is gone? But after forty-eight years there was nothing else to do but laugh, and, besides, she had a clear conscience. She had discharged her vows. They'd had the lot, Minnie and Joe. Sickness (lots), health (hardly any), better, worse, richer, poorer (mostly), and they had loved each other all the way through it, in their way. 'Mah Joe,' she'd say. 'You never knew him, not really, not when he was fit and strong. Oh, he loved to laugh, and talk, and go out. He loved to get yer mither all dressed up when she was a wean and take her out. But she doesn't remember that now.' What my mother remembers is Joe getting all dressed up to go to the cards on a Sunday afternoon, but memories are selective. It's one of life's luxuries.

Amanda looks up and gives me a cool, nervous glance. She still needs me, even if it's just to prompt her to start passing plates. She begins her maidenly dance of the sandwich, her fair hair brushing wrinkled faces, her blue eyes sparkling into their dull old orbs. They reach out to touch her, to stroke her unlined cheek and tight, downy jaw. Beautiful little goddess. She's her father's daughter. She'll have this valued in pounds, shillings and pence before the day's out and already be looking forward to Christmas.

The doorbell rings again. Hannah's form is motionless through the frosted squares. My heart thumps slow and hard until I think it will explode through my ribs, my dress, through the L'Aimant and onto Peg's precious fur, hanging where Amanda has thrown it on the banister. I'm broken before the door is fully open. She looks up at me. Hannah is flushed and wet, bare of make-up and clean of perfume, free of everything. She is round and triumphant with new life. I reach down to her and she cradles me. My tears roll off her shoulders and drop onto the wet path. I close my eyes.

The memory is so clear it's like gazing through new glass. Hannah and me sitting on the couch together at her show of presents and her saying to me, 'Yes, but you wouldn't swap it though, would you? I mean, you wouldn't change it, would you?' And I said, 'Well, I don't know.' And I looked across the room at you, swinging your car keys and impatient, mouthing off to John about the Celtic and I thought, *I have already. And he doesn't know it. Because this isn't what I wanted. It's not how I thought it would be.* And I looked back at Hannah and she was still gazing at me although her smile was fading, and I said something reassuring. Like Father Devine.

With Hannah here I can stop trying to produce tears. They pour out of their own accord. They have somewhere to go. Like when she came to me: freezing and wet on the step, black cardigan sleeves pulled down over nail-bitten hands; clutching two stuffed Asda bags that held whatever she had pulled from the drawers while dodging the blows. I would have taken the bruises for her; perhaps it would have made me feel alive. I drew her in and over tea, then Southern Comfort, the words spilled out of our mouths. We held onto each other and wept and rocked, then we drank some more and said to hell with them all. Then the next morning, Peg on the doorstep, demanding to know why Hannah had left John without so much as his piece made. Hit her? If her John had hit her she must have done something to des –

I slammed the door in her face and never opened it to her again until today.

There is someone at the door again. A man in professional black eyes the widow with a wary glance. I'm leaning against Hannah, weak with relief. Maybe he thinks I've been at the sherry.

'Mrs McLean?'

I toy with the idea of saying no.

'Yes.'

'We've come to . . .'

'Yes, I know. Through there.'

Will they get you through the living-room door? We always meant to have it widened. Well, of course they'll get you out, what am I thinking of? You were delivered in it. I am ridiculous, I was ridiculous. I am sorry now.

The cups and saucers are tidied; hats are straightened. The room is tense, expectant. The priest starts praying. He produces this – thing – that he starts shaking over you. Sarah has collected up all those mass card things and starts putting them down the sides of the coffin. There is water coming out of the – thing – in fat drops and it sputters onto them. Get me out of here. The voices rise and fall, the prayers are said in grating unison, then they start a hymn, get me out of here, and Peg's warble soars over the mixed bass and sopranos of this old steel-town choir and I think that I won't be able to stop the scream that's gathering right down inside of me. So I look at Hannah to keep me steady but she's looking awful pale and it's some instinct that gets me to her side before she crashes back into the TV.

I missed the rest. But I expect they all had a good time. Better that it was just you and them anyway, I was never any good at all that ritual and mass stuff. I always stood up at the wrong bits and then Peg would get cross and scowl over at us. Hannah and I had a lovely time, kind of, after the sweat and the pushing and the blood and the stitches and . . . well, I have to tell you all this because you weren't there when I was having Amanda. Anyway, by the time I got back only the pattern was left on the plates, so they must have worked up an appetite. Amanda scowled at me from the couch when I got back. Sometimes she looks so much like your mother that it makes me want to laugh.

Easter

David Pettigrew

Both set out with the best of intentions, but by the time their car drew up the sandy track they had stopped talking altogether. Throughout the journey the temperature had dropped and the cottage windows sparkled in the headlights. Spring was late that year and Easter had come early, but the freeze was unexpected. They unpacked the car in silence and she went straight to bed while he stayed up, trying to light the fire in the living room.

In the morning she lay in the high bed, watching her breath rise above her in pale little puffs. At first all she could hear was the wind and a slow wash of waves from the beach, but then the living-room door creaked and his heavy tramp came down the hallway. He passed by and went into the bathroom. The water tank rumbled and the pipes, which seemed to run under every floorboard and through every wall, began to wrap the building in their familiar whine. She pulled the quilt over her head, thinking how typical it was of him to sneak into the shower first.

The noise of the pipes didn't let her lie long and she sat up and reached for the radio on the cabinet by the bed. It was Good Friday and there was a programme of pieces from the *St Matthew Passion*; the next was to be an aria, *Mache dich, mein Herze, rein*. Bach was not one of her specialities, but the announcer provided a translation. At this she gave a slight snort and turned the volume up. Then she slid off the bed and shuffled to the window with the quilt gathered around her shoulders.

It was so cold that a thin layer of frost had formed on the glass on the inside. She scraped at it with her fingernails, but her breath misted over the gap so she rubbed at it again. The beach was very close, but she found she could see nothing because of the ice on the outside. Meanwhile, the music began: a reserved introductory passage, followed by a bass voice delivering the title line. The orchestra was unhurried and it was soon clear that the tempo would not increase. The singing was also restrained, but occasionally there was a hint of urgency, especially when the title phrase was repeated. The music pulsed slowly and the voice quietly pleaded. She contemplated the opaque white in front of her nose and after a few minutes a small hole cleared on the other side.

Later, she moved into the kitchen and shivered near the stove. Throughout the process of washing and dressing they had managed to avoid each other and now he was back in the living room, methodically ripping a newspaper into strips for the fire. She sat at the kitchen table with an open jotter in front of her. The cream pages were printed with musical staves and, sitting on one hand to keep it warm, she carefully marked red symbols over the lines with a pen she held in the other.

Next door the ripping came to an end and she heard him groan as he got to his feet. The living-room door creaked and once more he thudded into the hallway. It was not clear where he was heading, but she prepared herself by furrowing her brow and staring determinedly down at the page.

The kitchen door opened and his footsteps halted at the entrance. Obviously he hadn't expected her to be there and she could feel him hovering behind her, trying to decide whether to come in or not. She continued writing and eventually he stepped in and walked over to the wall cupboard above the sink. There was the clink of a mug on the draining board and he coughed. 'Would you like a coffee?'

She scored out a symbol and placed a new one on a lower line. 'No.'

He sighed and took the kettle from the stove; water poured into the mug. From the extremity of her vision she was aware of him shuffling at the sink, but then he stepped to the table and sat down on the chair opposite her. The pen moved across the page and he sipped slowly from his mug. Finally, he said, 'Is that new?'

She could feel him bend forward to try and see what she was writing so she pulled the book away with her fingertips. He leaned back and put the mug down on the table.

'I thought we came here to talk,' he said.

She kept her eyes down. The water in the kettle bubbled and outside the waves lapped on the beach. Her pen scraped across the page. He bent forward again, but this time grunted in surprise. The mug tumbled into view and coffee slopped out, swimming over the page.

She dropped the pen and jerked back, her chair falling over as she jumped to her feet. She grabbed the book by its edges and poured the fluid off onto the table. Now she looked at him. 'You did that deliberately.'

'No. It was an accident.' But he was still sitting, watching the coffee flood over the table.

The open book dripped from her hands. The bottom halves of the pages were untouched, but the red ink at the top was smudged and running. The pool spread over two-thirds of the tabletop and the mug lay on its side.

'No. You did it deliberately.'

Their eyes met and he sighed once more. Then he reached over and righted the mug. 'I'll get a cloth,' he said.

The following day she stayed in the bedroom while he slumped in an armchair, listening to the wind brushing over the windows. The cold had lessened overnight, but the panes were still white and layered with frost.

When the morning passed he rose from the chair and moved to

the upright piano. He sat down on the worn cushion of the stool and tapped a couple of keys. The piano was old and not used often. It needed tuning, but he thought it could bear something delicate so he picked out a tune, hoping to lure her back through. His fingers trickled through the piece but she did not appear. He rubbed his chin. Evidently the choice had been unimaginative, too obviously romantic. He could see her lying back on the bed, sniggering, and the image made his cheeks burn.

So he thought of another tune, an aria with which he was not too familiar. In fact he had only heard it the other morning, coming from the bedroom as he dried himself after his shower. It had been performed by orchestra and solo singer, but it was a slow piece and he thought he could summarise it by chords. He was sure she had heard part of it, but she would never expect him to be plodding through such a thing on the piano.

He began with a low hum, trying to translate the melody through to his fingers. From a frame on top of the piano her face bestowed a half-smile and he repeated the initial phrase over and over. His hum became louder. The treble keys were going off pitch, but he thumped on, trying to find a way in. His voice rose tunelessly, struggling for the words. *Mache dich . . . Mache dich . . . Mache dich . . .* but that was all he could manage before lapsing back to a drone.

The door of the room swung open and knocked into a chair. There was no half-smile on her face, just a grimace. She was wearing her cagoule and held his in her hands. His fingers stopped and he looked up at her, offering a coy smile. But her expression remained stern and she threw the cagoule so that he had to stretch back to catch it.

The wind blew into their faces and the sand cracked underfoot. By this time the tide was out and the waves were far away. They still hadn't spoken, but as they moved their arms sometimes touched. He could hear the papery rub of their cagoules' material and as she didn't move away he assumed détente was setting in.

Eventually they reached a favourite spot, a dune which jutted out in a dog-leg from the main barrier of sand between the beach and the frostbitten grass behind. The dune formed a small cove, a snug from the winds which harried the sands. Without hesitation both moved into the cove and crouched to collect the sticks and bits of board which gathered at its edge when the tide was in. This was what they always did and wordlessly a pile of wood was created. Then he dug in his pocket for matches and she reached up to pull at some of the long grass which sprouted like white hair from the top of the dune. The longer strands were frosted, but underneath these the short ones were dry. She thrust the grass under the pile, he lit it, and the fire was made.

They sat on the same side of the flames, but he was careful not to get too close. Time passed and the shadows began to gather, but when the flames started to die down she got up to collect more sticks. Later, he took his turn, and this way the fire kept going until one of them was ready to speak.

In the end it was she who broke the silence. '*Mache dich, mein Herze, rein.*'

He turned his head away so that she wouldn't see he was pleased. 'So, what does it mean?' he asked.

She looked into the flames, unsmiling. 'It means, "Purify thyself, my heart." '

Moments passed before she spoke again. 'Why did you think of that?'

He tried to sound nonchalant. 'Well, I thought it was appropriate.'

Now she looked at him, eyes narrowing. He thought he could see the corners of her mouth turn upwards, but perhaps it was just the flickering light because then she stood up. She kicked sand on the fire. 'Come on,' she said, 'let's get back.'

On Easter morning the wind pushed at the front door. With each gust the handle rattled and finally she opened her eyes. She sat upright and listened, but apart from the rattle there was no other sound, just the wind and the waves. The curtains were half open and she noticed that her breath was invisible. She looked to the window. The frost had started to recede and the upper panes were clear. Backlit by the sun, thick, grey clouds rolled through the sky.

She reached for the robe heaped at the bottom of the bed and pulled it around her shoulders. Then she stretched over the side and picked up the jotter from the floor. The previous day she had dried it in front of the stove and the pages were rippled and stiff. Some of the red markings were smeared and where the coffee had spilled the paper had turned an ancient brown. But the sequence was still legible and taking the pen from the bedside cabinet, she started to write.

Without hesitation, notes continued uncoiling over the staves. When she heard the living-room door and his footfalls in the hallway she did not even pause. Predictably, he went into the bathroom and the water tank rumbled. She shook her head when the pipes began to whine, but she continued to write, working on as the sun appeared through the window and spread over the page.

When she entered the living room he was taking his bedding from the sofa. He kept his back to her and she did not speak as she moved to the armchair. Resting the jotter on her lap, she looked out of the window on the opposite side of the room. On this one patches of frost still reached up the lower panes, but they had a heavy, crystallised look and their grasp was beginning to slip. From her position she could see that the grass had become green, but not enough of the ice had cleared for a view of the beach. Only the waves could be heard, foaming on the shore.

He pulled off the last sheet and held it before him as he moved to the clear area in front of the window. He had to face her as he stretched his arms sideways to open out the sheet, but he avoided her eyes and then raised his arms slightly so that his face was obscured. Outside the clouds swept by and for a moment the sun broke through, illuminating his body and his outstretched arms behind the sheet. Then he shook it and wound it up in his arms. The sun disappeared and he moved away to the piano, dropping the sheet on the sofa as he passed.

For some time he leafed through a pile of music books which sat on a hard chair next to the piano. Then he opened the lid and dragged his fingers firmly along the keyboard. He started to do this again, but broke off when she put her hand on his shoulder.

His body flinched and he looked round sharply. She pushed a strand of hair from her eye and smiled at him, but he turned his face down and tapped the keyboard with his forefinger. She opened the jotter and set it on the ledge above the keyboard. 'Try this,' she said and, pushing the music books off, she sat on the hard chair.

Before him he saw the cream pages of two days before. The coffee stains were heavy, but the red notes were clear. At the top of the piece were the scribbled words 'Purify thyself, my heart' and for a minute or so he scanned the music, but made no reaction. He stretched his fingers and began to play.

When he finished he put down the lid and placed his hands on top of it. Neither of them spoke and slowly she reached out and put her hand on top of his. She resisted squeezing and he did not pull away. Sunlight burst into the room once more and he turned to look at the window. Finally, she spoke. 'Do you like my transcription?'

He kept his eyes on the window. 'Well, perhaps the piece is a little slow.'

She looked at the back of his head. Beyond him, the glass shone. 'But my interpretation . . . is it okay?'

The room darkened as the sunlight moved on. He turned back to face her. His lips carried a half-smile and rain tapped on the window. She looked past him. The last crystals of frost had slipped down and now the view was clear. On the beach waves washed over the sand.

Precious Cargo

Ruth Thomas

My health visitor tells me to get out. 'Wrap the baby up and get out,' she commands, circling my child's head with a frayed tape measure.

She thinks I am post-natally depressed because I sit in the flat all day. It doesn't occur to her that I stay in because it is snowing; it's a blizzard out there. And it's so much prettier in here, the rooms still full of flowers and congratulations cards and helium balloons. Even if a little wilting and shrivelling has gone on in the last couple of weeks, the balloons keeping pace with my stomach.

'There are dozens of groups around now,' the health visitor says. 'I think you should join one.'

I look at her and my mind goes blank. It is three weeks now since my daughter was born. Perhaps I am experiencing *post-natal drift*? Perhaps I am just wallowing in a dream of nappies and milk-laden breasts and maternal love.

'I'm not really a group person,' I say.

'This is different. New Mums need to get together.'

It's funny, because I still find it hard to see myself as a New Mum. I can hardly believe it, the way life slips along. The way you are a girl and then suddenly, you are a mother.

The health visitor weighs Amber and she cries, wriggles and is asleep, her face upturned like a flower against my shoulder, her mouth a tiny pink O.

155

'What a life,' I say, brushing her cheek with the edge of my little finger.

'At least get out for a walk this afternoon,' the health visitor barks, frowning and packing her bag. She hands me a piece of orange A4 paper. It is a list of all the new mother and baby groups in town.

When she has gone I look out at the snow, falling thick and soft past the window. February. I have not been out since January 8th. Maybe this is something to worry about. 'Okay,' I say. I look at the sheet of A4 paper. There is a New Mums and Babies Group at 3.15, about twenty minutes' walk away. It is now three o'clock. 'Okay,' I say again. I change Amber's nappy, dress her in a bodysuit, a sleepsuit, a snowsuit, wrap her in the blanket my mother knitted for her, put her in the pram, fold another blanket over her and leave the house. Outside I feel strange; unable to walk properly, my feet clomping monster-like down the pavement. It is like opening your mouth to say something and gibberish coming out. The sky is enormous, boundless, and it makes me feel that I shouldn't be outside beneath it. It seems like trespassing, as if someone is going to put their hand on my shoulder and say, 'Oi, New Mum, what are you doing out here?' But after a few minutes I am beginning to get used to it. I am remembering how to walk on pavements again, how to walk past people without trampling on their toes. Quietly I slide the pram through the snow to the smart end of town, where the skips contain good-quality furniture and pieces of frozen garden turf; where the houses are detached and have long, gravelled front paths. These are the kind of houses that always make me curious; these are well-adjusted houses, containing well-adjusted lives.

We stop outside number 15. It is obviously the right house because there is a little bronze cast of a baby's foot attached to the gate. Snow has gathered between the toes, making me want to cover it up with a baby's sock. Amber is still asleep, blissful beneath her knitted blanket, and I envy her all the lifting and carrying, all the softness and warmth. Now we are here I feel like running away. But I don't because we have probably been observed. So I push the gate-latch down, open the gate and try to push the pram-wheels over the step. They seize and won't roll, so I turn, yank the pram backwards over the step, turn again and drag it behind me up the path.

Before I have pressed the tiny-hand-shaped bell, a woman opens the door. She is wearing expensive-looking trousers and a clean white sweater, appliquéd with a balloon motif. Her make-up has been applied with a professional hand.

'How funny', she says. 'People don't usually pull their prams.'

'I didn't pull it all the way here. Just up the path.'

'Oh.'

'I'm still getting the hang of it, really.' In fact, this is the first time I have used it.

'Isn't it cold?' says the woman, after a tiny pause.

'Yes.'

'I'm Libby.'

'I'm Kate.'

'And who's this?' Libby asks, peering into the pram.

'Amber.'

'What an unusual name,' says Libby.

I don't know what to say. I have still not got used to people saying that.

'We like it,' I mumble, and a little smile flicks across Libby's face.

'You can leave the pram in the front room,' she says, turning and leading the way up the corridor. Her flat is warm and clean and smells of peach air freshener. I wheel after her, snow falling off the pram in clumps onto her pristine carpet. Amber has opened her eyes now. There is a tiny, resigned expression on her face. It is like the face of an old man sitting outside a pub. I lift her out and push the pram into a room which seems to contain nothing but small bronze hands and feet. On the floor, on the table, on the windowsill.

157

'Here we are,' Libby says from the far end of the corridor. 'We're in the sitting room.' She pushes another door open.

Five women are in the sitting room, with five corresponding babies. The women sit on geometrically patterned sofas. The babies lie on playmats and stare up at dangling plastic toys. One of them has a shock of ash-blonde hair, like a Gonk.

'Hi,' I say.

'Hi,' reply the women. Two of them are wearing identical shirts. Breastfeeding shirts; I recognise them from the catalogues.

On a small table in the centre of the room is a tray bearing five teddy-bear-decorated mugs, a small milk-jug, a cafetière and a plate of chocolate biscuits.

'This is Kate,' Libby says.

'Hi,' I say again, feeling already that I am encroaching on something. Feeling that I am not wearing the right kind of shirt. Amber and I are twenty minutes late. All the other women already know each other. Smiling, I carry Amber over to a flowery playmat, place her on her back and sit down in a nearby armchair.

'I'm really pleased,' one of the women says after a small silence, 'Chloe only woke up twice last night.'

'What times?' asks someone else, timidly reaching for a chocolate digestive.

'Midnight and 4.30. I was really pleased.'

There are mumbles of approval. Once, none of us would have been pleased about being woken up at midnight and 4.30.

'Coffee, Kate?' Libby asks.

'Thanks,' I say, enthusiastically. I feel it is best to sound enthusiastic. Libby holds out the plate of biscuits and I say 'thanks' again and take two. Since giving birth I have never eaten so many chocolate biscuits in my life.

'So,' says Libby, sighing and sitting down on a very Hoovered sofa. In the alcove behind her head are serried ranks of baby photographs in gold frames. It looks like an altar. At the far end of the room is a table bearing more examples of bronze feet and hands. 'So,' Libby says again.

I am struck by the difference in size between the babies, considering they were all born within a month of each other. Short-legged, long-legged, big-headed, odd-shaped-headed. Of course, I think Amber is the prettiest. After a few minutes, the one with the odd-shaped head begins to wail, and a woman picks him up, leans forward to undo her bra and puts him to her breast. The wailing stops. Libby hands round more biscuits. Somebody starts to talk about jaundice. A clock chimes the half hour.

'Our cat keeps jumping into Amber's cot,' I say, thinking it is about time I shared a worry. Everyone gasps and looks at me. This was not the correct thing to say. So I don't say any more. I look down at Amber, lying in front of me. She has just learned how to smile.

I am the only person in my circle of friends who has had a baby. They were all a little shocked when I told them I was pregnant. 'That's great,' said my best friend, Rebecca, who wears expensive trouser-suits every day and works in a legal firm. 'Was it planned?'

'Not exactly. But, you know, there's never a perfect time for having children.'

I am beginning to sound like a woman I met once who kept saying 'Children Are The Enemies of Space. Children Are The Enemies of Space.' Over and over. This is what happens when you become a parent.

Now my friends keep sending me emails asking me what it's like being a mummy. 'Is Joseph actually changing nappies?!' they ask. We have all spent so many years being flippant about babies that I don't know how to respond. I email Rebecca at work, trying to think of something urbane and witty. But I can think of nothing. I sit and look at the letters on my keyboard. 'Joseph's quite an accomplished nappy-changer these days,' I type. 'And Amber's beginning to look really pretty now. She's lost her wrinkly look.' What will Rebecca make of that? Will she even know what I'm talking about? I imagine her sitting in her office, case-notes in front of her, Marks and Spencer's Mexican Wrap waiting for lunchtime in her desk drawer. Then I look at Amber over the keyboard and smile. Sometimes I'm so happy that my eyes blur over. I drip with emotion, my heart swelling until it is painful.

My friends came round to see Amber when she was four days old, and they were all too frightened to hold her. 'Oh God, what about her head?' Rebecca asked, sitting there in her Jaeger suit. 'It's all wobbly.'

'You just support her head with your hand,' I said sensibly, like some milky Earth Mother. Maybe that is how Rebecca sees me now. I have floated into a new orbit: a galaxy of mothers.

'She's cute,' she said uncertainly. 'She doesn't look much like you.'

'Thanks.'

'No, but I mean, she doesn't look much like Joesph either.'

'She just looks like herself,' I said, and then I thought, *That's what they all say. That's what all new mothers say, in that awful droney voice.*

Then Amber started to cry and I took her and held her up against my shoulder and made those crooning noise that you hear mothers make. Rebecca looked a little alarmed.

'You're making funny noises,' she said.

'Am I?'

I haven't seen Rebecca since then. We've both been busy.

'Is this your first baby?' I ask the woman sitting on the sofa nearest me. She has a long plait and very clear blue eyes.

'I think they're all our first babies,' she replies.

'Yes. I suppose this is a New Mums and Babies group. Stupid question really.'

The woman smiles and does not disagree.

'Would you like a biscuit?' I ask, picking up a plate of foil-covered Caramel Logs and offering it to her.

'No, thanks. I've already had four.'

'You sound like me,' I say. 'I'm just addicted to chocolate at the moment.'

'Awful, isn't it?'

And I'm wondering: *is this it? Are new mothers supposed to bond over chocolate biscuits?* I can't remember how I used to do it, how I used to make friends. The last time was when I went to university, and it was so much easier then; you just drank too much and said provocative things and made shy arrangements and occasionally went to bed with boys. I've lost touch with all those boys.

'What's your little boy's name?' I ask the woman.

'She's a girl, actually,' she says. 'Her name's Emma.'

'Oh, sorry. I just thought because of the blue . . . Emma's a lovely name.'

'Thanks. How about yours?'

'Amber. And I'm Kate.'

'They're both nice names.'

'Thanks.'

And then we run out of steam. There is something there; there is definitely something there, but neither of us has the energy. Two of the other women are talking about abdominal exercises '. . . and you have to do twenty lotus leans and twenty sitting twists . . .', and it makes me feel exhausted.

'Have you started exercising yet?' Libby asks, turning and fixing me with her impressively mascara-ed eyes. I mumble something about not quite getting round to it yet, and reach for another biscuit. '*What did you do today?*' Joseph will ask me tonight, and I will say 'I changed ten nappies. I breastfed eight times. I ate five chocolate biscuits with six strange women.'

The conversation moves on from post-natal exercises to mastitis and how you can put cabbage leaves on your breasts.

161

'Oh, look, it's snowing,' the woman with the plait exclaims quietly but nobody seems to hear apart from me.

'I love it when it snows,' I say.

'Me too,' says the woman. 'It makes you feel . . . I don't know . . . happier.'

At a business meeting this would be the moment to exchange cards. But we have no cards. We don't even have diaries or scraps of paper. So we do nothing. We just sit and look at the falling snow. Then, just after the clock has struck four the woman pulls herself off the sofa, picks her daughter up off the floor and says she is leaving.

'Yes,' I say abruptly, 'I ought to get going too.'

Because I can't stand it any longer. I have to leave; I have to. I stand up and lift Amber off her flowery mat.

'I've actually got an appointment at half past, so I ought to go really,' I say.

The only appointment I have is with my living room. There is obviously something wrong with me. Maybe my health visitor is right.

Libby springs up from the couch almost at once, looking relieved that two of us – four of us – are finally going to vacate her living room. She smiles.

'Before you go,' she says, 'I wondered if you'd like one of these.'

She turns to the alcove full of baby photographs and takes a leaflet from the top of a little pile. She hands one to each of us.

'Thanks,' I say. There is a photograph on the leaflet of more bronze baby hands and feet. Above the picture is the name of a company: Libby's company, I realise, with a little jolt of comprehension. Libby's company is called Pitter-Patter. And there is a sentence under the title: *Have your baby's hands or feet cast in bronze, for a lasting memento of those precious first weeks.*

'My children are three and five now,' Libby says, 'and I'm

really pleased I've got casts of their feet. They grow up so fast. Their feet are enormous now. You have no idea.'

'Right,' says the woman with the plait.

'Right,' I say.

'We use plaster of Paris,' Libby says. 'It only takes a few minutes.'

'Right,' says the woman with the plait.

'Right,' I say.

I look down at Amber, at her tiny feet in their sleepsuit. 'Well,' I say, 'I'll have a think about it.'

And then we are all out of there as fast as we can put our babies in their prams and wheel them through the front door.

At the gate we look at each other.

'Well,' says the woman with the plait, 'it was nice to meet you. I expect we'll meet up again at some point.'

'Yes,' I say, 'I expect so.'

'Take care,' she says.

'You too.'

And we turn and push our prams away in opposite directions.

Rebecca and I used to have this joke. She wanted a baby one day but she didn't want to go through all that pain. Meanwhile, I was intrigued by the whole process of pregnancy but wasn't sure about spending years of my life bringing up a child. So I was going to have the baby and she'd bring it up. I'd be out there in the world of work and she'd be a brilliant mother, taking her kids to the park every day and helping them make castles out of toilet-roll tubes. When you're eighteen, you never quite see yourself in your thirties. You never know how you're going to be.

We are nearly home when an old lady in a hat suddenly rounds the corner, stops and peers into the pram.

'Precious cargo,' she says.

'Yes,' I reply, wanting to tell her about all the bronze feet and the way I nearly made a friend but didn't – maybe she would understand what I mean; she has an understanding face, like some old oracle. But I just say, 'I'm still not used to it.'

'You have to learn how to do it, dear,' the old lady says. 'People don't tell you that.'

'No,' I say, 'I—'

But she has walked away. So I just stand for a moment, in the snow, and look into the pram at my sleeping baby, my *precious cargo*. My daughter. There is a sort of electricity in the air. It feels as if someone is about to call my name.

Wonderful Age

Ruth Thomas

Joseph is a little like a child himself. Shy, but given the chance, an exhibitionist. And he wears cheerful maroon shoes. His girlfriend usually loves his shoes, but today she snapped and called them 'childish'. He is thirty-four now, after all, with a child of his own.

This afternoon Kate is at the dentist's, having two fillings, so Joseph has to take their daughter to the birthday party on his own. He has taken the last couple of hours off work; two hours on a Friday afternoon to be at a baby's birthday party. It is being held in Jumblies, on the outskirts of town. Through the big plate-glass windows there is a ploughed field and sheep.

'Look at the sheep, Amber,' Joseph says, holding his daughter up and pointing through the window.

'Ba ba,' says Amber, waving at them. 'Ba ba.'

'Yes,' says Joseph, pleased, 'sheep.'

He puts her down again, and watches her walk. He has hardly got used to supporting her before she can do it on her own.

Slowly they walk the length of the building, towards a green door that says PARTY ROOM. Almost obliterating the doorway is a bouncy castle, a rigid, purple and blue structure sagging and creaking like some dreadful sea monster. Amber stops in her tracks. 'It's okay,' Joseph says, steering her on. He wonders if one-year-olds are perhaps a little young for bouncy castles. But some of the babies are already being posted through the entrance. And after a moment, Amber regains her confidence. She runs forward and begins to clamber over a mountain of foam blocks.

'Shoes off!', commands a woman in a lilac sweatshirt as Joseph plods across the rubber matting.

'Oh,' says Joseph, 'sorry.' He bends, unlaces his maroon shoes and puts them in the corner of the room.

'You'll certainly find those again, won't you?', the woman says.

'Yes,' says Joseph, disliking her.

This is not his kind of party. It is usually Kate who takes Amber to these events, and most of the parents are mothers. There are just two other fathers, slinking around the corners of the room, clutching onto their children's possessions. A balloon shaped like a poodle. A cardigan.

'Hi,' Joseph says, approaching the one with the cardigan, 'which one are you attached to?'

'That one,' the man says, nodding towards a small, almost hairless child sitting in a ball pool. 'Bethany.'

'Oh,' Joseph says. He doesn't know what else to say. At adult parties, he might attempt something deadpan or clever. But here he just says, 'I'm Amber's dad. She's the one with the brown hair.'

There are actually a lot of children with brown hair, he notices, but he doesn't bother trying to explain which is his daughter. The man doesn't reply. He looks as if he really doesn't want to be there. 'This is women's work,' he says, with no detectable irony in his voice. After a moment, Joseph sidles away, across the rubber matting. Looking down, he notices he has a hole in the toe of his left sock.

He has never been so happy since the birth of his daughter. He just has to look at Amber, and it feels as if all the space in his heart has finally been filled up. What a beautiful, beautiful little girl! He can't believe how he and Kate could have created someone so perfect. Even changing nappies is not the awful task he thought it would be. The ritual of disposing and wiping, the application of zinc and castor oil, is not so bad. It is only the secondary things that are not quite so good – taking the bin-bag full of smelly nappies out to the wheely-bin in the evening; constantly picking bits of toast off the kitchen floor; arriving home to find Kate exhausted and bad-tempered and surrounded by mess. 'I'm going to have a really nice, relaxing time at the dentist's,' she had said that morning, and she had sounded as if she meant it.

'Joseph!', says a woman, padding across the floor towards him in her stockinged feet.

'Hallo,' Joseph replies.

'Emily's mum,' the woman explains. These days, the women he meets are always *somebody's mum*.

'Of course,' Joseph says. He can't remember who Emily is either.

'No Kate?'

'No. She had to go to the dentist's.'

'Oh, that's a shame. Shame to miss the party.'

'Yes. She had to have two fillings.'

'Hmm,' says the woman, this information not seeming to sink in. 'Amber's certainly having fun,' she says, looking across at her as she reaches towards another child and enquiringly tugs her hair.

'Amber!', Joseph calls, but she doesn't look up.

'Selective deafness,' says the woman. It is one of the things parents say.

All the other women are sitting in groups on the foam structures. They are talking, laughing, rescuing their children from hazards, and Joseph realises that he has already become one of the orbiting fathers. One of the misfit men in lugubrious shades of green and grey. He looks across at the man he has not spoken to, but he is staring down at the poodle-shaped balloon as if hoping that it will float him upwards, out of the room, away. So after a moment Joseph goes over to Amber and kneels beside her.

'Having fun?'

Amber picks up a yellow ball and begins to chew it with her four teeth.

'I don't know if you should be chewing that,' Joseph says.

'Oh, they're all chewable,' says a woman, the one who had instructed him to take off his shoes. 'You're going to have a tough job getting her not to chew things.'

She smiles pityingly as if she thinks he is one of those fathers who knows nothing about their own child's development.

'She's just exploring, isn't she?' she smiles.

And an expression of Kate's comes into Joseph's head. *Brilliant Mother.* This is a Brilliant Mother. A professional; a woman who has read all the books, who has given birth in the most profound and moving way, who knows exactly how to bring up her own and other people's children. Kate has, she says, met a lot of them since Amber was born. At nursery, in parks, at the baby clinic, at Mother and Baby Coffee Mornings. 'I met a Brilliant Mother today,' she says sometimes, and until now Joseph has wondered exactly what she meant. He has been worried, to be honest, that she has grown a little cynical in the last year. Cynicism and motherhood – should they really go together? For instance, today he has brought his mobile phone with him in case she wants to ring, in case she is worried, but all she said was 'I'm just going to have a nice afternoon at the dentist's. I might go for a swim afterwards if there's time.'

'So when is it Amber's birthday?' the woman asks.

'Actually, she was one a couple of weeks ago.'

'Oh. Didn't you have a party?'

'Not as such. We went out for a meal.'

'Just the three of you?'

'Yes.'

'That must have been nice.'

'Yes. It was really nice. Pizza.'

The woman looks annoyed, as if she's thinking, *Why the hell should I fork out on balloons and party bags? Why should I be left hoovering crisps off the floor if other people are just going to swan off to a restaurant?*

'Amber liked the waiter,' Joseph says.

'They respond to black and white at this age,' the woman snaps, springing up off the floor and pulling her sweatshirt straight.

His mobile phone is silent. Kate's afternoon at the dentist's seems suddenly to have taken on a kind of glamour; a dangerous, adult edge. Maybe she is already at the swimming pool. Maybe she is changing into her bright-green swimsuit, hurrying down to the pool, getting into the water. Maybe she is floating there, lying on her back, staring up at the beautiful blue sky through the glass roof.

His own afternoon has been going on for hours. All he hears is the sound of a bouncy castle generator, exploding balloons, babies cottoning on to words. All he is is a father watching his daughter.

At four o'clock it is time to cut the birthday cake.

'Everyone downstairs,' the Brilliant Mother shouts from the doorway. She is now carrying a baby in a striped romper suit. 'You can put your shoes back on,' she adds, as an afterthought.

Joseph picks Amber up and goes to the corner of the room to find his shoes. But they are not there. They are not where he left them. What? How can they not be there? Who would go off with his shoes? Maybe some child hid them, he thinks, looking around the room. Or some parent. Or a janitor? A deranged janitor with a hatred of outdoor shoes on his clean linoleum?

'Lost something?' one of the orbiting fathers asks as he leaves the room.

'Shoes.'

'They're always pulling them off, aren't they?'

'Ha!'

He goes to the bouncy castle and peers inside, wondering if

his shoes are sitting forlornly in there. But they are not. Neither are they in the bin, hiding under coats, perched behind a foam structure.

Now he and Amber are alone in the room. Everyone else has gone downstairs to eat cake. He is reminded of school days, when he was always last out of the changing room.

'I've lost my shoes,' Joseph says. He has a picture in his head of his beautiful maroon shoes. The ones Kate has always loved. He feels ridiculously bereft.

Downstairs at the far end of the room all the parents are wedged into tiny chairs around a low table. Their children sit on their laps, some wearing gold-foil party hats. 'These are the sort of parties we go to now,' Kate had said, when the invitation had arrived in the post. 'Do you remember the parties we used to go to?', and Joseph had smiled at her, remembering darkened rooms, smoke, prolonged kissing, nausea, a vague melancholy. There was a lot to be said for children's parties, he had said; they were a lot less depressing, really. And Kate had sighed.

Now, losing his shoes: that was something he might have done at one of those former parties.

In his socked feet, he finds the last empty chair and perches on it, the sides jutting against his sitting-bones. They are just in time to sing 'Happy Birthday'.

> *Happy Birthday to you*
> *Happy Birthday to you*
> *Happy Birthday, dear Maximill-i-unn,*
> *Happy Birthday to you*

Under the table, his feet feel cold.

'Would Amber like a chipolata?' the Brilliant Mother asks, appearing suddenly at his left shoulder with a paper plate full of small brown sausages.

'I expect she would,' Joseph mumbles. He takes two, one for

himself and one for his daughter. He peels the wrapping off Amber's and hands her the sausage-meat. She puts it in her mouth, considers, and then takes it out again, neatly, between her small fingers.

'Oh, wonderful age,' the woman trumpets, and she is about to sail on with the plate when Joseph says:

'Have you seen my shoes?'

'Shoes?'

'Yes. I couldn't find them. The maroon shoes.'

'The maroooon shoooes,' the woman repeats. 'Surely you can't have lost them?'

'Yes, well, I have.'

'How funny. It's usually the babies who lose their shoes, isn't it?

'Yes.'

'So you're shoeless?'

For a moment he thinks she says *useless*.

'Yes.'

'How funny,' she says again, pushing on with the chipolatas.

The birthday cake is covered with very sweet blue icing. Amber's piece has the X of Maximillian on it. Joseph decides not to give her any, the words *tooth decay* appearing automatically in his head. *Tooth decay, toothbrush, strawberry-flavoured toothpaste.* He thinks of Kate at the dentist's, at the swimming pool, and envies her. These parties, if you take your child to too many of them, are really not that much fun. You begin to wonder.

He is about to take a sip of tea when Amber reaches forward, picks up a plastic cup and pours diluted orange squash all over their jeans.

'Amber!', he says.

'Someone's having fun!' exclaims the Brilliant Mother on her way past yet again, this time with a plate full of Cheesy Wotsits. Joseph looks down at the wet stain covering his crotch, and thinks, *I don't even care.*

'This kind of party is really designed for older children,' he mutters to the woman beside him – a quiet woman who has been sitting there for the past quarter of an hour, her daughter gesticulating in her arms.

'I don't think one-year-olds really know what it's all about,' he says.

'Does anyone?' replies the woman.

He looks at her.

'Did I hear you say something about maroon shoes?', she continues. 'Because I put a pair of maroon shoes on the windowsill upstairs . . .' She pauses. 'Because a little boy was playing with them and I didn't think it was very . . .', she pauses again, '. . . hygienic.'

'Are you implying that I have unhygienic shoes?' Joseph asks, flirtation creeping into his voice, the way it did at parties he used to go to. Like the party he met Kate at.

The woman smiles. 'I thought they looked like very nice shoes,' she says. 'Very . . . exuberant.'

'Thank you,' says Joseph.

'I bet you'd like a pair of shoes like your dad's,' the woman says to Amber, her nerve collapsing suddenly, at the novelty of flirting with an adult male.

Shoeless, he goes to find the Brilliant Mother. She is standing at the sandwich table, trying to operate a tea flask. Struggling with the black plastic lid.

'We're off now,' he says. 'We're going to go and meet Kate.' He can't keep the excitement out of his voice. He feels as if he hasn't seen Kate for weeks.

The Brilliant Mother looks at him.

'I can't get this thing to work,' she says.

Quietly, he carries Amber upstairs, past the cafeteria and back to the crèche to find his shoes. There they are, sitting on the windowsill where the woman said she had put them. His old shoes. His faithful old shoes, like something from a former life. 'Reunited,' he sings. And still in his socks, he starts to dance, his daughter in his arms.

The Selkirk Oscillation

Brian Hennigan

I t is a well-known scientific fact that no two scones are the same. While doughnuts and the occasional pancake might rise with perfect similarity, it is understood within the baking communities of the Scottish Lowlands that it is in the very nature of scones to be individually apart.

From an early age my eldest sister, Elspeth, sought to confound this truth, sweating through the night over the family hob while the rest of us tossed and turned under the family duvet. Not that Elspeth's investigations came to anything. As time went by she became simply one more of those dark, peripheral figures who pepper every small town's back alleys, their eyes alive to the promise of each passing pedestrian.

Occasionally Elspeth would make a nuisance of herself outside one of the many baker's shops to be found in our home town of Selkirk, preaching her vision of symmetry to the lunchtime queue for crusty baguettes. A polite telephone call would bring my mother, who would take her daughter home to the fire and a calming bowl of fatty mince. For my part I was able to endure the resulting playground taunts. The rock-hard products of Elspeth's never-ending quest proved more difficult to digest. But then – on a day now so mouldy with years but so fresh of mind – something happened.

It was a brisk October morning, one of those when the clothes cling as the wind presses them onto the body, like the discomfiting grip of an elderly relative. The first duffel coat of winter had appeared that very week and the streets had an air of icy anticipation. Already there was talk of stockpiling newspapers to see us through the winter, when the roads would often be blocked and news is hard to come by. At the school each room rumbled with the sound of the awakening oil heaters.

My class had only that moment begun its Latin lesson when there was a short sharp bang some distance off. As the grammatical conjugation ground to a halt, the excited tones of a woman's voice could be heard approaching, heavily tacked boots cracking off the cobbles. And although our eyes were to the front, where the stern gaze of Mrs MacFee dared us to waiver in consideration of the verb 'to peel', there could be no doubt where our hearts and minds were, as all present felt the approach of a force from beyond the natural world. With a sharp visceral cry the door to the schoolhouse was punched open. 'Behold!' boomed an uncomfortably familiar voice.

Shamefaced, I lowered my head in embarrassment. This time my sister had gone too far. Yet even as my brow came to rest on the traditional vandalised contour of the Formica desk, I became aware of a general gasp around me. Raising myself, I found that every one of my classmates and even Mrs MacFee were looking in wonder at what Elspeth carried. I strained my neck to see through the jungle of mottled grey pullovers. And there, sitting on one of our best plates, were two identical scones.

At first tentatively, and then in a tremendous rush, the room gathered round, eyes newly widened by the sight before them. Many hands reached out to bathe in the aura of those wondrous products, yet none chose to touch their rocky surface. It was as if all concerned realised the unworldly nature of these creations.

Nothing is bigger than bakery in the Scottish Borders. Word of Elspeth's achievement swept like a swollen river through

Selkirk, bringing chaos to the town as people sat on the High Street in bright-orange dinghies. As the climate of unreason rose ever higher, answers were demanded, even before questions had been asked.

My sister was duly brought before the town council. The two identical scones sat by her side, playing the combined role of guardian, witness and mid-afternoon fancy. To the demands for information, Elspeth was succinct.

'The random crystalline nature of the flour atoms has been curtailed through the application of oven-based oscillation.'

Then she fell silent and would say no more, not even when they poked at her belly with a sharp stick.

Just then a voice broke through the rabble. It was my mother.

'The secret of the scones is to remain with Elspeth. We shall form a co-operative for the town and, following my daughter's recipe, build an empire of scones on which the sun will never set.'

That very evening the good people of Selkirk began to make their plans, while the bad people of Selkirk joined them later in the pub. By the end of the night, everything looked rosy.

The rivalry between the southern towns for dainty supremacy knows no limit. As the story of this miraculous development seeped through the region, the burning envy of all those it reached could be seen hovering above the valleys, like smoke from the battles of yore. It was not long before emissaries arrived, bearing the obligatory gifts of food, wine and stationery products.

'We've heard about the scones,' said the man from Hawick.

'These developments must be shared,' said the man from Galashiels.

'What time is the last bus?' said the man from Kelso.

But through all these queries the women of Selkirk kept their counsel and offered no sharing of the new reproductive technology. The plenipotentiaries left empty-handed, having been relieved of their gifts on arrival. How could we have guessed that, in this brief exchange, we had turned our backs on peace?

At the time, thoughts of ruination were far from our mind. We knew only that our innovative products would pave the way to riches. Absolutely identical foodstuffs are much coveted by the fine ladies and gentlemen of Edinburgh, Glasgow and – to a lesser extent – Aberdeen. In such heady environs any difference between baked goods can lead to debate, prevarication, even fistfights. Identical scones would do away with such teatime torpor. Ours would be the comestibles of choice.

By dawn of the following day, the layout for the new industrial baking complex had been meticulously paced out near the rugby pitch. A heli-pad would be provided for the high-flying senior executives of the top stores; plans for a direct link to Europe were underway and all schoolchildren were taking lessons in Japanese business etiquette, apart from those who brought a note from their mum. The entire town was on a mission, which perhaps explains why no-one noticed an under-cover act of devious daring.

We were gathered at the town hall to witness the unveiling of the new mouse pad, when the reverent hush was broken by the arrival of my mother, her eyes betraying a level of distress unknown since the invention of coleslaw. Still panting, she addressed the expectant people of the town.

'They've taken Elspeth.'

As the words dripped like fusty porridge from her frightened lips, words that but three days before might have been the cause of much joy, we descended as one into a wild rage. Who knows what might have happened had Mrs MacFee not realised that the edge of sanity was approaching? With a loud crack of her knuckles, she pulled us back from the chasm that all but one of our feet had already crossed. Breathless and sweaty, we listened to her timeous address.

'Now is not the time for anger. Now is the time for intelligent thought and effective action.'

The room nodded urgently, eager for further guidance.

'Few things were unknown to the ancients and it is to them that I propose turning,' our teacher concluded, a finger already leafing through the text in her left hand. Slowly, deliberately, she flipped it opened. Mesmerised, we gathered greedily round, as the light of cunning shone brightly through the window.

How the pastry was kneaded deep into the night as the town worked. To the chill of the air our limbs were immune as every inhabitant did their bit to make what history would surely prove to be our, and my sister Elspeth's, salvation.

We were aided by knowing where we should target our countermeasures. Shortly after my mother had broken the news, a messenger arrived, bearing a note from the people of Galashiels.

'You have pushed us too far. Stop. We only want to share. Stop. If you give us the formula then we will give Elspeth back. Stop. Then peace will reign and a new era for us all can start. Stop.'

We listened to the messenger then sent him on his way. Little did he know that we had been expecting just such an ultimatum and that by revealing their identity, the kidnappers had sliced the bread for the sandwich of their undoing.

By eleven o'clock the following morning we were ready. On a typical Scottish winter day, a handpicked team of commandos made their way towards Galashiels under cover of darkness, armed with the very latest in military hardware. By nightfall, we had reached the outskirts of the town.

No true Scot can resist the allure of a good pie, however hot or cold. Lips will burn on flaming crust and teeth will break on frozen meat before any pie goes untouched in a Scottish household. So it will come as no surprise to know the shape by which we came to enter the heavily walled settlement.

It must have been shortly after the first change of the guard that word of our arrival began to circulate among the sentries. Certainly it was around then when, through a carefully concealed listening hole in the pastry rim, we heard the alarm being raised.

'Hurry! Come quickly! There's a giant pie at the gates!'

But the succour that this vision brought to the stomachs of these unfortunate guardians could never rival the sense of impending revenge that it heralded in our own hearts. As we listened to the approaching footsteps, we were naturally apprehensive. There will always be those who, quite properly, doubt the promise of the uninvited gift from above. With obvious trepidation the pie was encircled and we felt ourselves the centre of intense debate. While the majority wished to bring the gargantuan offering within the town whereon to feast, there were still those strong voices that urged caution.

'Listen,' these voices said, 'we must take care. Anything could be inside it.'

They were right to be suspicious. While in bygone days the pie was unfailingly a host to traditional fillings, nowadays it's not just mince. Everyone had heard the rumours of pies filled with potato, beans or even macaroni. Under such circumstances, their caution was surely justified.

But they were not cautious enough. For within minutes of this initial hesitation we felt ourselves being hoisted onto the shoulders of the town's menfolk, while the town's womenfolk danced round our generous base, banging tins of beans and waving well-read copies of *The Female Eunuch*. Clearly they had a party in mind.

Sure enough, once inside the stone fortress of the town, the gigantic pie became the centerpiece of a festival of merrymaking. How were they to know that, while they drank on cherry ale and mutton brandy, the Selkirk commandos were already within their bosom, biding their time, nurturing their anger, knitting their jumpers.

We sat and waited for many hours. While during this period there was the occasional attempt to extract a chunk from the massive pastry offering within their midst, for the most part the inhabitants were happy to dance, sing and do crosswords. And eventually, once the last chunk of marzipan had sunk into the gloom of the fondue and the citizens' fervour had been drowned into stupor, it was time for us to act.

With the most careful of movements the roof of the pie was pushed back, until the light of the stars was visible to us all, encircled by a magical ring of pastry. One by one we abseiled down the hard-baked walls. Around us lay the erstwhile triumphant revellers, now asleep and awash in the assorted debris of party hats and Polaroid cameras.

It did not take us long to find Elspeth. She was secured in the living room of a newly built bungalow. Those who had been charged with watching over her had soon deserted their duties to participate in the town's impromptu glee making, leaving my sister alone and afraid by the light of a luminous clock radio. We united her from the sofa and were soon on our way. A number of us wished to take some revenge on the sleeping trespassers of Galashiels but Mrs MacFee would not allow it.

'Halt,' she cried, as one of our number headed for the local bakery with a flaming torch. 'The tigers of wrath are wiser than the horses of invention. Let them have their bread that they will not lust after ours.'

At that we fell silent and no further damage was visited upon the town.

Upon returning to Selkirk, Elspeth never more spoke of identical scones, or of the process by which they had arisen. Having seen the world of anger, fear and jealousy they created, she chose to put aside the search for perfection in favour of the bringing of joy to people's lives. She can still be found on the High Street, dispensing buns to needy tourists, often having to force her kindness through the half-opened windows of their passing automobiles. The rest of the town, if not understanding, is certainly supportive. That we might be wealthier is not in any doubt; that we would be any happier remains a topic for nightly discussion.

The Caponisation of Edgardo De Pucci

Clio Gray

I grip the eel by the gills and slap it hard onto the carving block. With a swift chop of my knife I slice off its head. The feeling is not unpleasant. Beneath my glove, the skin slithers and halts, the writhe of its cold body ceasing. Like the hangman's noose that morning, it stretches and grows taut, jumps a little before swinging into a pendulum and altogether quits its life. It was fifteen minutes after the clock struck eight. The minister's lips twitched into silence; he closed his book and turned away. A collective sigh escaped the crowd as they surged forward, their bodies' momentum causing the rope to twist a little and the corpse to turn. Dogs snuffled and whined at the edge of the piazzale, the dust still dew-damp, cooled by the shadow of the church. Inside, at the oak, hands tugged at boots and buttons, fingers pinched at shirt and shift, handkerchiefs swabbed blood from cuts and broken bruises. A single finger was severed from its joint, cut off from its body and the promise of resurrection in the Land of Light. This last was the deed of Pina Cavellini, whose second-born son bought her much dismay. He had one leg short and one leg long, a hand which curled like a crab in its shell. His skin had the colour and clamminess of a dead limpet. And he fitted, sometimes three times a day. His breeches were always soup-splattered, stained with a week's-worth of dinners all spoilt and spilled. He was thin as a stick, and most of his teeth had been knocked out, but, still, he was a cheery lad and good for the gossip, hanging around as he did all day, sitting on his mother's stoop. We all turned a blind eye when the pouch appeared the morning after, swinging around his neck, smelling of lavender and sweetbrier, and something less savoury half-hidden underneath the pokes of straw. It is well known that the corpse-peelings of executed criminals can heal everything from clogged lungs to toothache, and are particularly efficacious in the cure of epilepsy. The district's only doctor had been canvassing the mayor for years to tighten up the law, and to prosecute thieves and blasphemers to their mortal extent.

'Bring back the sword!' he could be heard muttering as the bodies piled up in his hospital. 'Such a clean way to go, and think of the benefits – why, the condemned sinner is cured of his sin, and his redemption guaranteed. His blood buys his salvation and can be mopped up by the bucketful to heal those he sinned against. It's the perfect solution to the rise in wrongdoing, which, God knows, is a plague we all bear. The Barons sit on their arses, their chests stuffed with gold and we all get poorer. And poverty, as we know, by common observation, is the bedfellow of dissolute living and disease. That one causes the other is indisputable; that consequences of treating one should be the treating of the other is natural law.'

The poor Doctor has been disappointed these last twenty years, for nobody has offended public conscience badly enough to be deprived of his life. After all, we all knew each other, grew up together, and it doesn't seem right to chop the heads off those you played Kill-The-Rat and Marble-Jacks with. And then came Edgardo De Pucci, riding into the village with his handsome black stallion and his fancy leather boots. He clattered down the streets, dismounted outside the tavern and hitched up his fine horse. Instantly he was covered in a clamour of young

182

boys who sprouted from alleys and doorways, and each was given a coin and assigned a task – comb the mane, wash the tail, polish the straps, shine the saddle, guard the bags. He had arrived precisely at the right time – had waited at the crossroads outside the village so as to create just such an entrance – and the bar was filling with men coming in from the fields, closing their shops, clearing out of the tanneries, bringing their stink and thirst with them. Edgardo flung a purse of silver florins and papal piastres on the counter and announced his intentions to the world.

'Greetings! *Salutati amicóni*! I am returned home! Let us celebrate for a week, or as long as it takes!'

I watch the eels swirl in their bath – a vast structure of marble slabs built into the neck of the Bracciano Lake. Below it, the shelf drops into darkness, the water closing its eyes against the light, shivering from blue to green to blindest night. The eels down there, my *capetoni*, are giant creatures, thick and dark as tarred ropes coiled on a sunken deck, slowly unwinding through their domain. They are as liquid as the water in which they move, strong and secret, black as the blackest of men. The trap beneath the boathouse cannot catch them. I go out in the icy heart of winter when they rise a little from their depths. It is early and the mist whispers on the water, the paddling of my boat sending echoes from shore to shore, sounding loud and intrusive, making the ice in the air hum and sing. I bait the line and lower it in, finger by finger, slowly, slowly, so as not to alarm, gently breaking from one world into the next. My honour is dependent on my patience and skill; I must outwile the wiliest and catch my eel: the bigger it is, the greater the honour, both for myself and my village. It will be dressed into steaks, thick as cobblestones, packed into ice and sent to the Pope. It is our Christmas Gift, our Trust, our reminder that the Rock of Peter can be hurled into Hell with the best of us, as was his predecessor, Martin IV, exiled and alone in Perugia, whose belly will burst throughout eternity, trying to release its surfeit of eels.

Having been at the smoke-house by the lake the last few days, I had missed news of Edgardo's arrival. Stepping into the second night's carousing at the tavern, I recognised him at once, and in my shock tripped over the unconscious body of the cobbler, who never could hold his drink. Edgardo was as ever he was, flat-faced, bony-shouldered, with pockets as deep as his short legs allowed. We embraced like the brothers we had once sworn to be when we were ten, and he smothered my cheeks with a grease-ridden bristle of kisses. He waved aside his companions, staggered to a table, which he swept clear with his arm, and sat me down.

'Platter of buttered pig's trotters and a bottle of finest brandy!' he called to the barman's youngest daughter, the only sober one left in the entire family, excepting cousin Gianelli, who never drank, considering it a finer art to chew tobacco all day and dribble. Edgardo told me his tale: how he'd sought and found his fortune in Rome as he had always said he would; how he'd loved and lost a wife, who'd born and buried three children before departing to Naples with a pox-ridden bastard of a silk-merchant who was tight as a bolt of his own slippery cloth. How he'd come back home to settle down, spread his riches around the village, live among old friends. Tears dripped over the forgotten trotters, and a trickle of spilt brandy seeped through the table-seams and onto the dirty floor.

'Find me a good country wife is what I'll do,' sniffed Edgardo, dreaming of rosy-cheeked milkmaids and a tribe of strapping sons, 'They'll know a good man when they see one, not like the trollops and whores you find in the City. The only work those bitches know is how to lift their skirts.'

We commiserate over more brandy, lamenting our respective bachelorhoods, discussing possible proposals, me enlightening him to the martial status of each girl he remembered, Edgardo sniggering and arguing with himself about long-forgotten fumbles in barns and haystacks, the mowburnt ardour of his youth.

'Now now,' his beer-breath is wet and pungent as he slips from an elbow and confronts me face to face, slurring a little, his mind beginning to jumble.

'Here'sh one not forgotten . . .' he lifts a finger and prods the air. 'Wass her name? Wass her name? Worked in . . . Where's it? Always smelt of fish. Good looker, though, always a bit ripe for it.'

He meant Bellastidda, and he was right. She was pretty and plump, good hips, walked straight and square, had breasts full and white as if already primed and warm with milk. She came to the lake a few times, after Edgardo had left. Asked me if I thought he'd come back, if he'd come back as rich as he'd always said he would. I would shrug, and pass a pot of smoked eel. Asked her to the Midsummer Dance one time, but she had refused. She still came every now and then, dipped her pale round ankles into the eel pools, sending sunlight shimmering across the marble base, silvering the backs of the eels.

No-one could understand it when less than a month later he had killed her and sauntered back into town like he owned the place. Pina Cavellini's son, sitting on his stoop, had seen them heading off to the woods, hand in hand, laughing and cuddling. That afternoon, Edgardo had come back alone, and Bellastidda, well, she never came back at all. Of course, Edgardo denied it, said he'd left her in the top meadow so she could cut across the fields and tell her father she was going to get married after all. She was happy as larks in spring, said he, but everyone frowned and shook their heads. Even me, his oldest friend. Who knows what can happen to a man when he leaves for the City?

'Why had he ever come back?' it was muttered in the tavern. 'To show us all up as poor and provincial, stuck in our ways? Weren't we as good as he, that he should come back bragging and lording it over the rest of us, thinking it his right to pick the best olives from the barrel?'

It was a sad tale. Poor Edgardo came home to find happiness and ended having his neck wrung like a rabbit, eleven minutes of choking and kicking in front of family and friends, his thin prison-issue shite staining his pants, no-one to hang hard on his legs and shorten his agony. Bellastidda was never seen again, her body never found. It was presumed she had refused his advances and that he had taken what he wanted anyway, paying her with the back of his hand and burying her in the woods. It was saddest though, for Pina Cavellini's son, still sitting on his stoop, suffering the stink of that finger rotting round his neck. For it shan't cure him. Edgardo was a braggart, it's true, but never a criminal, and Bellastidda lies at the bottom of the eel pond, feeding the Pope's Pies. She'd come to ask my advice that afternoon, you see, and I, being an honest man and true, gave it.

The Caged Bird

Alan Mackay

Just along from our rooms, further along the quayside, is the smallest ouzeri on the island, if not the world. A single room with a small gas-fired stove – two burners, small for Greek coffee, large for frying – behind a counter a wash-hand basin, a few shelves bowed with the weight of bottles of ouzo and a refrigerator the size of a privy. Outside there are six tables and eighteen uneven chairs lop-sided, askew. There is also a bird cage on a pole. The cage is tied off at eye level and safe from the octopus mezes-crazed cats that gather round our feet in the evenings. In the cage a lark hunches in one corner.

On the first evening we walked the quayside from the ferry-pier to the children's playground, counting the bars, counting the restaurants. As we passed the smallest ouzeri the bird shifted on its perch with a flutter of its wings.

She said – Look. Isn't that a lark? How sad.

I said – I suppose. And we passed on.

Later, when we had settled on the smallest ouzeri as being the one with the best view and charging the least for its ouzo, and taken our seats outside, we chose to ignore the lark in the cage.

She said – I suppose we shouldn't judge. After all, it's their country, their culture.

I said – If that makes you more comfortable.

She said – It's not a matter of comfort, it's about acknowledging the validity of difference.

I said – That's fine by me. And ordered another pair of ouzo.

She said – You mustn't think me callous.

I said – Why should I feel you are callous when you choose to suck on the comfort blanket of compromise? I remember now that we had tried several other ouzeries before this, and that we were embarking on another round. It didn't excuse, I suppose, but it does help explain, I think, my flippancy.

She said nothing.

We stared at the harbour for some time, sipping ouzo and chewing on tentacles of grilled octopus. Above us somewhere a church bell began to ring out its single-note summons to prayer. The ouzeri's owner, a silent though smiling man of middle years and corresponding girth, came out of the shop and untied the cord from which the lark's cage was suspended from the pole. As the church bell rang out he slowly pulled on the cord and the cage rose gradually higher up the pole until, at a certain point, the lark became animated and began to sing its ascending chorus. He raised the cage to the very top of the pole and held it there, the lark now in full vocal flight, until the bell ceased. Then, he slowly lowered the cage back to its original position, tied the cord off and returned to the inside of the shop.

She said – Did you see that?

I said – Yes, let's go and eat.

She said – But you have to admit it was an extraordinary thing for the lark to do, as she forked another congealed block of moussaka into her mouth.

I said – I suppose so.

She said – Do you think there was any connection between the church bells ringing and the bird?

I said – We'll have to wait until tomorrow night and see if it happens again. We should treat it as an experiment. I poured us the last of our first bottle of retsina and waved the empty at the waiter. If it happens again, there is a likelihood that there is a connection. But not a certainty.

She said – How many observations would you need to be sure?

I said – Seven to be absolutely sure, unless the pattern is monthly, or annual, and thanked the waiter for the next bottle.

She said – Seven? How long are we staying here?

I said – Eight days, by the look of it. Over by the ferry-pier a boat laden with gravel was tying up, ready for unloading in the morning.

The next evening we sat at the smallest ouzeri and watched as the owner hoisted his bird cage up the pole in time with the church bell. We nibbled on small deep-fried sardines, some boiled potatoes and bread smeared with tarama, washing each plateful down with the ouzo.

She said – There, does that prove it?

I said – Not to my entire satisfaction. The two events may still be coincidental. We need more evidence.

She said – I'm not sure I want to sit here to find out. It makes me somehow complicit. I mean, the poor bird. I mean, larks are put on earth to sing, and this one only does it once a day.

I said – We can't be sure of that. We will have to accumulate more evidence.

She said – Well, you'll have to do it on your own, I don't want to be part of it. I'll join you after the bells have stopped.

I said – But you'll still hear the bird, half the island's population hears the bird. You won't be able to avoid hearing the bird.

She said – But I won't be an active party. I will hear the bell and a lark, to me they don't have to be that bell and this lark. It increases the possibility of chance for me if I remove myself from the immediate vicinity.

I said – That's bollocks, but she said nothing.

That evening, while we sat at the smallest ouzeri sipping grainy coffee and the sweet Greek brandy that the owner pours from a barrel on the counter, the moon began to rise from behind the church with one bell. A great white orb raising itself above the horizon and spilling its light over the harbour. At one point it positioned itself directly above the blue dome of the church, mocking its humble splendour with its iridescence. All around us people leapt from their tables to take photographs, jockeying for position to keep the moon above the dome, flanked by the bell towers on either side. All around us flash bulbs popped and motor drives whined another frame into place behind the lens. All around us.

She said – Do you think that the flash bulbs will reach as far as the moon?

I said – probably not. Would you like a photograph too?

She laughed out loud and attracted far too much attention. Behind us, in its cage, on its pole, the lark stirred with the unexpected light, but did not sing.

A few days later, on the beach with the two tavernas, where they put grated carrot in the tuna salad, and with the aubergines in the Special, we talked about the lark again. I began to feel that she was becoming obsessed.

She said – Of course not.

I said – It seems to be all you ever talk about.

She said – That isn't true, I talk about lots of other things. I talk about which beach we should walk to tomorrow, which taverna we should eat in tonight. I talk about the books I'm reading and what a bad choice I've made this year, again. I ask you about the books that you've brought. Whether you are enjoying them and whether I would like any of them. And, I am patient with you when you patronise me in reply. I talk about the contents of the three-days-ago copy of the *Daily Telegraph* that you wouldn't let me buy because you don't wish to fill the coffers of whoever it is that owns the bloody paper. I talk about how good it is to know what is going on in the world no matter which paper it's in, that it keeps us in touch even if we are three days late in finding out that Margaret Thatcher has just died.

I said – Has she?

She said – No, she hasn't, that's not the point. I'm only trying to say that I am not obsessed by that poor bloody bird, that it is not the only thing I ever talk about.

I said – Well, it just seems that way sometimes.

She said – Well, it's not. It's not. But it is a shame. And I do feel sorry for it.

I said – Well at least it gets fed and watered. At least it is safe from harm. At least it has . . . at least it has a nice view of the harbour.

She said – And that bloody boat unloading gravel from seven thirty in the morning to eight at night! It can watch that too.

I said – If you want to move rooms we can do. It's not a problem. The woman will understand. It is very noisy.

She said – No, that doesn't matter. I don't mind the noise. Really I don't. It's part of the atmosphere of the place, I suppose. Anyway, how is your experiment coming?

I said – Well, it's been four days now, and the correlation is steady at 100 per cent. I'm getting more and more confident that there is a clear connection between the bell being rung and the lark ascending. Quite clear. I looked out to sea, in a faraway sort of way and saw the hydrofoil from Samos cutting its way towards Leros. No sound to hear from here. Just like a toy in a bathtub.

And on the seventh day the lark ascended. From my vantage point at the foot of its pole I toasted it with ouzo in celebration. And, as I sat there, I was struck for the first time by just how beautiful its song was. No longer a curiosity, a game even, the game was over, my bouts of solo drinking, my head-start, had been vindicated. Six days shall you labour and on the seventh it's up to the top of the pole and have at it again. But beautiful, yes, surely beautiful. The bells stopped, the cage descended, a most curious silence descended upon the ouzeri. The lark and I exchanged glances and I ordered two ouzos in anticipation.

She said – Well?

I said – We can leave tomorrow. The lark and the bell are joined at the hip. I remember that I slurred that line, though whether from emotion or the intake of ouzo I cannot recall.

She said – You're drunk.

I said – Not yet, but I expect to be.

That evening we ate at the fish taverna right on the front, the one with the red and white gingham tablecloths. We washed the fish down with too many crown-caps of retsina and discussed the cooking at great length.

She said – This is the best swordfish I have ever had in Greece.

I said – Do you mean this is the best piece of fish you have ever had or that the cooking is the most proficient of any that you have had? And stuff like that.

After that we returned to the ouzeri to say our farewells and drink a last drink, though God knows we did not need one. The owner gave us free drinks when we said we were catching the ferry the next day and embraced us, on our departure, as if we were long-lost relatives not tourists. We promised to return one day and made our way back to the room, slowly, with very deliberate steps. She fell asleep almost as soon as she lowered her head. I lay with my eyes open and watched as the ceiling revolved slowly above my head and thought about larks in other people's cages.

At about two o'clock I was standing, trying to pee as quietly as possible, and looking out the small ventilator window in the bathroom at the harbour below, when the idea came to me. It was dazzling, as all retsina ideas are, in its simplicity: I would set the bird free. Seven days I'd sat and watched the whole barbaric ritual, the obscure vendetta or whatever it was acted out between the ouzeri owner and, presumably, the priest. The game of proving the correlation having run its course I was none the wiser as to the reason behind it, but I knew it had to end; the innocent must no longer suffer.

I pulled on my shorts and a dark T-shirt as camouflage and flip-flopped out of the room and down to the quayside. Only the lapping of the water and the skulking of a few cats disturbed the still of the night. Above me the waning moon, still almost two-thirds in size, lit the scene with a brilliant clarity. At the ouzeri all the tables and chairs had been taken inside, the awnings rolled up and the doors locked. Only the cage, tied to its impossibly high pole marked the building as unique.

The lark stirred at my approach, I could see its eyes flash the reflected light of the moon like tiny diamonds. I spoke softly so as not to scare it, shushing words, comfort words, do-not-be-afraid words, I am-here-to-set-you-free words. The lark dropped from its perch to the floor of the cage, its head slightly cocked in curiosity. I reached up and fumbled at the catch, nicking the tip of my finger as I did so. I stifled my tiny pain.

I said – There now, as I let the door swing open and stepped back. There now, you can get away.

But the bird refused to move. No amount of persuasive talk could coax it out of the cage.

I said – Come on now. You don't have to stay here any longer. Come on, you can escape, I'm giving you the chance to be free.

Strangely, I didn't feel stupid talking to a Greek lark in English at two thirty in the morning. It seemed the most natural thing in the world to be doing. I did wonder if it may have been better if I'd spoken in Greek, but was sobering up just enough to laugh at myself for that. I sat on the ground beside the pole and leaned back against the ouzeri wall, suddenly exhausted by my efforts.

I said – Oh, come on, you stupid bloody bird, fly away, for God's sake, and let me get to bed. The lark ignored my plea and resumed its position on its perch.

The cage door swung gently in the breeze from the sea,

making the tiniest creaks on its rusty hinges, and the cord tapped lightly against the pole. The two sounds began to have a soporific effect on me, my eyes fluttered and my head rolled forward onto my chest then snapped back again.

I said – Shit! This is getting beyond a joke. Come on, your future awaits you.

I struggled to my feet, bracing my back against the wall and pulling myself up by the pole, careful not to pull the cage up the pole by the cord. The last thing I needed was a cacophony of lark at three in the morning.

I said – Now, come on, you've had your fun. It's time you took to the skies.

I slowly put my hand inside the cage and the bird fell from its perch in a panic and dropped to the floor where it scrabbled into a corner. Suddenly gripped by a panic myself, that it would die from fright if I was not careful, I withdrew my hand to let it calm down. Eventually its frantic movements subsided and I once again, slowly, ever so slowly, inserted my hand.

I said – There now, I'm not going to hurt you, there now, and inched my hand towards the palpitating creature. There now. I wrapped my hand around it and gently withdrew it from the cage.

I said – There now, as it peeked from my fist, its heart panic-hammering against my palm and fingers. There now – I kissed its tiny beak – off you go. And I tossed it lightly skywards, watching, made suddenly immobile by the unfolding horror before me. For, in a flutter of clipped-wing panic, it fell to the ground and began to hobble brokenly in frantic circles as a ring of cats began to slowly close around it.

Radar Bird

Jules Horne

S o this is the pitch, right? It'll be a stonker. Believe it.
Right from the opening credits, popcorn will sit un-
scoffed, Coke unsooked, sweetie wrappers unrustled. One-film
stands in the back row will remain unsnogged.

Women will laugh, men cry, couples argue and break up and
make up and make love, and maybe live just a wee bit better for
having seen it.

When they go out into the night to the trams and the tubes and
the car parks, chips will be the last thing on their minds. They'll
walk through the dark with an empty soreness inside for all the
loves they killed and lost. But deeply, bittersweetly happy.

Playing she: let's go for Juliette Binoche – sweet, mysterious,
passionate, vulnerable. Outfits by Ghost. Simple, effortless, with
a touch of whimsy.

Playing he: how about Michael Douglas? Grim-chinned,
baby-eyed, a veneer of dimpled innocence masking innards
of the purest evil. Costumes by someone stiff and square-
shouldered and very *Eighties*. Possibly Next. He's the baddie,
right?

The basic plot is girl-meets-guy, girl-loses-guy. There isn't a
happy ending, a froth of white and invitations, unless you count
the fact that she had a narrow escape from a life of unspeakable
misery. Which is something to be grateful for, though not
fantastic box office.

But the first bit, the meeting bit, the strings-and-roses bit, doesn't count. That's the prequel. It's a prequel that will never be made, since the events of the main feature recast the whole past in a horrible, sordid light that make any vestigial mirth from before sound pretty hollow. Hindsight. That old spoiler. That old killer of all unravelled joy.

So let's ditch the prequel. Let's cut to the chase. What we've got in front of us is that classic favourite, girl-loses-guy.

There are two problems with this scenario, you say:

Problem one: it sounds careless. What did she do? Drop him at the checkout? Chuck him in the bucket with the tattie peelings?

The truth is, she wasn't careless at all. She cared a lot, and did her best to show it, often, with all the affection she could reasonably spare.

Problem two: it sounds as if she played an active part in what happened. Sadly, she didn't. It would be more accurate to say that she was lost.

Lost? Where? In the woods, you say? Did she mislay her trail of breadcrumbs? Drop her compass? Or was she lost metaphorically, in a vague, mind-body-spirit sort of way? You're right. Let's have facts. Let's have stats. The truth is, she was *losed*.

Ah, the passive. It won't go away, will it? You're right. She isn't the agent at all. He is. Let's turn them round again. Him then her. That order. And find a verb. Yes, all the euphemisms in the world don't make it any easier. Dump. Ditch. Discard. Chuck. Abandon.

So here's where we're at. Guy-dumps-girl. This is a hump-and-dump film. A fuck-and-chuck, if you'll pardon. A new genre. A new, unforgiving realism is about to hit our screens. Millions will connect. Millions will cry. Millions will find release and move on.

So. Over the opening credits we see her at the airport, waiting anxiously at the head of a long queue as he comes haring up, case in hand, tie and jacket flapping. City guy. Busy busy. Perfunctory peck and apologies.

Cut to plane interior. He is loosening his tie and wriggling irritably. She is looking out the window, crying.

Why is she crying? Because she doesn't understand. For weeks, she's been doing everything wrong. Flashback: chopping onions, booking holidays, folding clothes, choosing shoes. The wrong shoes, for chrissake. She can't even choose her own shoes properly. She's cracked it to a T, the art of reliably and flawlessly doing everything wrong. Which is odd, because before that, she'd been doing everything more or less right.

On with the dialogue:

> HE:
>
> What's wrong?
>
> SHE:
>
> Nothing.

She continues looking out of the window, crying, but in an aesthetically pleasing way that doesn't smudge her make-up.

You're right to raise the issue of cliché. Much appreciated. That exchange crops up in pretty well every film about relationships ever shot. Though often, if you'll forgive, with different personnel.

> SHE:
>
> What's wrong?
>
> HE:
>
> Nothing.

Or

> PARENT:
>
> What's wrong?
>
> CHILD:
>
> Nothing.

Or

HUMAN:

What's wrong?

ANDROID:

Nothing.

But yes, it's always the same general sub-text:

HE:

Everything, but don't imagine for one instant that I'm going to talk to *you* about it. It's such a painful can of worms that I don't know where to start. You're distant, I'm depressed, we're not communicating, we've stopped loving, it's all crumbling slowly about our ears and we're afraid to press too much in case it collapses. And there's no point in starting a scene right now cos if we're going to embark on a row it will have to be the mother of all rows and that's a thing I'm putting off as long as possible. Now bugger off and leave me alone.

So you see, it's the best available line in the circumstances. Crisp, short, economical. But we can look at the alternative. The truth.

HE:

What's wrong?

SHE:

Everything.

HE:

For God's sake, don't start. Cos if you're gonna start, I'm getting off this plane right now. I'm not spending a week with you snivelling on like a tragedy queen. Jesus, we're on holiday. Blow your nose, there's people looking –

CUT! See? It's not attractive. Not filmic.

They arrive at the main location. The setting is a Greek island, generically blue (sky) and blue (sea) sandwiching a paradise of heat and beaches. Montage: taxi, bare white hotel room, stripping off the thick layers of London. She puts on a long yellow dress; he wears unlikely British shorts. They collapse separately onto the separate beds and look at the ceiling. He cracks open a bottle of beer.

How much time do you have? Ah. Yes, let's cut to the chase. Not that there's a chase as such. After all, it's an island. No room. And too expensive. Always an eye on production costs.

Anyway, the key scene, the scene it all revolves around, is this:

Guy-tells-girl-he-has-found-someone-else.

This concept is first introduced with a scrap of dialogue. Setting: outside the restaurant, in the twinkling dark, after the first meal out, the first bottle of wine, the first unwinding.

HE:
It's not that I don't love you.
SHE:
???

The ??? can be expressed in various ways, depending on the skill of the actress. Eyebrows, mouth, the horizontal lines across the brow – all can be used to great effect. It's a gift, really. A chance to show a wide emotional range of huge complexity.

For him, too. Yes, it's a great line. An awful line, too. Great in its awfulness, both grammatical and emotional. Two negatives, for a start. 'Not' and 'don't'. You can be forgiven for thinking they make a plus. That they cancel each other out. That he loves her. That would be a mistake. The same mistake *she* makes, in fact.

What a line! Is it an apology? A confession? A reassurance?

What is he saying in that moment? It's clear the words didn't come about by chance. Such crushing banality can only be achieved with an unusual effort of thought, precision and practice.

The full subtext would take at least half an hour to express:

HE:

It's over but I'm too much of a coward to tell you straight. Look into my eyes and read them. It's all in there. I posted the message there weeks ago, big and clear. Why won't you read it? Why are you so obtuse? Make things easy, please. Don't make me say things directly. I don't know how. I have the words but they hurt in my mouth. They're sharp and bitter and ugly and don't suit me. Don't force me. I want *you* to say them instead. I want *you* to take the initiative. Why do you think I've been treating you like that? Criticising, nit-picking, niggling? It's for your own good. I want you to hate me. Then you'll come to say the words that I can't. Believe me, it'll be easier. For me, at least. Oh, and there's someone else.

You're in a hurry? Yes, I appreciate that. I just wanted to give you a flavour of how deep this thing goes, despite the apparent shallowness of the dialogue.

The problem is she doesn't crack the code. Her ??? is a genuine ??? She isn't feigning incomprehension in order to gain time.

The other problem is he thinks he's said something meaningful. He thinks he's told it like it is. He thinks he's been big, bold and incisive. He's feeling relieved, therefore. That it's all out in the open. That she Knows.

In fact, she knows sweet shit. That's why she says ??? And

when he starts crying, from relief and possibly the strain of thinking up such an immortal line, she says ??? again, and gives him a comforting hug. Therethere. A warm old motherhug for the little lost boy. You're all right. It's OK. Therethere. I understand. Shhhhh. It's OK. Ad lib ad inf.

How can she be so selfish, you ask? Is she doing it deliberately? Pretending not to understand? Forcing him to say the ugly words? Is she entirely incapable of subtlety? Of imagination? Of compassion? Self, self, self, always self. And here he is, trying so hard to be kind. As illustrated by:

HE:

I'm sorry.

Oh dear, you say. That old chestnut. That catch-all cover-the-cracks. That handy self-absolution.

Stay with it. It's a challenge, especially for Michael Douglas. Here's what lies beneath:

HE:

I'm sorry that you exist. That you were born. That you can't be unmade. That you can't be deleted by simply shutting my eyes. And, particularly, that you have a toothbrush in the glass by my sink. And I apologise for all the painful things I've ever done to you, and, while I'm at it, for all the painful things I'm about to do, especially in the very near future. Beginning in just a few moments. Beginning now.

You see? Much more to it than meets the eye.

You're getting impatient. That's great. You want to see how it ends. You're hooked. Stay with it.

The point is, love stops. There's nothing you can do. It's not intrinsically a problem. A love that's puttered to a halt without a fuel stop in nearby reach is not necessarily in trouble. You can get out, relax, take a breather, enjoy the view. It might be a pleasant view, you never know. Peaceful. Familiar. Comfortable.

The problem isn't usually the stopping of an old love. You can live with that. People do, by and large. No, it's the starting of a new one. A huge, red, shiny sports job zooming into the layby, headlights flashing, horn beeping, offering you a lift somewhere. Somewhere new. So you're going places. Not stranded on the verge.

It's a metaphor. It doesn't have to be a real car.

And when that new love zooms off into the sunset, or the new dawn, or whatever looks most scenic, what we're left with is a great big hole. A gap in the story.

You want to follow the new car? Shame. That's so obvious. This is not about obvious. The new love is probably pretty much like any other: soaring hyperbole for the first few weeks, or even months if they're lucky, then flattening out in time, till you'd be hard pushed to call it a hummock.

And the ending? Not pretty. Malaria, perhaps. Or bourgeois boredom. Or even bridge. The day they find themselves playing bridge – oh dear, that will be a day to look in the mirror and weep. And death, of course, ultimately. That goes almost without saying.

But that's way off the track. This isn't about the new car, if you'll forgive.

Have you time? Just a minute? Then let's cut back to where she's still standing, having uttered her ???, and offered her therethere hug, and having heard his 'I'm sorry' mumbled tearfully into the shoulder of her long yellow dress.

Wait! Hear me out! Let's cut to after he's said the ugly truthful words and magically, in a moment, transformed his guilt into her nausea, and a rushing in the ears, and a protective disbelief all in one.

Or cut to the swim? Yes, let's cut to an island shore. Albania is out there somewhere. Warships sailing, grey distant silhouettes up and down the Ionian Sea, if that's technically possible. Small sailboats dotted about, maybe. A deepening sunset.

Don't go! Nearly there! Into the water she slips, from a barnacled rock. Into the picture-blue water bloodied by the sun. A shock of awakening. A numbness cleansed. It's a dream-like place. Down goes her head, below the water, where there's only her and deafness and her heartbeat and her bursting lungs.

Wait! Listen! Up above, somewhere in a tree, a bird sings. It sounds like a radar, softly pipping across the water.

This is what it sings:

You see? The bird song, pipping in the almost dark. And the crickets. A rhythm section, if you like. This is what the crickets do:

Can you hear it? And the engine, away in the distance, a moped changing gear:

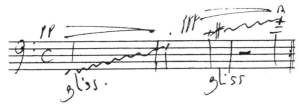

And that's the world above the water, while she's swimming down below. The stillness and the promise of that quiet noise.

If she could hear it.

Alasdair's Angel

Cathy McSporran

Alasdair tried to explain: it was his salvation that had come about, on that day, the day it all happened – the hottest day of the year. But the doctors just said: *The scissors. How did you get hold of the scissors?*

So Alasdair told them about going to check his pigeonhole. He had been late again, but the College in its wisdom had located the staff pigeonholes in the Chemistry building, so he had to cross the road to pick up his mail, and now he would be later still.

He didn't care. It was too hot. His wife's separation papers were a thick warm wad in his breast pocket. He had tried to read them when they arrived that morning, but the words had begun to squirm on the paper like insects. He would look at them again later, in his break-time, perhaps. When it was a little cooler.

From his pigeonhole he took a long Jiffybag marked 'STA-TIONERY OFFICE', and tipped it into his hand. Luckily for the skin of his palm, the scissors slid out handle first.

Stationery had got it wrong again. He had asked for paper-scissors – but these were steel shears, twelve inches long, sharp and gleaming. Later he would reflect that it was asking for trouble, giving out things like that to a man who had to work with Billy Innes. At the time he just put the scissors back in the Jiffybag, and headed out into the hot white daylight.

The street was baking. Only the roaring traffic stirred the blood-warm air. Rave music thumped from the open window of a jeep. A scarecrow figure on the corner, whose gaze Alasdair had learned to avoid, whispered about 'spare change'. Alasdair crossed the road, skin already prickling, and went down the shaded side street.

It was quieter here, and cooler. He passed the post office and the baker's and the chip shop. Only when he was outside the corner shop did he look up, to see if the little girl was there.

She was. Every morning of the school holidays she stood there, under the awning outside her parents' shop, a child about five or six. She was as immaculate as ever, gold sandals gleaming, long black hair brushed till it shone. Most local kids wore shorts and T-shirts in shrieking acid colours; this little girl was dressed, as always, in a miniature version of the *shalwar kameez* her aunts and her mother wore. Today, her outfit was white cotton, fresh as a crocus.

The girl was eating a big green apple. Her parents' shop sold sweets of all kinds, but Alasdair had never seen her eating any; perhaps she had a sugar problem. She held the apple carefully in both hands. When she saw Alasdair her face split into a big grin, mushed apple pushing between her teeth.

Every morning this kid smiled and waved as if she were delighted to see him. She was the only person, nowadays, who could be relied upon to acknowledge his existence.

There was a flash of peacock-blue behind the girl, as Mrs Ali came to the door. She eyed Alasdair dubiously; there was something about Alasdair's large bulk and morose features – particularly since the Prozac had made his face heavy and jowly, and his Easycare shirts began to strain at the buttons – that made parents regard him with suspicion. Mrs Ali drew her daughter inside, and Alasdair walked on.

He crossed through the blaring traffic, and turned into the College's concrete square. It blazed in the sun like whitewash. The 'ornamental lake' (a pond scooped out of moulded concrete) was brown and shallow today. Alasdair scurried from one patch of shade to another, into the Admin Building.

The lobby was dark and cool, but when Alasdair opened the door of his own office, the stuffy heat took his breath away. The light was as bright as if he'd wandered outside again. The Registry was all windows, each with a Venetian blind permanently jammed at the top. It had never been roomy, but this was Admissions season, and piles of application forms teetered on every spare inch of worktop. All summer the forms would stack higher and higher, leaning tipsily against cabinets and printers, and flapping into flight if anyone was stupid enough to switch on the fans.

Christina and Rachel, already stripped down to tank-tops, were tapping away at their keyboards. They glanced up at Alasdair. One of them – Christina? – mumbled a greeting as he went past. Otherwise, they ignored him. The girls had worked in the Registry only a few months; to Alasdair they were not as real, somehow, as the two older women they'd replaced. Lately he had started to forget which was Rachel and which Christina, although they did not look alike.

Before Alasdair could boot up his computer and try to look as if he'd been there for hours, Hugh Pirrie emerged from the side office marked 'Registry Manager'. When he spotted Alasdair, his vague smile became fixed. 'Alasdair, ah – can I have a word with you? I have a meeting now, but – about twelve?'

Alasdair nodded dumbly. Hugh Pirrie disappeared again. Alasdair sat at his desk, letting the Jiffybag clunk down onto the surface. The scissors slid out. Right on cue the main door was kicked open, and Billy Innes backed into the room.

Christina and Rachel looked up at Billy and smiled, as he dumped the armfuls of copier paper on his desk. The sleeves of Billy's Warehouse shirt were rolled up, and his youthful face was flushed, but heat and exertion did not seem to trouble him much. His dark hair was perfect. His long-lashed, rather girlish eyes were bright and clear. Parents never watched Billy with suspicion; he looked more like a children's TV presenter than an office clerk.

'Morning, Alice,' Billy said, to Alasdair. 'Or afternoon, I should say.' His eyes met Alasdair's for a moment then flicked away. Something about Alasdair – his polyester shirts perhaps, or his clown's-wig red curly hair, or his wide mournful face – seemed to offend Billy very much.

When Alasdair didn't reply Billy added shortly, 'File system's down again. We need to produce the graduation reports today, in case you forgot.'

Alasdair turned to his computer.

The student files should be in his directory. But they weren't. Perhaps the College network manager had moved them. Alasdair dialled the Computing extension. It rang and rang. After a while Alasdair put the phone down, and stared at the blank space on his screen. He didn't know what to do. He was so hot.

Beyond the monitor, he could see Billy settling down to open a vast pile of mail. He was looking for a distraction, and Alasdair knew what that would be. 'You're looking rough there, Alasdair,' Billy announced. 'Out last night? Out clubbing?'

One of the girls giggled. Billy was encouraged. 'No? In with the girlfriend then? Up all night giving it whay-hey?'

Rachel pulled a face, maybe at Billy's crudeness, maybe at the thought of Alasdair having sex. Then she said, 'Alasdair, any chance of those reports now?'

Alasdair stood up. His head hurt; he would go out, sit by the lake. There was always some fresh air there, surely he would feel better . . . 'I'm taking my tea-break,' he announced, and left the room, closing the door on the mutterings behind him.

When Alasdair emerged into the College square, he found that the ornamental lake was on fire. Some Chemistry students had poured on something black and oily, then dropped a lighted match. The air shimmered over the flames. The square smelled of burning tar.

Alasdair sat on a concrete bench. There was no fresh air here, not a whisper. But at least he was out of the office, so he pulled out the separation papers and found a pen. He'd already decided he would not try to read them. He would just sign them and send them on their way.

But the jagged line that appeared by the cross was nothing like his curving signature. He smoothed the paper out on the bench, tried again – a spiky A, then a long flat line. He scored it out, tried again, and again. But still his proper signature would not come.

The Chemistry undergrads had taken to their heels, pursued by security guards. A group of girls were laughing uproariously. Janitorial staff appeared, shouting for buckets of water. Alasdair sat amidst it all, his face scorching. He shut his eyes, but he could still see the fire. The concrete all around, the high buildings, even the sky, were all burning.

When Alasdair returned to the office, he found it was after two, and Hugh Pirrie was waiting for him. 'Come into my office, please, Alasdair.' Alasdair followed him in, Billy Innes whistling a funeral march behind him.

The tiny office was even stuffier than the main Registry. Alasdair sat down and watched Pirrie launch into his prepared speech. 'Alasdair, I'm sorry, but I have to give you another formal warning. Your timekeeping has not improved . . . and – ah – your attention to detail has been slipping, quite badly. The application files are full of errors. I've had to rework them myself.'

No wonder they're full of errors then, Alasdair thought. But he said nothing, and watched a cloud of black smoke rise past the window. Someone had put the lake out. Eventually he heard Pirrie say, 'Alasdair, are you still . . . *happy* in this position?'

Alasdair wanted to laugh. Yes, he nearly told Pirrie, he was overjoyed. His wife had left him, apparently because he hadn't grown enough as a person; and once he had dreamed of writing verse about angels in their flight, but instead he was writing Data Management reports for a second-rate college. But he said, 'I've just been a bit distracted lately. I'll make sure it doesn't happen again.'

'Very well.' Alasdair took this as a dismissal, and left.

Billy and the girls watched him coolly as he went to his desk. He began to search the computer network again, but after a moment realised he couldn't remember what he was looking for. He ended up flipping randomly between directories, trying to look busy. His burning face eased at little, but his head still ached and ached.

The Registry clock showed three-fifteen, but the day was stoking up rather than getting cooler. Alasdair, giving up on the network, found himself staring at Christina – a lock of her bright blonde hair had come loose and was brushing against her bare neck. But then Christina looked up and met his eyes; her look of furious disgust sent him hurriedly back to his computer.

Billy, of course, had noticed. He was dealing with another mountain of mail, and his vicious boredom was growing. 'Still no new girlfriend then, Alice? No? That's not good for you. Going without. Bad for the health. Rachel should know, she never goes without, do you Rache?'

'Shut your face,' said Rachel, smiling.

'You should get yourself a new woman, Alice.' Billy was watching him with wide, mocking eyes. 'Or a new man, whatever turns you on.'

Alasdair turned his back on his tormentor. Billy was quiet for a moment – probably planning a fresh line of attack – so everyone heard the hum of the printer turn into a long tortured squeal, followed by silence.

'Printer's down, Alasdair,' said Rachel, as if it were all his fault.

Alasdair's head was still throbbing. The mechanical shriek

had left a whining sound in his ears. Closing his hand around the big steel scissors, he advanced on the silent printer and used the scissors to prise up the lid. Warm air puffed over him. He pulled out some crumpled sheets of paper, closed the lid and flicked the switch a couple of times. Nothing.

Behind him came Christina's voice – or was it Rachel? no, Christina – with the indignant snap of one at the end of her patience. 'Alasdair, I need those data files *today*. Where in God's name are they?'

'I can't find them,' Alasdair said. He dragged the printer away from the wall and opened the back. There was no paper in there. The printer was as hot as an oven. The scorching heat had come back to his face.

Christina got up angrily, and flounced into Pirrie's office. A moment later she returned. 'Hugh says you've to get those files right now.'

'I can't get them.' Alasdair took the roasting machine in his arms and heaved it around again. Sweat trickled down his forehead. He used the scissors to lever open the bottom tray. 'The system's broken down.'

'Give it one of your Prozac, then,' Billy said quietly but clearly.

There was a hiss of breath, laughter or shock, from one of the girls. Even Billy, sensing perhaps he'd gone too far, fell silent.

Sweat was running into Alasdair's eyes. He couldn't see. He stood like a dummy, still poking the scissors into the machine. He was thinking to himself: It's over. There's no more. It's over.

Then his eyes cleared, and the whine in his ears cut off. Alasdair began to move quickly. In two strides he had crossed the room to Billy's desk. The scissors glittered in his hand. Rachel or Christina screamed as he raised them high over his head and brought them down.

The blades thudded into place, bang on target. Billy leapt back, half-stumbling over his chair, shrieking and swearing. His face, Alasdair noticed with some satisfaction, had gone grey and shiny. He looked as if he was going to throw up as he stared down at the long shining scissors, still clutched in Alasdair's large hand, their points embedded in the fake pine veneer of the desk.

Billy backed up against the wall. He was still cursing, in the same high-pitched voice. Rachel-or-Christina screamed again. Alasdair was vaguely aware of Hugh Pirrie appearing in his doorway and stopping dead.

Alasdair let go of the scissors. They teetered and fell with a clatter. Alasdair looked at them sadly. He couldn't even do *this* right. If he'd planted them in Billy's chest, then . . . well, that would have changed things forever. There would have been screaming, and blood. There would have been sirens and radios and overpowering hands. They would have taken him away, and he would have been surrounded by fear and awe and revulsion forever. Things would have changed.

Instead, he was still here. Still in hell. Nothing had changed. He was afraid that any minute, someone would burst out laughing. So he left. Pirrie backed away from him as he went past, but it was of little comfort.

Alasdair left the College square. The sun grilled him like a piece of meat. But it didn't matter.

He knew now what to do. He would go home, tidy things up, and then he would take all the Prozac at once. The sleeping pills, too, just to be sure. He had tried for so long. He couldn't try any more.

It was a relief, to have made up his mind. But still, he wept as he turned the corner into the side street. For his family and his friends and, mostly, for himself.

He cried, but no tears came. His eyes stung with salt he could not wash away. But soon it wouldn't matter, he told himself. And that was for the best. It was all for the best –

'Mister. Mister.'

He stopped, confused by the light voice, aware of no-one nearby. He looked into a pool of shadow under the shop awning. Whiteness floated there, cool blue-whiteness like snow.

He stepped closer, blinking hard. It was the little girl, standing outside her parents' shop watching him. After the long dry day, her hair was still shining and her white clothes were still spotless. In one small hand she clutched the neck of a clear plastic bag, as if she were taking a goldfish home from an old-fashioned fair. But there were no fish in the bag – it seemed to be full of bizarrely huge glacier mints, clear colourless cubes.

The child's deep-brown eyes were bright and curious. 'Are you feeling poorly, mister?' she said.

Alasdair tried to speak. His throat was parched. 'I'm hot,' he whispered at last.

The little girl nodded. She took one of the cubes out of the bag. Water dripped from her hand, Alasdair noticed; the squares in the bag were swimming in water. 'Here y'are,' the girl said.

Alasdair knelt in the pool of shadow, his head level with the girl's. 'Open wide,' she ordered.

Alasdair opened his mouth, and shut his eyes. The girl placed the ice-cube on his tongue.

At first, it was like burning. Then his tongue and mouth were numbed. And then cold water began to trickle down his throat. Alasdair swayed slightly as it reached his stomach. He felt the chill seep into his blood, and spread all around his body, lastly to his burning aching head. His skin cooled. His sweat began to dry.

At last the water rose to his eyes, and the salt was washed away. He opened his eyes, and saw the little girl smiling happily at him. He put his arms around her and drew her close, burying his face in her thin shoulder. He felt her hand, still damp and cool, patting at his back. She said something, to Alasdair, or over his shoulder into the shop – he didn't understand and didn't try. He just cried and cried until the soft white cotton was soaking.

Even when a woman shrieked somewhere behind him, he didn't stop. Not even when angry male voices were all around him. Only when a fist struck his head did he let the girl go, so she wouldn't fall down with him.

Then the rough hands he'd imagined were dragging him away. The furious voices still babbled. Pretty soon there were radios, too. And sirens. Lots of sirens.

Shunting

Paul Brownsey

I am wondering again why I am here when it is announced that there will be a slight delay before we can enter the chapel. I picture staff squirting Glade everywhere, trying desperately to disperse smoke that reeks of burning flesh, though of course I know that crematoria do not function as one imagined them in childhood.

The delay adds to the risk that one of the family will speak to me. I stare fixedly at a notice about bereavement counselling far longer than is necessary to read it. It is framed, as though this gives it appropriate dignity in this place.

'There's a funeral every half-hour. I expect people are still leaving from the last one.' The lone woman who has addressed me is wearing red shoes and a silky orange trouser-suit. Not one of the family, I guess, though these days people wear anything to funerals. Maybe she can tell me what I want to know.

'Probably, yes,' I say. 'I don't know who the family exactly are. It was such a brief notice, just mention of him and "All friends welcome at the crematorium", nothing about his being, you know, "husband of" and so on . . .'

Beneath auburn pageboy hair her face stiffens as though I'd slapped her. I babble on, 'I suppose I count as a friend, just about, though I've not had any contact with him since I was ten.'

Her face relaxes into a smile; of approval, I think, though it's hard to tell because her make-up seems misaligned, like a layer of colour printing slightly out of sync with the rest of the photograph. I discover it would be gauche to persist with my enquiry.

But now a door has opened, a black-clad usher is beckoning us inside. Piped organ music enfolds us softly. Somehow I am separated from the woman; she is at the back. I take a chair in the third row, which will have a good view of the chief mourners. Its secular shape and blond wood call to mind the phrase 'office furniture' and its padded seat is of a far too vivid blue. But suddenly I know that I have a place at this funeral. I realise with astonishment that the colour is the very same peacock blue as the blazers of the Buccleuch Dogs.

His voice at the door, apart from him, sounds just like a man's. 'Is Bobby coming out?'

I am playing with my train set, trying to think of it as really great, though it is only clockwork.

'It's Alistair, Bobby.' I can't quite catch my mother's tone as she admits him and disappears, whether it is approving or disapproving. I have heard her say, 'Of course, in a village like this there are so few their own age.'

Alistair is smiling his soppy V-shaped smile, the one that makes my mother say, 'If he smiles at the girls like that they'll just laugh at him.' I am making my head circle in parallel with the boring motion of the train around its circular track. A proper train set would have loops off and sidings.

I say, 'This is a really great train set.'

As though this is an invitation he crouches down so that our heads are on a level. His hair is gingery and crinkly, in waves like corrugated paper. It is a coup to have a big boy as your friend, but I still don't turn my face towards him, not even to inspect the Kit Carson Cowboy Comic he produces from behind his back, not even when I see from the corner of my eye that it is one I haven't got.

'Thank you,' I say indifferently.

'Good, Bobby, you should always say "Thank you".'

Waiting for his coffin to come in, I wonder whether he said it loudly for my mother to overhear.

He adds, 'I've got a lot more somewhere that I bought when I was a little kid.'

Then: 'Guess what.'

'My name isn't Wat.' One of Robin Hood's men was Wat o' the Whip.

'I've found a pithouse.'

My eyes are on Alistair's before I know it.

I leave the clockwork train running endlessly in its little circle. At last to have found one of the dugouts of the Buccleuch Dogs! This is what the local children call the boys at the posh boarding school just outside the village. They are reputed to be all English; the border is not far away. Sometimes, unexpectedly, you come across them en masse on their mysterious outings, their swarming peacock-blue blazers vivid and clean against nature's greens and browns. People say they dig secret subterranean houses on Millgarva, but none has ever been found. Until now.

The elusive music fades, the minister bids us be upstanding in a voice that seems determined to maintain an earthy Glaswegian accent, the coffin is borne in and deposited in the recess. Three of the bearers bow in unison and exit: undertaker's men. The fourth takes a seat in the front row, next to two women too old to be the possible widow. He is tall, long hair swept back, the confident face of a bird of prey. He is about my age, so cannot be a son. There wasn't a brother.

The path up Millgarva passes our garden. Looking into it from outside the fence, I feel I am someone else.

When we are a long way past our garden Alistair says, 'It's ever so hot.'

He stops and unbuttons his shirt. He does not have a vest on. He takes his shirt off. He smiles in my direction. I think of my mother's look as she waits for me to be thrilled with my birthday present.

Again I see it's true, what I have heard my mother say: 'He gets so brown, that Alistair. Always with his shirt off. Very healthy.' I hear her laughter: 'I think he wants to be a film star. Like Tarzan!'

We are high above the village, which looks to be sinking among the encroaching hills, a scattering of low cottages along the minute disappearing road. I try to experience the lovely view that visitors tell me I am lucky to have so near my home, but it is just ordinary, nothing like the Grand Canyon.

Alistair is saying, 'It feels lovely, being bare.'

He says, 'Why don't you take your shirt off?'

'My shirt is Aertex: it keeps you nice and cool. I've got a weak chest.'

He takes my shirt between finger and thumb as if making a diagnosis and says, 'Yes, you do.'

'My train set just goes round and round on the same track; it can't do shunting.'

'It's wrong to complain, Bobby. Your parents might not be able to afford a better one.' He's not a playmate, he's a grown-up. Something else my mother has said: 'Well, he'll be going out to work soon, anyway.'

We are approaching a bushy reach: clumps of low trees, lots of broom still flecked yellow with shrivelled blossoms. The boss would come out and give the driver his orders: you've got to shunt these trucks from this siding to that siding and back again. Purpose didn't come into it: it was in the nature of a train driver to do shunting.

Alistair is pushing between close-grown branches. I think of thorns ripping across the smooth chest. When I imagine a bleeding tear across one of the dark spots I do not yet know are called nipples I call out, 'Don't.'

218

'It's in here.' I can't see him. 'Push through like I did. Don't be a coward as well.'

My legs in short trousers, my arms, my face are scraped by branches and prickles. I try to find it enjoyable, like the jets in a shower bath I once had. And here is a grassy clearing. Trees and bushes enclose it like a secret. The summer afternoon is concentrated here, its heat and smells. Everything outside this clearing is a very long way away.

'See it?'

I run to branches lying too casually on the grass: the turf beneath is yellower, sits higher than it should.

'Well done, Bobby.'

We haul the branches aside. Like a grown-up, Alistair allows me to do the honours. I scrabble where the turf does not sit right, my hands touch something hard, I find an edge and pull. A plywood square comes away and there is a dark hole. I think of the entrance to the underworld, where Pluto rules over the dead.

My absent mind has been monitoring the minister's funeral address. There has been no reference to widow or children. I wonder whether other people are imagining the inside of the coffin. Alistair lies there in darkness, bare-chested, in long khaki trousers, his soppy smile on his face. We sing a psalm, the usual one, and I wonder if the little clearing counts as a green pasture.

'What if there are snakes down there?' I picture the pithouse full of interlaced snakes, a solid mass of innumerable snakes knotted, writhing.

'So you *are* a coward.' He's kicking away turf to find where the roof meets the earth walls. I start jumping up and down on the roof, willing destructive force into my feet.

Then I jump feet first into the dark entrance-hole. There's no squirming or slithering; my feet hit hard earth. It's like I'm protruding from the vent of a pie, enclosed nearly up to my neck.

While Alistair lifts beam-branches from where the Buccleuch Dogs socketed them into the earth, I enlarge the entrance-hole, flinging off lumps of turf, pushing back branches. 'You can get in, too,' I call. I picture us back to back, the same height, my back against his bare one. We are back to back in firelight and darkness, tied to the same stake by Buccleuch Dogs, who in their peacock-blue blazers caper around us like Red Indians, making horrible faces, howling, shadows and flames flickering. Alistair's chest is still bare. A branding-iron is heated red-hot in the flames, a Buccleuch Dog grinning like a devil presses it lovingly against his bare chest. But Alistair does not cry out, and because of his courage they let him and his friend go.

Alistair stops his wrecking, stands upright, puts his hands on his hips, faces me. He says, 'I'm so hot I wish I had my shirt on so I could take it off again.'

He is smiling his soppy smile. The sweat is visibly trickling down his chest. He holds the pose. For the first time when he has had his shirt off with me, his trousers waist has slipped below his belly-button, from which a line of hair descends. I stare at it from my pie vent.

I say, 'You look like an Indian.'

Suddenly he is kneeling before me on the ruins of the roof, holding my shoulders. 'Just a scratch, nothing to worry about.' The hanky he has taken from his trousers pocket has a red spot on it when he removes it from my face. He still kneels there, his eyes moving over me as if he is looking for more scratches. Tarzan, who is always bare, is tending the boy who lives with him in the jungle. I think about where Tarzan keeps a hanky.

I say, 'It's right to not like snakes. They brought evil into the world, in the Bible. Adam and Eve in the Garden of Eden.'

I say, 'God put Adam and Eve there without any clothes on.'

One hand remains on my shoulder. His eyes aren't meeting mine. We are both motionless. I'm still protruding from the pithouse opening. I think I can actually see the skin of his back sizzling a deeper brown in the sun.

I say, 'So we can take all our clothes off. God wouldn't be angry.'

I laugh, imitating a child that says things for no reason.

His grown up voice: 'Bobby, you shouldn't say . . .'

I reach a hand to his chest well away from the nipples. My fingers experience something which isn't me.

I have I jolted Alistair backwards on his heels Trying to save himself he crashes through the skeletal roof, sprawling against the disturbed earth at the edge. When he gets to his feet beyond the pithouse, slapping dirt off his trousers, there is earth all down his back, stuck to the sweat. He hitches his trousers up above his belly-button. He says contemptuously, 'You couldn't not wear clothes. You've got a weak chest.' Without waiting for me to clamber out, he pulls away vigorously at the remains of the roof frame. Moving branches scrape and scratch against me.

When the roof is completely gone we survey the shallow pit dug by unknown boys for a lair to feel safe in, dirt recoiling from the pure colour of their immaculate blazers. Ashes in the centre show that the entrance-hole doubled as a chimney.

I say placatingly, 'If someone put the cover on while they were in here with a fire they'd all have burnt.'

'Don't you know fire needs oxygen to burn? The fire would have gone out.' He speaks as a big boy who knows things; his knowledge is lodged in huge caverns that I am not yet allowed into. He is kicking hard at the smoothed earth of the pithouse walls, he is jabbing again and again at the rim with a branch that was once a roof beam. He brings down great clods.

Two little planks have been lodged in one part of the walls, the earth between them scooped away to create a wee recess. There's a handle-less cup at the front that I conscientiously smash with a stone. I catch a metallic sheen further in and pull out an unadorned biscuit tin.

Inside there's a scattering of stamps, cigarette cards, candles, some old newspaper cuttings on which I recognise Hillary and

Tenzing. Letters call to mind the startling fact that the boys of Buccleuch House live separated from their parents.

At the bottom is a Kit Carson. The cover is a heart-shakingly unfamiliar configuration of horses, riders, Indian feathers, faces engrossed by battle. Its promise of '64 action-packed pages' rises up like a beanstalk to another world.

'Oh, one of the comics silly little kids read.'

'I haven't got it.' My voice intimates I have many, many sources of Kit Carsons. It is defaced by the name of the Buccleuch Dog, Lachlan MacKinnon, but it's still a treasure. His handwriting, so different from mine, is a peephole to something unnameable.

'You're in luck, then.' Sneered as hard as he can.

'That would be stealing!' I turn the box upside-down. Everything falls and flutters onto the floor of the pithouse and I stamp and shuffle and grind my heels. The magical cover is ripped, dirtied, irrevocably. Our work is finished, the pithouse wrecked beyond repair.

Alistair is saying, 'You'll have to fight the Buccleuch Dogs for what you've done.'

'So will you.'

'Oh, no. I'm too big. They only bully little kids.'

He says, 'They'll capture you and torture you.'

He says, 'They'll cut off your ears. Your toes.' He picks up a creamy shard of the broken cup, advances with it, makes slicing movements. 'Your fingers.'

The line of hair shows, almost black, not gingery like on his head.

'Everything.'

He grabs an ear, hurting me; he lays the sharp edge of china against it.

He laughs, chucks away the shard, ruffles my hair. Still bare-chested, he plunges out of the clearing through the bushes. As I follow I am, of course, unaware that he will never call for me again, that if we encounter each other in the future he will just say, 'Hello, Bobby', in the breezy, distant way the grown-up men do, without ever mentioning his store of Kit Carsons.

The conviction in these memories is intensified as the funeral service reaches its close, the curtains jerk across the recess, and absolutely nothing has intimated wife or offspring in his life. The tall hawk-like man who helped to carry the coffin must be Alistair's partner. His grief spreads through me as though it were my own.

I look round for the woman in orange, but she is one of the first through the exit door and in the crowd I am trapped behind the two old women from the front row, moving very slowly arm-in-arm. Behind us the entrance door opens briefly; new mourners are crowded in the reception area where we waited half an hour ago. The piped organ music has been turned on again and now I recognise it: 'Memory' from *Cats*.

'She did come, then.' One of the old women.

'Well, they would have got married, but she wouldn't divorce her husband.'

I hear no more than that. Exiting, I glance for a last time at the curtained recess. Is the coffin is still there? Perhaps it has glided away and Alistair's body is already engulfed by flames as I imagined the Buccleuch Dogs roasting in the pithouse, though I think I have read somewhere that crematoria use a flameless heat. Either way, when I try again to picture Alistair inside his coffin as I did before, the image won't come. There's something shrouded in a, well, shroud. It absolutely resists being undressed. The shroud is orange and silky.

ABOUT THE AUTHORS

Suhayl Saadi was runner-up in the 1999 Macallan/*Scotland on Sunday* Short Story Competition. He is a Glasgow-based writer whose book *The Burning Mirror* (Polygon) was short-listed for the Saltire First Book Prize in 2001. His novel *Kings of the Dark House* is due out in 2003. www.suhaylsaadi.com

Dorothy Alexander was born in Peebles and now lives in Galashiels. Her publications include *Split Colours* and she has had stories published in various literary magazines. She has also collaborated with the book-binder Alison Allison and the sculptor Dick MacTaggart. Currently a student on the Creative Writing programme at Glasgow University, Dorothy is working on a novel and a long sequence of poems.

Iain Bahlaj: born in Fife, lives in Lochgelly. His stories: in *Chapman*, *Front & Centre*, *Fife Fringe* and *Shorts 3*. His first novel, *Tilt*: due for release since Woodstock, but should appear in 2003. Right now: short films, TV drama, stacking shelves, shunning second novel like leper.

Alan Bissett was born in Falkirk in 1975. He is author of the novel *Boyracers* and editor of *Damage Land: New Scottish Gothic Fiction* (both Polygon). His stories have been previously published in *Shorts 2*, *3* and *4*. He is currently Lecturer in Creative Writing at Leeds University and working on a second novel.

Paul Brownsey lives in Bearsden, a one-time newspaper reporter who is now a philosophy lecturer at Glasgow University. He has had stories published in most Scottish literary magazines and regular collections, and also in English, Irish and North American magazines.

John Dodds was born on the Isle of Lewis and now lives near Kelso. His fiction has appeared in various online and print magazines. A new story appears next year in the speculative fiction anthology, *Breaking Glass: The Best of Fantastic Metropolis*. He is currently writing his first novel, *Bone Machines*.

Angus Dunn, brought up in the Highlands, lives in the Black Isle. His fiction has been published in many literary magazines and anthologies and in 1995 he won the Robert Louis Stevenson Award. He has had writing residencies in Aberdeenshire (19979) and Scottish Sculpture Workshop (2002). He has written one unpublished novel and is work-ing on a second.

Clio Gray was born in Saltburn, Yorkshire, and now lives in Easter Ross surrounded by dogs, cats and clutter. She works at her local library and on the last novel of a trilogy set in mid-nineteenth-century continental Europe to be completed and (hopefully) published by the end of 2004.

Brian Hennigan's novel, *Patrick Robertson A Tale of Adventure* is 'Hugely entertaining it gets funnier and funnier' (*The Scotsman*); 'Only ten pages in I was reduced to a kind of delighted, giggly hysteria. Sparky and spiky and that very elusive thing original' (*The Observer*); 'A work of comic genius' (*Yorkshire Post*).

Alex Hetherington is an artist and writer. His writing has appeared in *Transmission, The List, Sculpture Matters, Stretcher* and 'The Glasgow Film Office'. At present he is developing work combining digital media and video, and is working on a collection of fictions. Born in Helensburgh, he is currently based in Dundee.

Jules Horne was born in Hawick and lives in the Borders, where she works as a freelance journalist and translator. She has had stories published in various anthologies and is working on a novel. She received a Scottish Arts Council New Writer's bursary in 2001 and won the Robert Louis Stevenson Award in 2002.

Hannah McGill lives in Glasgow and works as a journalist, mostly reviewing films. Her short stories have previously appeared in *Shorts 3*; the Canongate Prize For New Writing anthologies 2001 and 2002; and the *Edinburgh Review*. She tells people she is writing a novel.

Rachael McGill was born in Shetland in 1974. She now lives in East London. Her play *Butter Fish Parrot Fish* was shortlisted for the London Writers Award and her translation of *Nepal* for the Gate/Allied Domeq Translation Award. She is working on plays and pretending to write a novel.

Lorn Macintyre was brought up in Connel and Isle of Mull and now lives in St Andrews. A professional writer, television researcher and scriptwriter, he has had many short stories published and broadcast. His novels in the Chronicles of Invernevis series include *Cruel in the Shadow, The Blind Bend, Empty Footsteps*, and *The Broken Lyre* (newly completed); a collection of short stories, *The Dark Island* is pending.

Alan Mackay was born and raised in Edinburgh, and has lived most of his life in the city. He has been writing seriously for about fifteen years. 'The Caged Bird' was written at an Arvon Foundation course three years ago. His only previously published story appeared in *Chapman*, written under the name Alexander Innes

Carol McKay was born in Glasgow and now lives in Hamilton. Her short stories and poetry have been published in *Cencrastus, Northwards,*

Chapman, Cutting Teeth and *Mslexia.* In 2002 the Scottish Arts Council awarded her a writer's bursary to part-fund the writing of a novel.

Cathy McSporran's stories have appeared in *Chapman, Metropolitan, Nerve, Eclogia* and *Mslexia.* A graduate of the Glasgow/Strathclyde University M.Litt. in Creative Writing, she is now studying for a Ph.D. She is also working on her first novel, *Cold City.* Cathy lives in Glasgow with her husband and two cats.

Kath Murphy writes fiction and scripts. Her short stories have appeared in magazines including *Mslexia, Front and Centre* and *Tubthumping* (anthology). She received a Yorkshire Arts grant to complete her first novel, *West Country Girl.* She now lives in Edinburgh, where she is working on her second novel.

David Pettigrew was born in Kilmarnock in 1971 and lives in Glasgow. An editor with a publishing firm, he divides his working hours between home and an office in a village in Ayrshire. He has previously had a story published in the anthology *Glasgow Kiss.*

Linda Saunders was born in London and lived in England and Canada before moving to an uninhabited Hebridean island, which provided the inspiration for her current book. Having vowed that her next island home would have electricity, she now lives on the Isle of Skye. 'The Sheep' is her first work of fiction.

Frances Sessford was born in London, brought up in Lanarkshire and now lives in Perthshire. She has not had any fiction previously published, but her first novel is nearing completion. She works full-time as an editor for a technical publisher based in Stirling.

Fiona Thackeray was born in Edinburgh and has worked in therapeutic horticulture in Bristol, Brazil and Scotland. Her material has appeared in *The Guardian International, Woman's Own* and *Shorts 4.* Now living in West Lothian, she is working on a novel based on her Brazilian experiences.

Ruth Thomas was born in Kent. Her publications include two short story collections *Sea Monster Tattoo* and *The Dance Settee* (Polygon) and her work also appears regularly on BBC radio. She is currently completing a third collection. She lives in Edinburgh with her husband and two young children.

While every effort has been made to compile accurate information about the authors, *Shorts* is produced to a very tight deadline. The Publisher will endeavour to rectify any inaccuracies in any future edition.